# Elisheva's Diary

## RICHARD D. SMALL

*Relax. Read. Repeat.*

ELISHEVA'S DIARY by Richard D. Small
Published by TouchPoint Press
Brookland, AR 72417
www.touchpointpress.com

Publisher's Cataloging-in-Publication data on file.

ISBN-10: 1-946920-45-2
ISBN-13: 978-1-946920-45-4

Editor: Kimberly Coghlan
Cover Design: Colbie Myles, ColbieMyles.net


First Edition, 2018

Printed in the United States of America.

Dedication

For Eileen, Carrie, and Sharon

# AUTHOR'S NOTE

The story of Elisheva's time is adapted from texts thousands of years old. They were written in a fluid mixture of Hebrew and Aramaic with some passages in Greek—the languages particular to the era of the Second Temple of Israel before the birth of Jesus Christ.

I use modern terms to relate a story that occurred in ancient times, although I have retained the original Hebrew *Aba* and *Ima*, still used today, for Father and Mother. I have endeavored to capture the flavor and mood of the period; however, in places, meanings and emphasis may not correspond exactly to modern uses. The responsibility for any errors is solely mine.

Elisheva and her husband, Ariel, a wine merchant who also gathered intelligence for Queen Shlomtsion, were thrust into a world where powerful forces vied for control of the Levant. Elisheva includes in her diary, as faithfully as possible, the voices of the actors themselves as told to her by Ariel. Correspondence accredited to Queen Shlomtsion and the Roman Commander Lucullus is reconstructed from discussions between Ariel and her secretary, Eli.

Sometimes I feel this book is like viewing a dream. Perhaps this diary of Elisheva's life is a dream—after all, it is fiction.

Without question, the story of Elisheva could have happened. Perhaps most surprising is the peace, wealth, and turbulence of the era in which she lives and writes about with eloquence and passion.

The historical backdrop is true, even though many characters are solely my invention. King Alexander Yanai, Queen Shlomtsion, King Hyrcanus II, King Aristobulus II, Queen Cleopatra, Sulla, Pompey, Crassus, Lucullus, King Mithridates VI, King Tigranes the Great, and others, as well as all the locations exist and are portrayed as accurately as a historical record more than two-thousand years old permits. Many records of the period perished in the great Alexandria Library fire of 48 BC and in the destruction of Israel and exile of its people by Rome a hundred years later.

Only a small part of the once great city of Dan has been excavated. No doubt, diaries remain to be found.

Richard D Small
Metula, Israel
March 2016

# ACKNOWLEDGEMENTS

Authors traditionally acknowledge the contributions people made while they put their story in words. That I will do, as I owe a great debt to many. The greatest debt of all is to a culture that reaches back to the beginning of written history. Writing is a long-held and prized tradition. The most significant book of our times, the Old Testament, was written 3500 years ago in a fluid language whose beauty and wisdom still excite. The Psalms of David, written 3000 years ago, give solace to many, and the exquisite words of love in the Songs of Solomon touch the soul. All that is our inheritance, which I acknowledge with deep gratitude.

Throughout the creation and many drafts, Sharon Yael Small and Rachel Sylvetsky gave insight, encouragement, and advice. Elisheva's Diary would not have been possible without their help. Eileen Wolhar, Noreen Davis, and Michelle Buehring repeatedly offered comments that made the book better than it would otherwise have been. Arnold, Leonard and Herb Small read the manuscript several times. Their comments greatly helped the story. A very special thanks to my good friend Rochelle Wisoff-Fields who was always there to answer questions and gave freely of her experience. I am especially grateful for the insights of Melody Quinn and the skill and patience of Kimberly Coghlan who guided this book to publication.

# PROLOGUE

In the Hebrew Calendar Year 5728 (1966 AD), two Israeli Generals stood on an odd shaped mound assessing Syrian Army positions a few hundred meters north of the 1948 armistice line. The Syrian troops protected work crews diverting water from the Dan Springs—one of the major sources of the Jordan River. It would deprive Israel of a desperately needed water supply and doom the young country.

The senior general, Yitzhak, not taking his eyes from the Syrian troops, said to his ambitious subordinate, Amram, "We have to stop them. This mound is a good position. We can protect the springs, guard the approach to the northern towns, as well as block any force coming down from the Golan Heights. Make it happen. Move troops up tonight. Have them in position and ready to fight at first light. Include sharpshooters and a few mortars; later, if necessary, we'll reinforce with tanks and air support."

Amram, grim faced, nodded to his commander.

At nearby Kibbutz Dan, many suspected the mound was a Tel and possibly the site of an ancient city. Some speculated the mound hid the biblical location of the tribe of Dan. In an intensive effort to prevent damage to what might prove a valuable historical site, an archeological expedition led by Professor Avraham Biran undertook a hurried effort to survey the mound.

The team dug an explorative trench. They discovered the Tel concealed a major city first settled in the fifth millennium BC. The link to the beginning settlement of Israel forty years following the exodus from Egypt electrified the nation. Years later, it proved one of the more valuable excavations in Israel. It confirmed, for the first time, the existence of one of the most important Kings of Israel.

The violent clash of armies, in the 1967 Six-Day War between Israel and a coalition of four Arab countries, interrupted the dig. The work continued only after the Israel Defense Forces secured the area. The excavation team expanded to include archeologists from the center of the country, personnel from the nearby town of Kiryat Shemona, and the recently overrun Syrian Alawite village of Ghajar.

The story revealed by the Tel predates recorded history beginning a thousand years after Adam and Eve left the Garden of Eden. It was a time before years were counted in the modern calendar, a time when the Temple built by King Solomon stood as a beacon of hope for mankind. The ancient Hebrew calendar, said to begin with the creation of the world, is the natural measure for events recorded in the Old Testament and the city of Dan.

From the Tel, the archeologists had a commanding view of the Hula Valley and the streams flowing to the Sea of Galilee. The valley has been known by different names. Three thousand years ago, the Egyptians called the valley Samchuna. The Old Testament Book of Joshua refers to the area south of Dan and east of the Naphtali Range as the Merom Valley. Josephus used the Greek name Semechonitis. The modern name is the Hula Valley from the Aramaic Hulata.

*Know that time, enemies, the wind and the water*
*Will not erase you*
*You will continue, made up of letters*
*That is not a little*
*Something, after all, will remain of you.*
*Haim Gouri, 2015*

From *Though I Wished for More of More*,
Hakibbutz Hameuchad, Daniella De-Nur, 2015
[אף שרציתי עוד קצת עוד, Af She-Ratziti Od Ktzat Od]

Ariel's return to Jerusalem

Syria

Damaseq

Lebanon

Tyre

Kedesh
Hazor

Dan

Bashan

Merom Lake

Tsfat

Kinneret Sea

Tsipori

The
Great Sea

Dor

Jordan River

Samaria

ISRAEL

Jericho

Philadelphia

Jerusalem

Gaza

Idumaea

Dead Sea

**Ariel's Return to Jerusalem 3675 (85 BC)**

**Israel During the Reign of Queen Shlomtsion**
**Armenian Empire 3678 (70 BC)**

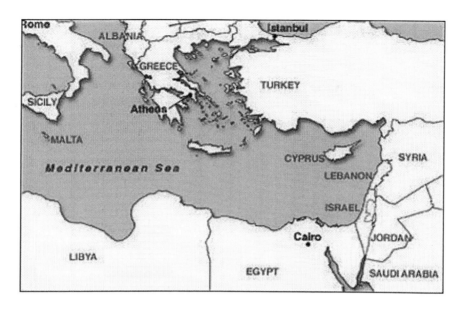

**Eastern Mediterranean 5777 (2017)[1]**

[1] Source: Israel Resource News Agency
israelbehindthenews.com/wp-content/uploads/2014/10/map.jpg

# BOOK ONE—ELISHEVA

I, Elisheva, daughter of Nadav and Noa, am starting my diary today, the day my best friend almost died.

It was a beautiful spring day bursting with energy. The air was cool as the last of the winter cold faded. Trees across the Merom Valley awakened with a magnificent profusion of pink and white flowers. The sky teemed with bees seeking the best blooms and birds scouring the ground for materials to build their nests. Life filled every corner of the fields around Dan.

I played hide and seek with my friends outside the city wall in the warm sunshine. Glancing up at Mount Hermon to the east, I noticed a hunter carrying a gazelle over his shoulders. Brilliant white clouds seemed to crown his head. I watched puzzled as he dropped the gazelle and started to run towards the fields surrounding Dan. He pointed to the south and waved his arms.

He appeared frantic, and we were tempted to laugh at the hunter's actions until guards on the city wall sounded the alarm. Then we understood. Looking to the south, we saw horsemen riding hard from the direction of Anafa toward Dan. Anafa, once a thriving town, had long since been abandoned. The bandit chief, Yosef, and his gang now occupied the town.

Farmers and travelers ran to Dan and safety. Everyone knew what it meant to be caught outside the walls.

The riders were fast approaching. We ran. Micah, born with a clubfoot, struggled to keep up. I slowed until he was next to me. He held my shoulder tight as I put my arm around his waist. He was drenched in sweat and out of breath.

Even though he was smaller than me, I soon tired, and we fell behind.

The riders closed. Micah pushed me away. "I can't make it; get help." When I hesitated, he pushed me again. "Go."

I ran to Dan.

Micah was alone. He limped onward dragging his foot. I saw him fall in the rocky field. Badly bruised and bleeding, he did not give up. He struggled toward the wall and safety. I was sure he would be captured and killed.

I reached the entrance to the city, out of breath and frantic. I screamed— "Someone help. Micah could not keep up. He is lost." I pleaded, "He is my friend; please save him."

Sobbing, I sat inside the gate trying to catch my breath. *Ima* came to me, put her arm around me and guided me through the inner gate to safety.

A stranger, standing with two boys near the outer city gate, heard the plea. He ran toward Micah.

Yosef raised his sword and spurred his horse. Half of his men followed him as he raced toward the city gate; half rode hard to the east to cut off any escape.

The stranger reached Micah ahead of the bandits. He threw Micah over his shoulders as if he were a small lamb and turned back to the city. Arrows, aimed by the mounted bandits, fell in front of him. He swerved to the east, heading for Mount Hermon.

Yosef yelled, "No arrows! No arrows! Do not injure the boy. The Jews will pay a huge ransom for a child—even a lame child."

Defying the attackers, the stranger reversed direction and headed straight for the city. Men, armed with bows and spears, stood on the wall and shouted, "Follow the wall."

An eternity passed. The man, with Micah still clinging to his shoulder, approached the outer gate. The bandits leaned forward and whipped their horses. Panting with fright, I felt faint.

Struggling to hold Micah, the stranger passed through the outer gate. Two of Yosef's gang followed with swords raised. I could hear the horses snort as they closed on the man. Foam dripped from their mouths. I held my breath.

*Aba* stood in front of the second gate. He threw his spear and killed the first rider; guards on the wall fired four arrows killing the second.

The man fell from his horse, blood pulsing from his wound. His horse, terrified by the smell of blood, ran back and forth between the walls. People screamed. I was stunned and could not move. *Aba* had killed a man.

The stranger passed the inner gate just as it started to close. He put Micah down and bent over taking deep breaths. The man fell to his knees. Sweat dripped from his face. Two boys ran and hugged him. I rushed to Micah.

With everyone safe inside the wall, the men relaxed. We were lucky this time, but two men were killed.

Someone asked, "What is your name, stranger?"

"I am called Gershon Ben Avraham. I am here from Jerusalem with my sons, Yoav and Ariel. I trade in spices, imported foods, and wine."

"We are grateful to you. Nothing we have can repay you for saving the life of a child who has an eternity yet to live."

Gershon, still short of breath, stood up, "Who killed the bandit closest to me?"

*Aba* stepped forward. "I threw the spear. You have done a great deed, friend. I would be honored if you and your sons come to my home for Shabbat dinner."

Gershon turned to *Aba*. "I am the one honored and accept your invitation with pleasure."

Silence descended on the people safe inside the wall. *Aba* took my hand. Alone with our thoughts, we slowly walked home. I was exhausted.

That night I could not sleep. A hundred thoughts raced around my head. The day started in brilliant sunshine and play. It ended in fear, a fierce struggle to live, and death. I had never felt such terror, such sadness, or such soaring elation.

I no longer felt like a little girl.

# BOOK TWO—DISCOVERY

Musa, a young man of marriage age, from the village of Ghajar, located at the junction of the Israel-Syria-Lebanon border, responded to an ad for jobs at Tel Dan. If accepted, Musa would use the money to build a home for a future wife and family. He had heard the rumors saying Israelis lacked compassion, did not treat Arab workers well, cheated, and could not be trusted. Yet, he wanted to start a family. He decided to take the risk.

Musa and several men from the village were hired to work at the Tel. Musa moved soil that the excavators scraped with great care to a waste area where archeologists sifted the soil for the tiniest pieces of previous civilizations. The work was hot, dirty, and monotonous under the searing Mediterranean sun. At the same time, he felt an unexpected excitement when the excavators removed layers of dirt and exposed remnants of past eras. Pottery shards sometimes hinted at a creative era and insights to typical foods, wine, seeds, and clothes. Outlines of long destroyed structures appeared from the excavations testifying to living conditions, granaries, warehouses, and life in a prosperous city.

Musa's fascination with this new world of archeology grew. As a child, he had been taught that the Jews stole the land. Yet, now he was part of an effort that revealed Israelite habitation for more than three thousand five hundred years.

What a great wonder the archeologists could identify houses, market places, defensive walls, and create a picture of life from this great puzzle. Often he remained after the workday and listened intently to the archeologists discuss the days' findings and the new understandings of an ancient people. The evidence of a high-quality life surprised him.

One day, Yigal, the site manager, asked if he wished to work on the excavation of new layers rather than debris removal. Musa heard the words, but the offer was so contrary to all he had learned about the Israelis, he did not know how to respond. Maybe it was a trick. He hesitated before answering, "Yes, it would be a great honor to join the distinguished excavators."

"Excellent." Waving his hand to indicate the Tel, Yigal told him that at first they did not know what to expect. "We now see that this Tel is of immeasurable significance."

Musa nodded. "What is so special?"

Yigal smiled at Musa and excitedly added, "We find evidence of a remarkable town, old in the earliest days of history. The lowest level dates from the Stone Age. The town flourished in the Bronze and Iron Ages and prospered under Babylonian, Persian, Greek, and Roman occupations." Yigal turned to the wall. "I am most impressed with the extraordinary well-engineered defensive wall." Enthusiastically he pointed in the direction of the city gates. "We have even uncovered the remains of stores selling exquisite glass and ceramic products, cosmetics, intricate jewelry, and metal tools."

Until that moment, Musa had not realized the broad scope of history being uncovered. The discoveries amazed him, and he felt proud to be part of such an important project.

"Congratulations, Musa. We need good people like you to dig through millennia of rubble to help reveal the Tel's secrets."

Musa's world changed when he became part of the discovery team. His whole life he believed this land was part of Assyria—forerunner of the modern state of Syria. At the Tel, he learned the Assyrians were the invaders. The Jews were tenacious and throughout history defended their land.

He was excited by his new job and responsibility. He was proud Yigal recognized his contributions, and he worked with extra enthusiasm.

His marriage, arranged by his parent's years ago, would soon be a reality. He had known his future bride, Aisha, since they were both young. She was beautiful with jet-black hair, black eyes, a smile that showed perfect teeth, and she moved with the grace of a young gazelle. Poems he learned in Arab literature spoke of such ideals. Without doubt, he was the luckiest man in the world.

The extra income from the promotion came in handy to buy building materials to construct the home he and Aisha would share. Hot and dusty at the end of a day at the Tel, he would work on his new home every evening except Thursday and Friday. No matter how tired, he would at least mix one tub of cement, and lay one or more rows of cinder blocks. On moonlit nights, he worked until late.

On Friday, he attended Mosque and sometimes, with his parents, visited Aisha. When he completed the house, he could marry. Sometimes after finishing a wall, he leaned on his hoe and dreamt about the future. He looked forward to a wonderful life with Aisha, enjoying with her the tranquility of long starlit nights and eventually, a house full of sons and daughters.

At the Tel, excitement, when an excavator unearthed pottery, jugs, coins, cloth remnants, tools, or a child's toy, interrupted the slow, tedious, and painstaking work. Musa uncovered a small purple glass vial stunning in its simplicity and delicate beauty. He marveled at the glass blower's skill and wealth of the ancient society that produced such a vial.

The excavators crowded around Musa as he brushed away a covering of dust thousands of years old. They cheered and pounded him on the shoulder. Yigal studied the vial. He speculated that it might have held a rare perfume or perhaps valuable oil used to flavor a "dish fit for a King."

The excavators worked through a long sweltering spring and summer. Musa continued to build. At the end of each month, he bought more blocks; each night the walls rose higher. Soon he would buy pipes and electric cable and install the plumbing and electric systems. He felt destined for a wonderful future.

One day, in the southwest corner of the Tel, his small spade hit something solid just below a thin layer of dirt. Alert and following proper procedure, he removed the loose soil. He was sure it would be no more than a worthless rock or a broken piece of pottery. At most, it might be used to date the layer. Even so, the archeologists said, "Every rock is important and has to be documented." He stopped to drink water using the moment to rest in the shade.

Yigal walked over and placed a hand on Musa's shoulder. "Any problem?"

"No, Sir. I work in an area with stones from the outer city wall. I am frustrated that I find so little. You must be very disappointed in me."

"You do a good job. I assigned you this area because you are careful and thorough. I trust you. Keep up the good work, Musa."

The unexpected compliment surprised him. "I try, Sir."

As he had guessed, he had uncovered another stone. This one was not from the outer wall of the city but shaped as if from a building—maybe a cornerstone. Brushing aside more dust, Musa uncovered pottery shards next to the stone. Perhaps in a long ago battle, the stone fell and crushed an important vase. Maybe the pottery would reveal a great discovery. The site photographer documented the location and then photographed the stone and pottery in place. Several days later, the laboratory dated the shards to within 10 years of 50 BC.

The days dragged on with few discoveries to cheer the archeologists. On Thursday, the last day before the start of the weekend, Musa uncovered a similar stone. Maybe this stone would be significant although he suspected, at most, it would be another small piece in the Tel's giant puzzle of history and space.

This time, a sudden rush of adrenaline sharpened his senses. As he removed the stone, he felt a smooth object with his fingers before he could see it. He had uncovered a jug different than any so far seen on the site; it seemed to be intact: oblong rather than round, it had a distinct blue lip. A goatskin covering tied by a leather thong sealed the opening.

He removed the dirt, brushing the dust to reveal more of the surface. Musa saw no decoration except for six letters in ancient Hebrew. Two-thousand-year-old air escaped as he uncovered an opening in the side of the jug.

He could see something inside the jug. Musa held his breath. Soon it would be time to quit for the day. Most of the archeologists and workers prepared to head home early for the Sabbath. A strange feeling overcame Musa. He felt compelled to continue. Whatever was in the jug, he had to unearth it now; it could not remain hidden another day.

Deft fingers moved sand exposing an opening. He could see a scroll with writing on it. He stopped and looked to see who remained. The photographer, sketch artist, and Yigal had already left for the weekend.

He was not sure what to do. Maybe leave it in place until Sunday when work resumed—maybe cover it with plastic to protect against the dew of the cool night air or possibly the rummaging of a wild dog or animal? "Perhaps I should take it home, protect it, and bring it back on Sunday. Surely, Yigal would not want something so valuable to be damaged." Without difficulty, Musa removed the soft parchment from the jug. Leaving the jug in place, he covered the scroll with a cloth and put it under his jacket.

CHAPTER THREE—GHAJAR—5729 (1969)

A loud knock on the door startled Musa.

"Who could it be at this hour?"

Musa shrugged and nodded to Aisha who rose from her chair to open the door. A tall Israeli dressed in jeans, a bright red flannel shirt, and wearing a beige Caesarea Golf Course cap stood in the entrance holding a package.

"May I help you?" she asked.

"I am looking for Musa. Is this his house?"

Musa, hearing the voice, came to the door. "Yigal, Sir please come in. Aisha this is Yigal from Tel Dan. Make our guest some tea."

Yigal reached out his hand to Aisha and said, "I have heard so much about you. It is my great pleasure to meet you."

Aisha lowered her eyes and mumbled, "Thank you, Sir. It is my honor to meet such a distinguished man."

"Aisha, the honor is mine."

Musa stepped forward. "Please, Yigal, sit here."

"Thank you, Musa. You look well; I see marriage agrees with you. I can't stay long."

"Please Yigal. Have some tea before you go."

"Only a few minutes and then I must really run off. We heard you married, and all the excavators chipped in to buy a wedding gift for you."

"Oh, this is such a surprise." His hands shaking, Musa opened the package. "Aisha, come look at the beautiful tablecloth and napkin set that Yigal brought us. Thank you, Yigal. Please thank all the excavators for me."

"Musa, we all wondered why you didn't return to work."

Musa felt the blood drain from his face and looked at the floor trying to

11

decide what to say. Yigal waited. Aisha stared at her husband wanting him to make the right decision.

Musa's hand twitched. Almost in a whisper, he said, "I needed to finish the house, and then after the wedding, my father-in-law wanted me to work with him. I could not refuse. I am so sorry, Yigal. I should have come back. I am so sorry."

"Musa, we all wish you and Aisha much happiness. Now, I must really go. Thank you for the tea."

After the door closed, Aisha started to say something but stopped. Musa leaned back in his chair as if crushed by a great weight. Aisha stood next to him and took his hand. Neither spoke.

# BOOK THREE—DAN

I was born in paradise three thousand six hundred sixty-five years after the creation of the world. Dan was well known when Abraham and Sara arrived from Ur. In the beginning, the city was named Laish, and only hundreds of years later did the Israelite tribe of Dan cross the Jordan, after 40 years in the desert, to settle in the city. Legend says Dan first arose a thousand years after Adam and Eve left the Garden of Eden. I am proud of my city; it has a grand history filled with triumphs as well as much sorrow and anguish.

I cannot imagine a more beautiful place on Earth than the Merom Valley. To the east, the Golan Heights rise to a high plateau. Across the valley, the hills, home to the tribe of Naphtali, frame the Merom Valley in the west. Every evening, I delight in the breathtaking harmony and beauty as the Golan glows a soft pink in the setting sun, while the hills of Naphtali darken to a deep purple. The valley floor accents the surrounding hills with a rainbow of colors from the orchards, fields, vineyards, and forests.

Twice a year, countless numbers of storks, cranes, egrets, pelicans, and herons fill the sky heralding a change of season. Vast flocks, tired from their journey, seek safety and respite in the fields around the small sea. In the morning, I watch amazed as they face the warm sun, capture its energy, and spiral upwards to continue their journey.

I have always taken the beauty of my city and its surroundings as normal. *Aba* often told me of his travels across Israel to the Great Salt Sea in the west, to magnificent cities along the coast, to inland valleys, and to the desert in the south. He said the desert holds a special beauty—siren colors at sunset and the tranquility of a seducing wind at night under a sky filled with countless stars. Often shooting stars, traversing the heavens in seconds, punctuate the night panorama. But surely, nothing compares with Dan.

From my home, I look east to Mount Hermon. Like a giant shielding us from a hostile world, it stands over Dan dominating the hills to the north and the plateau to the south. Clouds sometimes hide the peak's majesty, and swirling storms mask it in a threatening atmosphere. On clear days, sunlight reflects from the forests and valleys on the lower elevations and projects magnificence, breathtaking to behold. During much of the year, a blanket of snow covers the upper reaches of the mountain. It is the source of the icy pure water flowing through Dan. In the winter, the blinding white peak often mirrors the sunset's rainbow of pastel colors.

I am lucky to live in the most beautiful part of the most beautiful kingdom in the whole world.

I have listened to travelers talk about the Galilee. They describe marvelous towns and villages built in beautiful settings: sculpted valleys with plentiful water and rich soil. Their descriptions of Kedesh are so vivid I can almost feel the excitement of the big market. Farmers send produce from the fields around Dan, and our artisans send goods from our ceramic and metal workshops through Kedesh to the coastal cities of Lebanon in return for rare woods, glass, cloth, dyes, and manufactured goods that arrive in Tyre and Sidon from Greece, Egypt, and Rome. Kedesh itself is built on a large hilltop surrounded by a rich valley famous for well-kept vineyards and exquisite wines.

They speak of olive groves on the road leading to the Great Sea. The trees twisted and gnarled as generation after generation of growth is added to life drawn from the soil.

Travelers from distant lands tell me the Great Sea is a wonder. Salty to the taste, it contains strange fish and exotic creatures not found in the Merom or the Kinneret seas. They say, sometimes, like the tempests blanketing Mount Hermon, storms rage over the Great Sea, with relentless waters swirling in an angry rhythm and pounding the shore; sometimes the sea turns a deep blue hiding a mysterious depth, and sometimes it is tranquil.

They speak of a beautiful land beyond the Galilee: villages located across a varied geography, ranging from mountains rich in forests, tranquil deserts producing fine wines, a coastal plain with thick forests, abundant agriculture, and rich fishing: all with a well-developed ethical and cultural life.

And towering above everything, the crown jewel of Israel and the world, the magnificent city of David and Solomon, the location of our Temple, Jerusalem.

I went to the market today as I do every Thursday afternoon to purchase food for the Sabbath. Since I am now ten-years-old, *Ima* trusts me to select the best fruits, vegetables, meats, and cheeses for our family. It was a time I relished.

She chose a special dish for this Sabbath evening meal from *Rachel's Galilee Recipes*—a treasured scroll passed by her grandmother to her *Ima* and now to her. It is her prized possession. Although some argue *Zilpa's Idumea Favorites, Tirza's Coastal Recipes* and *Ruth's Cooking with Wine* have superior recipes, *Ima* prefers the simple Galilee dishes carrying the flavors of our rich soil.

She will prepare *Aba's* favorite: chicken marinated in wine and figs flavored with cardamom, and slowly cooked over a low fire. She will baste the chicken until golden brown and serve the chicken with a warm compote of green olives and roasted red peppers. As always on Friday night, it would be a special evening meal.

The market excites me. I marvel at the wealth of goods from the farms and workshops of Israel as well as from neighboring and far away kingdoms. Alive with a chorus of smells, colors, and people bargaining, yelling orders, singing, laughing, arguing, and shoppers rushing to finish their purchases and return home.

Merchants from the Galilee, Lebanon, Damascus, Shomron, Yehuda, Idumea, Greece, Egypt, and of late even Rome—dress in a variety of styles and colors from simple woolen or linen undergarments and robes to fine linens dyed and patterned with multicolored stripes or elaborate geometric designs. Precious metals gleam on necks, wrists, and fingers; tattoos decorate many from distant lands, and purple, red, blue, and yellow fabrics add a swirl of brilliant color to the frantic rhythm of the market.

Everything a person might desire can be found: domestic wines from the Golan, Kedesh Valley, the coastal plain, the Negev, and wineries throughout the Galilee and Shomron, alongside imported wines from Greece, Armenia, and Rome. One section of the market sells fish caught in the Kinneret, Lake Merom, and the Great Sea. Another part sells livestock slaughtered according to ritual.

In the fall, special caravans bring dates and balsam from Jericho. Any time of the year, I can choose from cheeses of every kind and consistency, all types of nuts including my favorite—pistachios grown in Persia. In the center of the market are cart after cart of vegetables, olives from the Galilee and Greece, and fruits picked from farms and orchards around Dan and valleys throughout the kingdom.

I enjoy stopping at the stands that sell rare woods from the mountain forests of Lebanon, glass vials, toys, jewelry, pottery, metal tools, cooking utensils, and beautifully colored cloth.

I cannot pass by the stands selling scrolls without purchasing a story to read at night, often not sleeping until my candle burns out. My favorites are plays that make me cry, laugh until I cry, or those that make me sing for joy. I linger over the recipe scrolls for preparing holiday feasts and Shabbat meals. There is a lifetime of scrolls that I want to read including histories of our kingdom, the recent books of Judith and Susana, and learned treatises on the Torah, philosophy, medicine, and mathematics. The most popular, and my favorite, is the poetry of our Kings, David and Solomon—most of all, the beautiful verses from the Song of Songs.

I saw Gershon in a shaded corner of the market. He had big shoulders. Muscles rippled in his arms as he moved the heavy baskets of spices. He smiled as he worked and exuded a joy that attracted customers to examine his spices and to ask where he was from. I could see that he enjoyed meeting people and describing the quality and origin of his spices.

His two sons worked with him selling rare spices purchased from caravans that left Petra for Avdat and Egypt. At first, I concentrated on the baskets of spices and paid no attention to the boys.

The younger boy, Ariel, stared at me. Taller than me, he had curly black hair, an infectious smile, and brilliant, alert black eyes shining with the joy of life. He showed a quick delight in observing people.

The spice section is one of my favorite areas of the market; the sculpted mounds of fragrant spices set out in a dazzling display of color and smell: deep purple sumac, golden turmeric, dark green thyme, pale green cilantro and sage, deep reddish brown cloves so tasty in soups and cakes, black peppers, ground mild reddish-purple chili peppers grown in Pontus, greenish-brown zatar and oregano, dark brown ground cumin, light brown cumin seeds, green, yellow and burning-hot red chilies, piles of light brown bay leaves, huge sacks of salt from the Dead Sea, brownish-black sticks of vanilla to flavor desserts, and *Ima's* favorite, deep purple-yellow saffron.

I selected small amounts of pale green-yellow cardamom that *Ima* would grind and mix with wine and the juice of crushed figs for a marinade, turmeric to add to the olive and pepper compote, and sumac to spice a mixture of onions and radishes. For dessert, she would warm crushed persimmons flavored with vanilla and pour over a simple yellow cake.

Gershon explained to me that some spices, such as the rare and fragrant nutmeg grow in distant tropical kingdoms. He had a wide selection of hot and fragrant spices called curries that came from far-away countries where people spoke strange languages and worshipped many gods. He said meals fit for Alexander, the Macedonian King, who conquered Israel and almost the entire world, were made with such spices. There were even stories of even more exotic lands and foods located beyond India. He had heard about worms that produce a special cloth that could be dyed any color and felt smooth as skin, but he had not seen such cloth.

Looking from the packages of food and then at me, Gershon asked, "How will you carry all these packages, Miss—what did you say your name is?"

"Elisheva. I am the daughter of Nadav and Noa."

"I remember you, Elisheva. You were very brave to help Micah. Your *Aba* invited me and my sons, Ariel and Yoav, for the Shabbat evening meal."

"You saved my friend's life. I am so grateful to you."

"I did what anyone would have done. I was closest to the gate."

"Well, I think you are a hero. Have you seen my brother, Itai? He is supposed to help me."

"I haven't seen him. My son Ariel will help you carry all this food to your home."

"Thank you so much."

"Ariel, bring these packages to her house and come right back. We still have much work to do before Shabbat."

"I will, *Aba*."

I needed the help. I wanted to get home and start cooking with *Ima*. I was glad Ariel carried my packages, and for some reason, I would glance over at him. Although my packages were heavy, he seemed to carry them with ease. Sweat on his forehead betrayed that he found the burden heavy. I saw all this without consciously knowing it. That night, his face, smile, and penetrating eyes filled my dream.

Friday night is a special time in Dan. The labors of the week complete, we honor the Sabbath with a day of rest that starts with the evening meal. I help *Ima* prepare the house and the Shabbat evening meal. Gershon and his sons were coming to our home.

I woke early while it was dark and the sky still held the sparkle of a million stars. I did not get up from my warm bed; instead, I listened to the birds as they prepared to announce the sunrise. At first, I could distinguish the chatter and song of individual birds and the different pairs. More and more birds joined the chorus until the whole community celebrated, with song and great joy, the sun, sky, trees, and the birth of a new day. I relished the awakening of the world. Soon the sun would appear over the Golan, shading the sky with streaks of pink and lavender before flooding the day with a remarkable golden light. I had a feeling today would be a special day.

I wanted everything to be perfect. I felt a little anxious: maybe because of the distinguished company or maybe because of the boy who helped carry my packages. That mystified me—why am I nervous about a boy coming for a Shabbat evening meal?

*Ima* has several cook scrolls and prepares tasty meals. She is teaching me the secrets of cooking. Often she invents new dishes using the meats, vegetables, fruits, and spices available in the market. I love cooking with *Ima*. Often I dream about cooking for my family. I want to learn everything. I write the ingredients and the method of preparation for many of her dishes in a scroll I keep in my room.

I am determined to cook and manage a house as well as *Ima*. Sometimes, I am overwhelmed when I think of the great responsibility I will have when married. Family is the core unit of our society, and I, as the woman of the house, will be responsible for the health and happiness of my home and family. My husband will learn the laws that combine all the families into a cohesive society. I hope to continue our long tradition and make a good home. I want to share everything with my husband, both in and out of the home, as my parents do. I pray we will have many children.

This Friday *Ima*, for the first time, let me prepare the marinade to flavor the chicken. I concentrated to make the best marinade ever. I was secretly proud that Ariel would know I helped prepare the Friday evening meal.

I squeezed the figs collecting the juice in a shallow clay bowl and then ground the cardamom. The aroma was intoxicating; after combining it with fig juice and a small amount of ground vanilla bean, I closed my eyes thinking this had to be a scent of the Garden of Eden. I then added white wine, from the large amphora kept near the cooking area, to the mixture and poured it over the chicken. The chicken would remain in a cool dark place to absorb the sweet flavors before being roasted slowly over a "cool" fire.

*Ima* prepared the roasted red peppers she would add to green olives before dusting with turmeric. I sliced onions and radishes. I crushed golden-brown persimmons. The juice was sweet, and often I licked my fingers. Near the end of the meal, *Ima* would warm the juice over the embers of the fire and pour it over a plain yellow cake.

Late in the afternoon, I set the table. I placed two different size fired-clay dishes with blue trim next to tin spoons and knives. A special board, made from olive wood, held the bread *Aba* blessed before we ate. I put a large wine cup in front of *Aba's* chair and regular wine cups for everyone else. Gershon, Ariel, and Yoav would sit opposite my brothers, sisters, and me. *Ima* and *Aba* would sit at opposite ends of the table. My sisters picked red sage blossoms for the table center.

Gershon, Ariel, and Yoav arrived just as my *Ima* prepared to light the Sabbath candles to start our day of rest. *Aba* greeted them at the door. "Welcome to our home, Gershon. You do my family a great honor by joining us."

Gershon took *Aba's* hand, "On the contrary, Nadav, you honor us.

Many have told me your wife, Noa, is one of the foremost cooks in Dan; it is a privilege to be invited to your home. I have brought a small gift."

Noa lightly touched the grains with her finger. "Thank you so much. I have never seen grain like this before."

"It is called rice. This appears a small amount, but when boiled in slightly salted water, it expands and will be enough for your whole family. I hope you will like the taste. It is tasty when cooked by itself or with herbs such as parsley, dill, and cilantro." Gershon touched Nadav's shoulder. "I am not exactly sure where it is grown; all I know, it is in lands far to the east. Traders that go to India brought me a full sack."

"We are looking forward to trying it."

As we did every Friday evening, the evening meal started with a prayer honoring *Ima* and the women of Israel, a blessing over the wine, and the simple but eloquent prayer thanking God for our bread. This Friday, *Aba* also added a short prayer thanking God for the rescue of Micah and our good fortune to have Gershon, and his sons, Yoav and Ariel, in Dan.

*Ima* asked me to help serve the meal. I was nervous and afraid I might trip or spill food on someone. First, I brought the onions and radishes in a large bowl sprinkled with purple sumac. It added a refreshing tang to the dish and a wonderful contrast to the red and white colors of the onions and radishes. I walked around the table while everyone took a small amount for their plate. Ariel in a soft voice said, "Thank you, Elisheva."

My cheeks burned. I am sure they turned red like a ripe apple. Why, I do not know. *Aba* excused himself to help *Ima* cut the chicken while I again circled the table serving the warmed compote of green olives and roasted red peppers. Again, Ariel looked at me and thanked me. Again, I blushed. This time, everyone at the table seemed to be looking at me. I was glad when *Ima* entered carrying a large bowl with the fragrant chicken dripping with the marvelous fig-cardamom sauce.

The meal ended in a flash. I am sure it was wonderful. I only remember being afraid to look up at Ariel who sat opposite me. Every time I glanced at him, he was intent on his meal. I was sure he did not notice me, although one time I thought he was staring at me and turned away when I looked in his direction. I was surprised at myself but comforted no one noticed.

After the final course of cake topped with the warmed persimmon sauce, *Aba* asked Gershon about news from Jerusalem. While we were all excused from the table, Ariel, Yoav, and I were allowed to stay and listen to the discussion.

*Aba* said to Gershon, "We are concerned over King Alexander Yanai's policies favoring the Sadducees and the aristocracy over the Pharisees. People in the Galilee are convinced the Pharisees represent the true spirit of Israel. The rift between the two groups worries us."

Gershon stared at his wine for a moment. "It worries everyone in Jerusalem."

That surprised *Aba*. "I thought it was only us in the Galilee."

"No." Gershon said, "It worries the whole country. In fact, the argument brings out the worst in both sides."

I could barely keep my eyes open as *Aba* and Gershon discussed what I thought must be something important. Ariel listened closely and seemed interested in the subject. Maybe, because he is from Jerusalem and has traveled everywhere, he understands politics. I would ask *Aba* to explain all of this to me tomorrow.

Almost in answer to my question, Gershon explained that the Sadducees favor the princes of Israel over the priests as guardians of the kingdom rather than the Pharisees who advocate political power corrupts piety. They believe Israel should be pious in daily life and observe the laws of the Torah. This difference has persisted for a long time.

*Aba* appeared upset. "I do not feel any better knowing the issue has not been resolved."

"Nadav, many oppose the brutal persecution of the Pharisees. Alexander's Queen, Shlomtsion, supports the Pharisees. She follows the law and traditions without compromise."

"Does the Queen have any influence on affairs of state?"

Gershon hesitated for a moment before answering. "Actually, she has quite a lot of influence. She is popular with the people. They agree that piety and effective rule of the kingdom are not contradictions. The aristocracy and wealthy merchants worry about losing influence. The conflict and uncertainty creates a sense of fear in Jerusalem."

I was now very confused. Even though we were supposed to listen and not speak, I asked, "Wasn't Queen Shlomtsion married to King Aristobulus?"

"Yes. But they had no children."

*Aba* looked at me. I should not have asked. However, anticipating my next question, he asked Gershon, "So, why is Shlomtsion still Queen?"

"After the King's death, according to levirate law, his brother, Alexander Yanai, married her, and she remained Queen. They have two children, so the succession is secured. I have met Queen Shlomtsion."

I could see *Aba* was surprised. So was I and we all looked at Gershon wanting to hear his story. *Aba* asked, "How did you meet her?"

"How I met the Queen is a long story."

"Before you answer, may I pour you another glass of wine?"

"Yes, please. Your wine is excellent."

I could see that the complement pleased *Aba* and he replied, "I usually prefer wine from the Galilee or sometimes from the coastal plain vineyards. In your honor, I bought a jug of wine imported from Armenia. The shop owner assured me his customers highly recommend this wine."

Gershon sniffed the wine for a moment before tasting. "This wine is wonderful."

"I am glad you like it."

"I hardly deserve such gracious hospitality from you and Noa. After all, you saved my life."

"You are too modest my friend. Now tell me how you met our Queen."

"I travel to Egypt several times a year to purchase and sell spices and wine. The Queen must have heard of my journeys and asked me to deliver a message to Queen Cleopatra. I felt greatly honored."

"Do you know what was in the message?"

"No. The scroll was sealed in a clay container that only Queen Cleopatra could open. A few days later, I was summoned to the court. Queen Cleopatra requested I deliver her response to Queen Shlomtsion in person. Nadav, please keep this discussion between us."

"Of course. Can you tell me a little more about Queen Shlomtsion? We had no idea she maintained relations with the Queen of Egypt."

"I wish I knew more. I learned that she knew Cleopatra's mother, also named Cleopatra and both consider her highly. I have the impression that Queen Shlomtsion involves herself in our relations with neighboring kingdoms."

"Do you think she would remain Queen if something happened to King Alexander Yanai before their sons are of age? Since he always leads the army, we worry he might be killed in battle."

Gershon scratched his head. "It is a frightening possibility. I think she would be an excellent ruler of Israel."

"Do you think the country would accept a Queen as the sole ruler?"

"I see no reason why not."

*Aba* glanced at *Ima* and said, "I agree completely. In fact, the Torah does not preclude a woman from undertaking a man's responsibilities or a man from a woman's functions. I think the important and respected role of women is well told in the books of Ruth, Esther, Judith, and Susana."

"Absolutely, my friend."

*Ima* smiled at me and rapped the table twice with her fist.

Gershon stood. "I am afraid I have lingered far too long at your table. I see we have bored our children to sleep. I thank you for your most gracious hospitality and a lovely Shabbat meal; it was extraordinary, and the warmth of your home wonderful."

"It was our pleasure."

"If you come to Jerusalem during a festival or any other time, you are more than welcome to stay in my home."

"We would like that."

"*Shabbat Shalom.*"

After I had gone to bed and had almost drifted off, *Aba's* voice woke me. He whispered to *Ima*. "Our little girl is growing up. She told me she does not want to marry me anymore."

*Ima* whispered. "Oh, and why is that?"

"She wants to marry Ariel instead. Noa, I am sure you noticed how they looked at each other."

"We all did. And, it is the same way I looked at you my husband once upon a time."

"And I you."

"Do you think Ariel knows she intends to marry him?" *Ima* asked.

"No, I don't think she has told him yet. I guess it is time we start thinking about a match for her. She is a smart girl and needs someone special to complement her. Ariel might be a good match. Gershon is a fine man, and his sons are well mannered."

*Ima* said, "It might be a good match. Then again, I always thought Amos is a perfect match for Elisheva."

"I think so too."

"I have the feeling that his parents would agree Elisheva and Amos would be good together."

"Noa, Let's talk about this another time. It has been a long day. Now let's sleep."

"Kiss me goodnight, husband."

"Goodnight, wife."

"Noa."

"What?"

"One more kiss."

*Ima* giggled. "Go to sleep Nadav."

***

What had been a perfect day was ending in disaster. My head was full of confusing thoughts. I could not sleep. How could *Ima* suggest Amos when *Aba* just told her how I feel about Ariel? And why would Aba agree with her?

In the middle of the night, I must have dozed off. At dawn, I awoke drenched in sweat. I dreamt that a lion was sitting on a hill observing a herd of goats. Silently, he crept toward the herd. Suddenly, the goats looked at the lion and attacked him. The lion disappeared.

Today started as all great days do: a gentle breeze, warm sun, and a brilliant blue, cloudless sky. I stretched and turned over. I wanted to hold onto the memory of last night's meal—and of Ariel. *Ima* called, and reluctantly, I rose to start the day.

After the morning meal, Micah came to my house and asked *Ima* if I could come out and play.

"Yes, of course, Micah, please come in while I call Elisheva."

As soon as I entered the cooking area, Micah said, "Miriam, Elisha, Ariel, and I will meet by the eastern section of the wall near the giant laurel tree. The one where we collected bay leaves for your *Ima's* cooking. Do you want to come?"

"Let me put on my sandals; wait for me."

***

Micah and I ran all the way to the giant laurel tree. I asked, "What should we play?"

Micah said, "How about David and Goliath? I'll be David and Elisha, who is bigger than all of us, can be Goliath."

Miriam glared at Micah. "What about us? Who will we be?

"Elisheva will be one of the Israelites. Ariel and you can be Philistines."

Miriam refused. "I don't want to be a Philistine."

Ariel then added, "I live in Jerusalem so I should be King David."

"Since my name is Elisheva, I want to be Bathsheba."

Miriam grinned and reminded everyone that David loved Bathsheba, and he saw her bathing naked on a rooftop. I wanted to laugh. Instead, I am sure I turned red from head to toe. Ariel blushed, stared at the ground, and was quiet.

I said, "If Ariel is King David, he has to recite some of his poetry. What is your poem, King David?"

Everyone looked at Ariel. Micah said, "Tell us your poem, King David."

After a long pause, Ariel raised his head, took half a step forward and said,

*"I live in a great city on a hill.*
*It is the center of the world.*
*I live there with my people.*
*I live there with my glorious past.*
*I live there with my beloved, and my beloved with me.*
*I will live there forever."*

We stood frozen in place—not a muscle moving. I was surprised. We were all surprised. Ariel had made up a real poem. I broke the silence saying, a bit more critically than I intended, "That sounds more like a poem of King Solomon than King David."

Micah acted bored. "This isn't fun, let's see what we can discover where we were digging last week at the corner of the wall near the terebinth tree."

Ariel asked, "What do you expect to find?"

"Usually we find some broken jugs or dishes. I once found a beautiful silver dish with intricate designs; it might have been King David's."

"Do you think it was that old?"

"Maybe. My *Aba* said a rich man might have lived there a long time ago and forgot it when he moved. Maybe it was a present from King David."

Ariel looked at Micah, "Do you always find something?"

"Usually. Sometimes all we find are rocks from old houses."

We all went to the corner of the wall, moved a few rocks, and dug a hole. Micah found a cup with part of the top broken. It could have been one recently discarded except the design was unlike our modern pottery—more like a cup from the old days. He stared at it a long time, moving his thumb over the surface feeling the design.

"What do you see?"

Micah, concentrating on the cup, hesitated before answering. "I admire the timeless beauty of the design and the workmanship."

Elisha stared at Micah. "It is just an old cup. Look at the arrowhead and metal spoon I found. It has the image of a lion on it."

Miriam held up a polished dear horn "I bet this held valuable cosmetics for a princess. Next to the horn, I found red beads, perhaps once part of a necklace or bracelet. They belonged to a princess from Egypt, maybe even from Queen Cleopatra's mother."

I did not find anything as valuable as Miriam and Elisha did, only a small box with two bronze needles. Although they were very old, I could still use them to sew tears in my robe.

Ariel found a ring and held it up for us to see. "When I marry, I will give this ring to my wife."

I was sure he looked at me. I blushed.

The day passed quickly, and it was time to go home. Ariel said they were leaving early the next morning, and he had to help his *Aba*. They would first travel to the big market in Kedesh before returning home to Jerusalem.

Micah spoke for all of us, "Ariel, we will miss you. I hope you will return soon. I know Elisheva wants you to come back so you can get married."

"I never said that." Softly, I added, "Come back, Ariel."

Ariel looked at the ground, and in an even softer voice, he said, "I will."

Since Ariel left Dan, I think about him all the time. I wonder what he is doing, if he remembers me, or whether I will ever see him again.

Sometimes I think meeting Ariel was a dream. One day he appeared and awakened a part of me I did not know existed. I felt in the midst of a dance written on our souls at the beginning of time. He bowed, I nodded, and neither of us looked at the other—except we did.

Ever since the day Ariel left, Micah avoided me. I was puzzled. One day, *Ima* asked if something was troubling me.

"Yes. Micah avoids me."

*Ima* stared at me for a few seconds. "Why?"

"I do not know."

"Can you guess?"

"Not really. I do not remember saying anything to make him angry."

"Maybe it is not something you said to him."

"What do you mean?"

"What was the last thing he said to you?"

"I remember. But why would he be angry at that?"

"He is not angry."

"What then? Oh."

I never ever wanted to hurt him. I think Micah finally knew we would never marry the day a traveler arrived at Dan and knocked on our door.

Months had passed since Ariel returned to Jerusalem. Every night before I fell asleep, I closed my eyes and pictured him in my mind. Maybe he forgot all about me. I was foolish to think we were meant to be together.

My parents invited Amos' family to our house for Shabbat dinner. I helped *Ima* prepare the meal just as I had when Gershon and his sons were here. I was mastering some of the cooking basics and enjoyed working with *Ima*. As before, I helped serve the meal. Amos seemed pleasant enough, and his parents were very nice. I suppose we could be happy together.

I saw Amos almost every day. We walked in the fields, picked flowers for Shabbat, and simply reveled in the grand display of life around us. Sometimes we watched the otters play in the water, or lying on our backs, we watched the birds circle, dive, and soar to great heights. We talked about our families.

Occasionally, on very clear days, I shielded my eyes with my palm and looked through the glare to the south.

Amos would ask, "What are you looking at?"

"Nothing. I only see the beauty of the valley."

"Oh. Me too."

"Amos, do you feel it?"

"Feel what?"

"The soil."

"Of course, silly. We are standing on it."

"No. I mean the land."

"I don't understand."

"It's us. It's our parents, our grandparents, our great grandparents."

Amos pointed to a grove of trees. "I'm hungry; let's find some figs to eat."

***

*Ima* was in the cooking area when I came home.

"Elisheva, I just made some sweet cakes. Have some tea and cake with me."

"I am not hungry. Amos and I just ate a lot of figs. Tea would be nice."

*Ima* tilted her head at my response. "Are you feeling all right, Elisheva?"

"I am fine."

"Well, you do not sound fine. Tell me what's wrong."

"Do you think I will be happy like you and *Aba*?"

*Ima* blinked. I thought I saw sorrow, worry, conviction, and resignation flash across her face. Maybe they were only my thoughts. She closed her mouth and frowned. Her lips started to move, but no words came out.

"Elisheva, I am sure it is your destiny to be happy."

"But what if it isn't?"

"People grow at different rates. A simple man today may be a great scholar tomorrow."

"Maybe it is not my destiny to marry."

She put her arms around me. I buried my head in her warm embrace and cried.

"Be patient, Elisheva. Everything works out for the best."

"What if it doesn't?"

# BOOK FOUR—TSFAT

CHAPTER TEN—AISHA—AUGUST 5731 (1971)

For the first time in months, Musa felt exhilarated. As he ran on the soft emerald grass under a cloudless sky, he could hear the murmur of the crowd. The player in front of him, with a big number three on his the purple shirt, kicked the ball hard. Moving by instinct, Musa leaped high, and the ball struck him on his chest. Tilting his shoulder inward, the ball slid down. He pushed the ball to his right. Reversing quickly to his left, he broke free of the defender and in a burst of speed moved toward the goal. The crowd roared.

Defenders converged to block his path. He sensed rather than saw his son on his right moving toward the net. Feinting left, he passed the ball to his right. Three strong players in purple jerseys crashed into the boy. The crowd screamed.

He sat up in bed suddenly wide-awake.

Aisha's face contorted as waves of pain wracked her body. She held her knees to her chest and moaned like a wounded animal. "Aisha, what is wrong?"

"My back. The pains are terrible. You have to help me. I think the baby is coming."

Blood soaked the sheets. Aisha was drenched in sweat and screamed again as another pain came.

"Isn't it too early for the baby?"

"Take me to the hospital. Something is wrong."

Musa tried to stay calm. He had no idea what to do.

"Musa, get the car. I must get to the hospital."

"Is it okay to travel?"

"Get the car now."

***

35

Musa brought Aisha a towel to stop the bleeding and wrapped her in a blanket. He helped her to the car and headed to the hospital at Tsfat forty-five minutes away. Aisha closed her eyes and seemed to be asleep. Her face was covered with sweat.

He drove fast. At Kiryat Shemona, the traffic light turned red. No one was on the road. Musa ignored the light and sped straight down Route 90. He drove through two more red lights.

Aisha suddenly screamed and thrashed her head from side to side, as sharp pains came in waves. Musa, now even more scared, drove faster. He drove through a red light at Rosh Pina. A police car came up behind him, his siren screaming and red lights flashing. "Pull over."

Musa drove faster. The police car accelerated, passed Musa, and forced him to the side.

The officer, gripping his pistol in one hand and a flashlight in the other, approached. "Is everything all right?"

"No. My wife is dying. I have to get her to the hospital."

The officer shined his flashlight on Aisha. "Why didn't you call an ambulance?"

"Please let me go."

The police officer hesitated. "Follow me. I will escort you. It will be okay. Let's make sure we get her there safely."

***

They pulled into the emergency room entrance at the Tsfat Regional Hospital. Musa ran in. "Someone help. My wife is dying."

Two nurses ran out to the car. Seeing the bloody towel between her legs, they yelled for a wheelchair. In seconds, they ran past the reception area to the Doctors' station.

The police officer took Musa's arm. "Park your car on the side and then register your wife." He stood with him as the receptionist filled out the entrance forms.

A male nurse came out and whispered to the officer. The officer turned to Musa and said, "Your wife will be fine. The doctors have examined her, and everything is under control. Good luck, Musa. In the future, call an ambulance."

The receptionist said, "Please wait here. I will check if you can see your wife."

"Thank you very much. I will wait here."

A few minutes later, she returned. "Come with me."

The attending Doctor was talking to Aisha when Musa entered. "Doctor, this is my husband, Musa."

"Musa, your wife will be fine. She started labor a little too early. We stopped the process. I want to run a few more tests before we make a decision whether to send her home or admit her. You were right to bring her tonight."

Musa took the Doctor's hand. "Thank you so much, Doctor. Why did this happen? Does she have a rare disease?"

"Actually premature labor is not uncommon. There are many reasons. It could be a kidney infection, a structural abnormality, or a genetic cause. Your wife is thin—she may not have gained enough weight during the pregnancy. I have ordered a series of tests and as soon as I get the results we will decide what to do. We may want to keep her here for a few weeks to ensure a healthy delivery. By the way, would you like to know whether the baby is a boy or girl?"

"You can tell? Please, is it a boy?"

"Yes. It is a boy."

Musa took Aisha's hand. "The Doctor says you will be fine. We are going to have a son."

Still holding hands, they closed their eyes and silently thanked Allah.

# BOOK FIVE—TRAVELS

*Ima's* hands were full of batter when we heard a loud knock at the door. "Elisheva, please see who it is."

As I opened the door, I almost jumped back. A giant of a man with a thick black beard stood holding his cap. His hands were huge. For a brief instant, I thought a bear stood in front of me. Then the bear spoke. His gentle voice surprised me.

"Good morning, Miss. My name is Caleb. Is this the house of Nadav and Noa?" He stared at me and smiled. A kind smile.

"Yes."

"Is Nadav at home? I bring a message for him." His eyes twinkled as he added, "and one for his beautiful daughter, Elisheva."

My mouth opened. I stood at the door staring at him. He waited. "*Aba* is home. I will call him." I turned to leave and stopped. "Where are my manners? Forgive me. Please come in."

\*\*\*

I sat in the cooking area trying to understand why this man wanted to see me. What could the message possibly be? He spoke to *Aba*, but I could not hear what he said. *Aba* listened intently and periodically nodded his head.

After what seemed a long time, Caleb sat opposite me. He furrowed his brow and bit his lip. Finally, he nodded his head and said a young man named Ariel Ben Gershon asked him to deliver a package to me. "I promised to put it in your hands."

I felt my heart beat faster. *Aba* reminded me to say thank you. *Ima* entered the room and stood next to me. She seemed just as puzzled as I was. My hands shook as I opened the gift. It was a beautiful blue stone. The letter took all the words from my head leaving a torrent of tears instead.

*Dear Elisheva,*

*I will soon leave Kedesh for home to my city on the hill.*

*I enjoyed very much the Shabbat meal you made with your Ima. Dan was the best part of my trip, and the best part of Dan was meeting you. I am sending you a stone from Elath I thought beautiful. I hope you will treasure it and remember me.*

*Ariel*

*Ima* put her arm around me. What happened? What is wrong? She took the letter from my hand. "Oh, Elisheva" and held me even tighter.

Caleb leaned back in his chair, a faraway look in his dark eyes. He then said, "I joined Gershon, Yoav, and Ariel at sunrise as they left Dan. I also traveled to Jerusalem and asked if I could accompany them. I suggested a route that had a perfect place to camp before the hard climb to Kedesh. The air was still and even though early, we could tell it would be a warm day. As we climbed higher the air cooled and we kept a fast pace. After a few hours, we stopped to rest the animals and looked back at Dan, now below us. Mount Hermon towered above the plain and to the north; we saw a range of snow-covered mountains.

"As we caught our breath, Yoav punched his brother in the shoulder and asked if he missed Dan. Ariel shoved him to the side and asked 'Why did you do that?'

Yoav grinned and said, 'Well, little brother, you seemed quite interested in someone.'

'So? She is a very good cook.'

'Anything else, little brother?'

'She is very pretty.'

Yoav asked, 'And...,'

Gershon interrupted the boys. 'Enough. We have a long distance yet to go.'"

My eyes opened wide. "Did Ariel really say I was pretty?"

Caleb winked at me. "Who else? Now where was I?" He scratched his head. "Oh yes. Late in the afternoon, as we approached the trade route to the Beqaa Valley and Dameseq to the north and the Merom Valley and Megiddo to the south, we came to the ruins of the ancient city, Evel Beit Ma'acah.

"Gershon studied the remains of buildings reduced to piles of rubble and covered with weeds and asked 'what happened here?'

"I explained that eight hundred years earlier, the Assyrians destroyed the city and the great city of Hatzor farther to the south. Ma'acah, King David's fourth wife and the *Ima* of Avshalom and Tamar, lived here a thousand years ago. The ghosts of the long dead city filled the air around us. We bowed our heads and stood for a moment in reverent silence.

"We stopped for the night in a narrow, steep ravine scented with the sweet smell of fig trees and colored by a profusion of wildflowers and thorny raspberry bushes. The low murmur of a gentle wind and the fast flowing water of a stream fed by a spectacular waterfall, narrow at the top and spreading out toward the bottom, created a soothing harmony. At the top of the ravine, a family of wild pigs paused in their search for food to study us as intently as, in return, we observed them.

"We made camp above the waterfall, built a fire and enjoyed the serenity of a clear sky brilliant with countless patterns of stars. As a precaution, we kept the fire burning all night to protect us from the wolves and bears that frequented the ravine."

Caleb rubbed his beard and waited until I looked at him.

"Daybreak came late deep in the ravine. The sky brightened to a pallet of pastel colors while we remained in the shadow of the night long enough to hug our memories."

*Ima* stood near the cooking area listening to Caleb's story. She asked him to pause for a moment.

"Sure."

She returned with a cup of wine, a few pieces of bread, and some green olives.

"Thank you, Noa. My throat is a little dry from all this storytelling." Caleb took a long drink. "We set off to the north climbing a narrow path and passing three more waterfalls. Leaving the ravine, we entered a small fertile valley surrounded by tall weatherworn mountains. Golden sunflowers that slowly followed the sun's movement across the sky shared the field with wheat swaying gracefully in the morning wind. Ripples, like ocean waves, flowed back and forth across the wheat field.

"Gershon purchased several jugs of deep-yellow oil pressed from the sunflower seeds. We loaded the animals and turned south for the steep climb to the crest of the Naphtali range.

"At first, the path was difficult. When we reached the crest, progress was rapid. Ariel and Yoav ran ahead stopping to view the Merom Valley on their left. They hoped to see the Great Sea to the west, but only a sliver of blue that might have been water was visible.

"The sun was setting when we first viewed Kedesh rising above a beautiful valley of vineyards famous for fruity and dry red wines. We pushed on and entered the city gates just before nightfall.

"Despite the short journey from Dan, Ariel, Yoav, and Gershon were obviously tired from the climb. I ached all over. My legs were sore, and my knees hurt. I tell you; it was hard keeping up with those youngsters. I fell asleep the minute I laid down.

"The next morning, Gershon woke us at sunrise to arrive at the market early and sell their remaining spices. The trading went much quicker than Gershon anticipated. One merchant, Hiram, an old friend from the coastal city of Tyre, bought the entire remaining stock of spices.

"Business complete, Gershon purchased several amphorae of high-quality imported wine and two large amphorae of Tyre's famous purple dye used to color clothes and prayer shawls. The purchases would slow their return to Jerusalem but bring a substantial profit."

Caleb tore off a piece of bread and drank some more wine. *Ima* brought more. "May I bring you something else, Caleb?"

"No thank you. Ariel and Yoav asked about the history of Tyre. I also wanted know more. I could tell that pleased Gershon. He told us, 'Tyre was built about the same time as the Exodus from Egypt. Alexander the Great conquered Tyre by building a causeway to the island city. It was a massive undertaking that still connects Tyre to the mainland. The Armenian King, Tigranes, now threatens the city and Tyre has appealed to Rome for protection.'"

I looked at Caleb trying to understand the importance of what he said. I do not know much about international affairs, but it seemed to me that Tyre is trading one bad situation for another. So I asked Caleb if he thinks Tyre is making a good decision."

"You are a bright one. I see why Ariel likes you. Gershon asked Hiram the same question. Hiram frowned and answered that bandits routinely intercepted trade from Kedesh to Bar Am and Tyre. Pirates that cruise the Great Sea threaten any cargoes that do leave Tyre. Trade with Rome and Greece is a fraction of what it once was. Tyre needs help otherwise an important part of its economy will be ruined."

It seemed to me there was fighting everywhere and that evil triumphed. I wondered what my future held in such a dangerous world. If only Ariel would protect me. If only. Then I would be safe.

"Hiram said the bandit gang at Anafa frightens everyone in the Galilee. King Marion feels that since the bandits are based in your territory, King Alexander Yanai should take action against them.

"Gershon suddenly understood what Hiram intended and said, 'Hiram, the people in Dan would certainly agree.'

Then Hiram asked, 'Gershon, would you agree to deliver a message to your King that King Marion is willing to join forces to put an end to this threat? We depend on the produce of the Galilee.'"

"What did Gershon say?" I asked.

"He didn't answer right away. Gershon is a thoughtful man. But he did agree. The two old friends hugged and wished each other safe travels and good trading.

"As he started to leave, Hiram stopped and told Gershon there had been trouble on the road thorough Samaria. 'You might consider returning to Jerusalem from the coast.'

"Gershon did not seem troubled by this news. 'I am glad you told me. I should like to see the Great Sea again.'

"Before turning toward Bar Am, Hiram added, 'I have heard that Jerusalem is the most beautiful and holy of cities; maybe someday in the future I will visit.'

"Gershon smiled, 'Please do. You are always welcome in my home. Good bye for now my friend.'"

This frightened me. On one hand, it was good news that King Alexander Yanai would learn about the bandit raids. As soon as he knows about our trouble, I was sure he would send soldiers to help. It had not occurred to me that Ariel's journey back to Jerusalem could be dangerous.

Caleb downed the rest of his wine in one big gulp. With the back of his hand, he wiped some that had drizzled down his beard. Setting down the cup, he stared at the ceiling and took a deep breath. "Before leaving Kedesh, Gershon prepared a message for Nadav saying that he would report the danger to the court in Jerusalem."

Smiling at me and with a twinkle in his eye, Caleb added, "Don't worry little one. Your Ariel and his family are safe. I suggested that Ariel send you a message."

Caleb grinned as he told me how he watched Ariel struggle to write something.

"You should have seen him. He walked in a circle stabbing the air with his finger trying to find the right words. I thought he would never write the note." Caleb stuck out the tip of his tongue and slid it to the corner of his mouth. "Like this when he writes. He's a thinker, that boy." Caleb's laughter echoed against the walls. He winked. "And we know who he thinks about the most."

That night before I slept, I whispered, "Oh Ariel. Don't forget me."

Everyone was still asleep when I woke. It was early, and I listened to the happy music of the birds. I looked again at the gift Ariel had sent me. I held it tight against my chest and stared into the dark trying to see the future.

I heard *Ima* in the cooking area and went to help prepare the morning meal. Her body swayed in a happy rhythm as she hummed a joyful melody. "Good morning, Elisheva. How did you sleep?"

I put my arms around her, held her tight, and said, "Oh very well. I had such a beautiful dream."

She kissed me and asked me to set the table.

Caleb joined us, and I poured him a cup of tea. I hoped he did not want to leave and would continue to tell me about Ariel's trip.

Caleb stretched his legs, and while sipping the hot tea, he continued his tale.

"We left Kedesh and after a tiring day stopped for the night at the ruins of Hatzor."

I remembered that Hatzor was one of King Solomon's fortress cities that defended the central approach to Israel.

"Early the next morning, sticking to the crest of the Naphtali range, we reached the city of Tsfat. We were high above the Merom Valley and could see forever."

I said, "We see Tsfat from Dan. Every month they light a fire to announce the new moon. I heard that the fires are set on mountaintops starting in Jerusalem."

Caleb patted my hand. "Yes it is a good system, except when the Samaritans put out the fires."

"So that is why some months we do not see the signal."

Caleb nodded and continued. "We stayed in Tsfat an extra day resting the animals, content to laze in the cool air with the pleasing views of the distant

46

harp-shaped Kinneret Sea. We were safe from bandits as long as we kept to the high country.

"From Tsfat, we descended to the former Greek town of Tsipori to the west of Nazareth near the spice fields at Beit Lechem. Tsipori, at the entrance to the lush Izrael Valley, was famous for the colorful mosaic floors celebrating the Greek god of wine.

"Our path now took us to Megiddo and the Sea Road—so often traveled by Egyptian armies heading north to combat the Hittites—that led to the ancient port at Dor. Gershon explained that the earliest trading by sea used the port at Dor and over the centuries, hundreds of ships had sunk in the bay.

"Ariel had never seen the Great Sea. We slept on a luxurious bed of pure white beach sand under a canopy of countless brilliant points of light. I slept far from the shore. Gershon, Yoav, and Ariel wanted to sleep closer to the water. I warned them it was a mistake. They insisted.

"During the night, the sea reached up the shore, and they were completely soaked. The next morning, I tried to not to laugh when I asked how they slept. They looked away rather than admit they should have listened."

I listened entranced as Caleb described how the well-traveled road from the coast to Jerusalem started on a gentle slope through a fertile plain leading to beautiful valleys sheltered by rounded foothills. Every day they met travelers and other traders along the road. At night, they camped together trading goods and stories of remarkable wonders in the world.

"Travelers spoke of distant lands around the Great Sea. They said in many lands, it rained in the summer. Your Ariel was astounded. He thought, just as written in Ecclesiastics, the first rain came in the fall and the last rain in the spring—and each had a special name." Caleb laughed—a loud booming laugh. "It never occurred to the boy that it could be different elsewhere."

I was so absorbed in Ariel's adventures that I had not eaten a bite. *Ima* gently reminded me to eat something. Caleb nodded and winked at me.

"We woke early and left camp after a quick meal. We entered a narrow gorge that would lead us straight to Jerusalem. Even though now it would be a hard climb, our pace quickened."

Caleb described the moment when above and before them they saw Jerusalem. "We felt the thrill every traveler to Jerusalem experiences when he sees the heart and soul of Israel and before him the history of a thousand years.

"None of us spoke.

"Gershon broke the silence. 'Let's go home.'"

Micah is my best friend. He will always be my best friend. It did not matter to me that his foot pointed in the wrong direction. I never thought him a cripple.

Many times, he would look at something in total fascination as if he just discovered the most amazing thing in the world. He often surprised me with what he saw. I saw a flower; he would tell me to touch it, feel how soft the petals were, and look at the intricate design and colors in the center. He wondered why all flowers did not smell the same.

Spider's webs frighten me. He tells me to look at the web's embroidery—when adorned with a necklace of dew, it has an exquisite beauty. After he explains what he sees, I feel like I am blind. I did not notice he limped.

I never laugh or make fun of him like some of our friends. It hurts me to see him smile and absorb the teasing. I am sure he wishes that he too could run and jump and not be left behind. I look into his eyes and see someone special. He has a gift and will accomplish great things.

Several months have passed since Ariel left and we all played together. I am sure that Micah saw an undertone of feelings between Ariel and me and sensed we spoke a dialect of an ancient language that only we understood. I am sure Micah hoped for a long time that Ariel would forget me and I him.

Today I went to his house and showed him the gift Ariel sent me. I was so excited and wanted to share my joy. Micah took the stone and held it for a minute. With a sad look, he placed it on my palm, squeezed my hand, and murmured, "It is beautiful—like you."

I squeezed his hand in return.

I broke his heart.

My brother returned from the market distressed. His expression frightened me. "Itai, what happened?"

"*Ima* sent me to the market to buy eggs."

"What is so worrying about buying eggs?"

"It is not the eggs, Elisheva."

"What then is the trouble?"

"Nothing you have to worry about."

Now I was even more curious. "Tell me, Itai. You must tell me."

"I must? Then I will tell you. Traders in the market discussed Rome's relentless conquest of countries from Spain to the shores of the inland Black Sea. A crowd gathered around to hear the news and opinions. The consensus was that Rome wanted to rule the world.

"A man from Crete said the Roman Consul, Sulla, completed a brutal subjugation of Greece and crossed to Asia to attack Pontus—following in the footsteps of the Greeks when hundreds of year earlier they defeated Troy. Many said there was little doubt that King Mithridates VI of Pontus and his son-in-law King Tigranes of Armenia would challenge Roman ambitions in Asia. A large war to our north is imminent."

I told Itai it was ironic that the men who founded Rome and now attacked Pontus descended from those who abandoned their families and fled Troy. Itai looked frightened.

He stared at me. "Do you know what would happen to us if thousands of well-armed and well-trained soldiers attack Dan? These men are taught to work together to kill anyone and everyone in their path."

"Won't King Alexander Yanai protect us? He wouldn't let an enemy attack Israel."

"I hope not. However, he does not always win his battles. It would be a catastrophe if he lost defending Dan."

"What else did the traders say?"

"One man suggested the endless conflicts attest to a constant struggle between good and evil. A trader from Egypt argued it has always been and will always be so. The only thing agreed on was that Israel is more prosperous and safer today than ever: relations are good with the Kingdoms of Lebanon and Egypt, and Queen Cleopatra is a powerful ally. That reassured me until a small man standing near a fruit cart struck a somber note. He said Israel's wealth and success make it an attractive target.

"So far, though, Israel is not in danger as long as Rome concentrates its efforts in the west against the tribes in Gaul and Germany and to the north in Pontus."

"Itai, for how long will we be safe? What do the people in the market say will happen to us?"

The tales of our defeat by Babylon five hundred years earlier haunted me. I did not want to leave my paradise for exile in a strange land. I wanted to stay with my family in the Merom Valley forever. I pray Israel will be safe.

"We are protected in Dan; aren't we Itai?"

It is a year since Ariel left. Today a stranger came to our door. For a brief moment, I thought it was Gershon. He introduced himself as Ariel's uncle, Amnon. He was neither fat nor thin. I sensed he was a very strong man. His neatly trimmed hair was a deep black. He appeared to be much younger than Gershon.

Amnon said he was in Beit She'an. He heard so much about Dan from his brother, he decided to extend his trip. Gershon insisted he deliver warm regards to *Aba* and *Ima*. He nodded to me and said he had special regards to me from Ariel.

I stood there with my mouth open like a complete fool. This was the best day of my whole life. *Aba* put his hand on my shoulder, "Elisheva, invite our guest in."

Out of the corner of my eye, I noticed *Aba* smile as I asked Amnon if he would tell me about Ariel. "Did he say anything about me?"

"I will tell you everything, Elisheva. First, I must speak to Nadav. I won't be long"

"I will wait in the cooking area." I tried to be patient. Minutes seemed like hours. Is it good news? Is Ariel safe? Did he make it to Jerusalem or did something happen on the way? I did not notice that I nervously twirled my hair. *Ima* took my hand and held it tight.

"Be patient, Elisheva. Would you prepare something for our guest to eat? I am sure he is hungry and thirsty."

"What should I prepare?"

"A small plate of cheese, wine, and some of the roasted red peppers we made yesterday would be nice."

When Amnon came to the cooking area, he sat opposite me. Looking at the food and wine, he asked, "Is that for me?"

"Yes."

"Thank you so much, Elisheva. That is very considerate of you.

"When Gershon, Yoav, and Ariel arrived home, the whole family wanted to hear everything about their adventure. Yoav spoke about the Great Sea. Everyone listened in disbelief when he said that in the middle of the night the sea reached to where they slept and soaked them with salty water. Ariel's sisters, Shulamite and Tamar, thought it strange the sea would rise and fall; they swore if ever they slept by the sea they would stay up all night to watch the water rise. Ariel told them about the day they arrived at Dan and how a young girl helped her friend run toward the wall. Yamima said the story of a lame boy rescued by a wine merchant reached Jerusalem several weeks ago."

Amnon paused. "Were you that girl?"

"Yes."

Amnon nodded. "I thought so."

Amnon had a huge grin as he described how his brother told Yamima the boys were a great help and that Ariel seemed taken with a girl in Dan.

My face must have turned the color of red poppies. Could this really be true? Did I hear right? Ariel really did look at me at the Shabbat dinner.

Amnon gazed at the pots hung on the opposite wall and did not notice my reaction. He kept talking.

"The next morning I went with Gershon to the palace to seek an audience with the King. The King's secretary, Eli, said the King could not see us this day, but that we should return tomorrow for an audience.

\*\*\*

"Yoav and Ariel went to the warehouse and spent the next few hours organizing the Galilee purchases. I met Ariel just as he and Yoav finished their work and like thirsty travelers, they went to see friends, breathe the air of the city, and feast on the noise and excitement of Jerusalem.

"Ariel spent the afternoon wandering the narrow streets of the upper city. Smells of the city—baking bread, onions frying with small pieces of lamb to be wrapped in lafa or pita, pungent waste from animals mixed with the complicated odors of people—flooded his senses. I am sure he relived memories of running through narrow alleys with friends, the laughter of young girls, and the frightening stench of fear and death when fighting broke out between the Sadducees and Pharisees.

"In the sunlight, Ariel noticed, as if for the first time, building walls shining a golden yellow as if the city was constructed of stone laced with gold. Bright colored awnings shaded rooms adding a sense of gaiety to the first city of the world. Sometimes, Ariel heard artisans, merchants, and every once in a while a brilliant women's voice singing songs and hymns to God. He liked best the songs of children at play."

I closed my eyes and visualized Ariel walking through the crowded alleys and breathing the smells of home. I could hear the songs and imagine the children playing in the streets. Jerusalem had to be the most wonderful place in the world.

Amnon paused for a few minutes as if recreating in his mind the images of walking with Ariel in Jerusalem. Amnon said people nodded to Ariel as they passed. He smiled in return. He sang songs learned in Dan and from travelers on the road to Jerusalem. Occasionally, people asked where he learned that tune. He told them about his travel to the north and the people he met.

"Ariel walked through his favorite areas of the city: streets filled with leather workers, glass blowers, jewelry artists, metal workers, weavers, furniture makers, tool shops, wine merchants, scribes, scroll dealers, and makers of farm tools. Each street had a special controlled rhythm of song synchronizing the pace of work. The bustle of the workers, the beat of hammers, and the frequent blessing of work spiced with an occasional curse added to the vigorous melody of creation.

"My nephew lingered by the furniture makers shop breathing in the sweet smell of sawdust. The work of the carpenters fascinated him as they chiseled, planed, sanded, and fit pieces of wood together to make chairs, tables, and cabinets. One of the carpenters, a big man with bushy black eyebrows, shouted, 'Boy, would you like to try to plane a piece of wood?'

"Ariel looked surprised. 'I would, thank you.'

'Hold the plane this way and lightly slide it along the wood.'

'Like this?' Ariel asked. A thin shaving peeled from the wood.

'Very good, boy. You have good hands. Would you like a job?'

"Ariel said, 'It looks like great work, but I am learning the spice and wine business. Tell me, Sir; could you make small boxes to hold spices or small jugs of wine meant to be gifts?'

"The carpenter thought for a moment before answering. 'That would be a challenge; I could try.' He took Ariel's hand, and said, 'I am called Moshe.'

'My name is Ariel Ben Gershon.'

'Come back again, Ariel.'"

I had not thought of Ariel as a craftsman. "Do you think Ariel wants to be a cabinet maker?" I asked.

Amnon said, "It is hard to tell. He seems to have many interests. I think he is more interested in the challenges of business."

I was not surprised and nodded my head. "Please, Uncle Amnon continue."

He looked at me puzzled for a brief minute. "Thank you, Elisheva." Amnon scratched the side of his head. "I left the City of David with Ariel, and we walked east and south toward the Siloam Pool and the Kidron Valley. Do you know why it is a special place?"

"No."

"It is where King David, a thousand years earlier, made Jerusalem the home of the covenant and the leading city of the world. Jews still come to this spot to enter the city on the three great festivals—Passover, Shavuot, and Succoth. So too do invading armies. A tunnel connects the pool to the Gihon Springs outside the wall. Ariel always wondered how the builders fixed the path to arrive at the springs. My nephew is curious about everything. He is a smart boy.

"Shining in the brilliant sunshine to the north of the springs stood the Temple. Rebuilt after the exile in Babylonia, it dominated the city. Ariel said he learned that the Temple King Solomon built was far grander. I put my arm on Ariel's shoulder and said, 'Maybe it was. But the beauty held in the soul of a people is never diminished or lost by the appearance of a building.'

"I stood with Ariel on the thick wall overlooking the steep ravines surrounding Jerusalem. Although the city appears impregnable, it is not. The walls have been breached in the past. Invading armies consider the holiest of cities and the house of God nothing more than a source of wealth."

Ariel and I had learned the same lessons. I saw the same history repeated in the Galilee. Invaders looted the wealth of many generations and reduced once thriving cities to rubble. I just could not understand why always war? I feared that our future too, like the past, would hold brutality and death.

"My nephew and I looked to the Temple. I asked him what he thought. He surprised me. He thought of the poetry and songs of the warrior King David, the erotic poems of King Solomon, and the writings on law, society, philosophy, and history."

Now Amnon lowered his voice so that only I could hear.

"Ariel told me how you taunted his poem as reminiscent of the Song of Songs rather than the psalms of King David. It really bothered him. I suspect he meant it that way."

\*\*\*

Amnon said he had to leave and thanked us for receiving him so graciously.

*Aba* said it was our honor and thanked Amnon for the message. *Ima* asked if he would stay and share our evening meal with us. She served a simple meal with the most delicious goat cheese I had ever eaten. She said the goat herder found a special field with the sweetest grass and most fragrant flowers. All the flavors melded into a fantastic cheese.

As we ate, Amnon said that Gershon told Yamima how Ariel and Elisheva 'secretly' looked at each other. Gerhson imitated Ariel and Elisheva glancing across the table and looking away quickly. The news startled Yamima. She screamed, "He is only twelve, still a boy."

Amnon laughed and said, "Without blinking an eye, Gershon replied that Elisheva is ten. Gershon winked at Yamima and said, 'It reminded me of the first time I saw you. I bless our parents for leading us to each other. Now it is time to lead our children. Maybe we can take a trip to Dan; you could meet Nadav and Noa.'"

I must have heard wrong. Did he say that Gershon and Yamima talked about Ariel and me? Maybe I am dreaming. Did he say that Gershon wants Yamima to come to Dan? Did Ariel's *Aba* want us to marry? Is his *Ima* against us marrying? Maybe she wants Ariel to marry someone in Jerusalem.

Amnon continued: "Gershon said Yoav is ready to take over much of the trading in Jerusalem. Meanwhile, Ariel can trade in the Galilee and center the northern business in Dan; not right away, Ariel still has much to learn. He is a smart boy, learns fast, and has the temperament to do well. In the end, our business will cover the whole kingdom. It would be a big step for our family.

"Reluctantly, Yamima admitted that now is the time to consider Ariel's future. Even Adam and Eve grew up and had to leave the Garden of Eden."

I twirled my hair with my finger as I waited for Amnon to tell me about Ariel's friends. My heart beat faster. I was afraid of what I would hear. Why would Ariel even look at me? His *Aba* met Queen Shlomtsion. His friends live in the most magnificent city in the world. I am from a small town, far from the center of the world. Probably, no one in Jerusalem ever heard of Dan. Ariel's friends probably laughed when he told them about a girl who lived in the north near the border. Still, I leaned forward to hear every word as Amnon resumed.

"Ariel went to see his best friend, Boaz. Arriving early, he waited on the step outside Boaz's house, content to watch people on their way to shops or hurrying home."

As Amnon paused to sip some wine, I asked if Ariel told Boaz anything about Dan.

Amnon patted my hand gently. "Patience, little one. Ariel told Boaz he saw places they had learned about in history. He spent time in Dan and made several new friends: one girl in particular."

My eyes opened wide. "What? Did he mean me?"

Amnon did not answer. "Boaz now paid more attention to his friend. Before Ariel could continue, he told him that Rachel asked about him while he was gone."

I crossed my arms and hugged my shoulders. I started to rock back and forth. I was right. It was stupid of me to think Ariel liked me. It was only play. I was sure he knew many girls in Jerusalem.

"Let me finish."

I looked up and tried hard to smile. "I am sorry, please continue."

58

"Ariel seemed not to hear Boaz. 'Her name is Elisheva. She is beautiful, slight of frame, and moves with a grace and fluid movements of a gazelle. Her eyes are brown with flecks of green and her hair a beautiful shade of auburn. She is quiet, observing and delighting in the world around her. Her face is enchanting. She has a beautiful mouth and lips. Her smile radiates warmth and a love of humanity. She is highly intelligent—reads, writes, and knows poetry. She moves in rhythm with the wind, the sun, and the music of the birds. I wrote her a letter and sent her a gift from Kedesh.'"

"Ariel said that about me?"

"Yes. I saw Ariel, and we talked for a while before Boaz joined us. I heard the whole conversation."

"Are you sure that is what he said?"

Amnon stared at me and did not reply.

"Please excuse me. I am just so happy. I will not interrupt again."

"Boaz was surprised. I think almost in shock. 'My brother, I believe you are in love. But what about Rachel?'"

I could not help myself. I had to ask Amnon about Rachel. Is she pretty? Does Ariel love her? I was afraid of the answer, but I had to know.

Amnon stroked his beard and sighed. "I have seen Rachel. Like her namesake, she is pretty with straight black hair, green eyes, good teeth, and well-balanced facial features. I understand she is good with her lessons even if not the best in the class. She often makes people laugh, loves to laugh herself, and sings well."

The room was suddenly hot. Rachel seems to me like a wonderful girl. If she lived in Dan, we might be friends. I could understand if Ariel liked her. She was pretty, lived in Jerusalem, a longtime friend of Ariel, and I am far away in Dan. It would not surprise me if Ariel wanted to be with Rachel and did not think of me anymore. I am sure she would make an excellent wife for Ariel.

Amnon must have read my thoughts. "Elisheva, my nephew is considered one of the best in his class. He excels in all his classes mastering, without difficulty, the study of our laws, culture, and heritage. He is ready to discuss or debate the latest story, portion of the Torah, history lesson, marvel at the wisdom of Moses, listen to any discussion on nature, and even write poetry. Without noticing, he is at the center of his group. Rachel often pretends not to see him or feigns indifference even though I am sure she wants him to notice her.

"As far as I know, my nephew and Rachel are friends—just as he is with everyone in his group. However, the way he talks about you, it is clear he thinks of you differently."

I tried to remain calm. I could not help myself. I did not want to cry. I tried not to. The tears came anyway.

Amnon leaned forward and covered my hand with his. I looked up at him. He blinked several times. "Elisheva, my nephew did not stop talking about you."

I could not stop crying.

Amnon now told me how he accompanied his brother to meet King Alexander Yanai. *Aba* and *Ima* stepped closer to listen. Ariel's *Aba* was such an important man. I was proud that I helped serve him the Sabbath meal.

"After morning prayers, Gershon and I went to the palace gate. A guard escorted us to Eli's office. He informed us that the King requested that Gershon deliver the message to Queen Shlomtsion. Eli brought us to the Queen's office and introduced us.

Queen Shlomtsion asked Gershon if he know what was in the message. 'No, My Queen.' My friend, Hiram, did say his King feels beset by many hostile forces. Sulla's army is to the north in Pontus. Bandits attack on land and pirates on the Great Sea. I myself witnessed a bandit attack in Dan.'

"Queen Shlomtsion opened the message. She thought for a few minutes, and then said, 'This is serious. Tell me more about the problems at Dan.'

"Gershon told her that bandits prey on the town: they steal crops, rape women, and capture farmers and merchants for ransom. The people have no means to fight back. The city walls are strong; once inside, they feel safe.

"The Queen asked about the people of Dan. Gershon said they are pious and live in rhythm with the Sabbath, the rains, and by the recorded times for planting and harvesting. They have great respect for their King and Queen; 'they value your piousness,' he said.

"The Queen thanked Gershon and said that she would discuss the message with the King. 'If the King wishes to answer, would you agree to deliver a response?' she asked Gershon.

"Gershon told her it would be a great honor."

I thought about everything Amnon told me. I wanted to believe him. Who knew if it was written at the beginning of time that Ariel and I were meant to be together?

Amnon looked at me and no doubt guessed what I was thinking. "Let me tell you about Ariel's *Ima*, Yamima. She is a lovely woman. Highly intelligent, pretty with green eyes and long black hair pulled back and tied with a strip of red string. She is short; Yoav and Ariel are already taller than her. You can talk to her about anything. She is an excellent dancer and writes poetry.

"Like every *Ima*, she wants her sons to stay in Jerusalem close to her; she wants her house filled every Shabbat with sons, daughters, daughters-in-law, sons-in-law and many grandchildren."

I did not understand why Amnon told me this. I sensed he was about to say something important. I could not begin to guess what it might be. "Did Ariel tell his *Ima* about me?" I asked.

"No. He didn't."

"Oh."

"Yamima liked Gershon's idea that Yoav manage the trading business in Jerusalem. She also thought it a good opportunity for Ariel to establish a branch in the north."

I did not know Ariel was coming to Dan to start a business. I wanted to ask when, how, by himself, with his brother. With great difficulty, I remained quiet and listened. I leaned forward not to miss a single word.

"Gershon received a message to meet with the King and Queen. This was the third time in the past two weeks. Both Gershon and Yamima understood that politics brings out the worst in people, especially in the

62

competition for favor with the King or Queen. They were naïve about the infighting and were drawn into a world with enemies they were not even smart enough to identify.

"King Alexander Yanai requested that Gershon return to Dan with a unit of soldiers after the fall harvest. Gershon would organize the citizens of Dan to support an attack on the bandits at Anafa."

I did not understand and could not even guess why Amnon was telling me all this. What did business, the palace court, political infighting have to do with Ariel?

"Gershon could not refuse the King. Besides, he told Yamima this trip comes at just the right time. 'Our son dreams a lot about the girl he met in Dan. She seems to me special.'"

I gasped. I could feel myself turning red from my ears to my toes. Tears came to my eyes. I smiled; I cried. *Ima* looked at *Aba* with a barely concealed smile. Amnon stared at the wall behind me.

"Gershon said, 'Yamima, come with me; meet the girl and her parents. If Ariel and Elisheva seem a good match, we could ask them if they would consider marriage with Ariel.'"

*Ima* smiled. *Aba* frowned. I jumped up and put my arms around *Ima*. She held me and then said, "Let us listen to the rest of Amnon's story."

"The idea shocked Yamima. Finally, she said, 'It is simply not possible to leave. Who would look after the children? It is too hot to travel now. The trip is too dangerous. What would happen to our children if we do not return?'

"Gershon said the plan is to leave in the fall with soldiers from Jerusalem joined by reinforcements from Jericho and return before the weather turns cold. 'Shulamite and Tamar are old enough to take care of Hillel,' he said. 'Yoav, Ariel, and our families would help, if necessary.' Gershon added that he could guarantee their help if he promised to bring back some fine Roman and Armenian wines.

"Yamima did not think long and agreed to go. She should meet this girl. Maybe it would be a good match. She asked if he had thought about a dowry. He had not, but was not worried. He told her, 'Business is good, and with Yoav and Ariel about to assume a greater role, it will only get better. Nadav and Noa want only the best for their daughter, and I cannot imagine a better match than with our Ariel.'"

Still crying, I hugged Amnon and ran from the room.

I hoped Yamima would like me. I hoped Ariel would not change his mind.

# BOOK SIX—GHAJAR

The civil war in Syria changed everyone's views. The people of Ghajar divided into several groups: some content in Israel; some supporting the Syrian President, Bashar Assad; and others arguing for a future Syria governed by the rebels. No one, though, could guess who would be the rebels' leader, or how a new regime would treat the Alawites and Druze. The future of Syria looked bleak no matter who prevailed.

A war-torn landscape, brutality, starvation, and death replaced the simple pleasures of a warm home and the laughter of children. Only survival mattered. Musa heard on the news that government and rebel forces fought without concern for civilians. They destroyed homes, looted shops and leveled villages. Musa feared for his relatives.

Musa was born and lived his whole life in Ghajar. Although he and most in the village remained Syrian citizens, they also became Israeli citizens. Over the years, Musa realized the Israelis were a compassionate people. Even now, without seeking acknowledgment, they brought wounded Syrian combatants and civilians, left near the border, to Israeli hospitals.

As the family patriarch, honor demanded Musa help. If he raised money to hire a good lawyer, he could appeal to the government to allow his relatives to settle in Israel. He could help them find work and establish a life in Ghajar.

He read in the newspapers that private collectors paid extraordinary prices for even fragments of a scroll. If the two-thousand-year-old scrolls found at Qumran were a national treasure, the scroll he found, written earlier, might bring enough to save his family.

As Musa sat on his patio and stared in the direction of Metula, he sipped sweet tea flavored with spearmint and planned how to sell the scroll. If the police caught him, it would be a great tragedy. Israeli prisons were not nearly as bad as Syrian or Lebanese prisons, but they were not pleasant either. His family would suffer. He would not see his sons marry.

There was a man, Ratib, from a village in the Golan, who smuggled contraband across the border from Lebanon to Israel. He would know to whom to sell a valuable scroll with ancient Hebrew writing. Musa hesitated to approach this man but could not think of any other way to raise the money.

Aisha pleaded with him not to dig up the scroll. "It is too dangerous— if you are caught what will happen to us? Musa, please don't do this."

She waited for him to answer. With a sad almost fatalistic response, he said, "I must do it. Our family's honor demands I help. I have no choice."

***

Ratib lived in a compound that housed his wife along with their sons and their families. He was short and rotund. It was hard to tell if he was fatter or taller. He wore black metal-rimmed spectacles that magnified his eyes. Many people would have laughed when they saw him—until they looked into his eyes and saw a ruthlessness that warned people to be careful. He was a man to be feared. He was also charming.

He received Musa in the salon, furnished with plush red sofas, pale Persian and blood-red Afghani rugs. Heavy drapes opened onto a magnificent view of the snow-covered Mount Hermon. The luxury of the room left Musa uneasy. Perhaps, Aisha was right and this was too dangerous.

Musa sat opposite Ratib who smiled and said, "I have heard of your family, and they command great respect in our village. You are known as an honorable man and it is my pleasure to welcome you to my home. May I offer you some tea?"

"Thank you, Ratib."

"How may I be of service to you?"

Musa took a deep breath. "I must help my family in Syria; their home has been destroyed; they are destitute, and I want to bring them here. It is a matter of life and death."

"Yes, it is a terrible tragedy for our people. We all pray this nightmare will

67

end and order will be restored. Tell me, Musa, do you wish to borrow money?"

"No. I have something of great value to sell. I hope you could advise me how to proceed."

Ratib now listened intently as Musa told how he found a most valuable ancient scroll at Tel Dan. "I only sell it to save my family."

"You are a good man to risk all like this," said Ratib. "But you should know that I don't get involved in illegal activities; the penalties for dealing in antiquities are severe. I do not want to go to prison."

"Of course, Sir, I do not want you to do anything illegal."

Ratib's eyes, dark and menacing behind thick lenses, pierced through Musa. He walked over to Musa and looked directly at him. He lowered his voice. "Musa, I will try to help you. I will ask if anyone knows dealers in ancient scrolls. Because such an undertaking is dangerous, I will require a fee of forty percent"

"I agree and appreciate your help."

"At some point, you will have to establish where you found the scroll and its age so we can determine its value; otherwise, I am afraid it will not bring a high price. I assume you will be able to provide such documentation." Turning to pour more tea, he smiled and looked at Musa. "May I offer you more tea; perhaps some *baklava*."

"No thank you."

"Are you sure? The *burma* is excellent."

"I am not hungry."

Shrugging his shoulders, Ratib licked his lips and put several pieces on his plate.

Sweat dripped down Musa's back. His leg shook. He hoped his voice did not betray the fear and the queasy feeling in his stomach. "Of course, I can tell you all you need to know. How much money will I get for my scroll?"

Ratib put his teacup down and stared out the window. Orange-red pomegranate blossoms dominated the center of his garden. "I cannot say before I see the scroll and certainly not without a professional assessment."

"Could you guess?"

"Perhaps a few thousand shekels, maybe less, maybe a bit more. We will see, my friend. First, let me make some inquiries. By the way, Musa, how big is the scroll?"

Musa hesitated. He had no choice but to trust Ratib. "I could not read the writing. It is unlike the Hebrew letters used today. It is long; it might be the story of someone's life or a history of Dan. Maybe like the Dead Sea Scrolls, it is a lost book of the Jews' Torah."

"If that is true, then Dan must be very old."

"It is. The archeologists have shown that Dan is thousands of years old and at one time was one of the most important cities in ancient Israel. They dated the excavation layer, above where I found the scroll, to the period 60-40 BC. Ratib, the Dead Sea Scrolls were a lot more valuable than a few thousand shekels. Collectors might pay hundreds of thousands of shekels for this scroll, maybe a million shekels."

"You are correct, Musa, but you do realize the Dead Sea Scrolls were unique verifications of the books of Moses? If you found something comparable, you will be a rich man. If the scroll is a simple collection of bills of sale, letters or an inventory, it might not have much value. Don't forget, without proper provenance, buyers will be reluctant to pay a lot of money. Before we can talk about price, the first task is to find someone willing to trade in an ancient scroll. If I am successful, I will have to show the scroll to an interested buyer. I assume you trust me to look after your interests."

Musa swallowed hard and with bravado he did not feel said, "Of course, I trust you. Your reputation is well known in Ghajar. I believe it safest for both of us to leave the scroll buried until a buyer is found. I have hidden it in a place no one would ever find." Musa's hand twitched as he stood and half bowed to Ratib. "I knew I could trust you to help me."

Ratib patted Musa on the shoulder. "I will be in touch, Musa. In the meantime, please know that I will make every effort for you."

# BOOK SEVEN—DREAMS

*Aba* received a letter from Gershon saying he would come to Dan with his wife Yamima. I was sure it could only mean one thing. They came to discuss marriage with Ariel. I did not know whether to shout or cry for joy. I did both.

As *Aba* read, he did not say anything about marriage. He only said King Alexander Yanai ordered Gershon to Dan with a detachment of soldiers. Gershon and Yamima did not plan to be in Dan for long. He asked if they could stay in our house. The letter did not say whether Ariel would come or not. I so hope he comes.

Gershon wrote he intends to start a trading business in Dan. Ariel will eventually manage the trading business in the Galilee from Dan while his brother Yoav manages the business in Jerusalem. In addition, at the request of Queen Shlomtsion, Gershon will report on the defense capabilities of Dan, Kedesh, and Bar Am.

*Aba* did not say if there was more in the letter. However, I know why they come. I just know. I pray his *Ima* will like me and want me to be Ariel's wife.

Tonight after evening prayers, the town leaders came to hear the message. Everyone remembered Gershon and his promise to report to the Palace about the threat to our trade with the Lebanese coastal cities.

We did not know then that Tyre and Sidon also worried about the constant disruption of trade. Nor did we know the sea trade suffered from pirate attacks. Sulla's victory in Athens and Piraeus promised some relief. The Roman navy was now close enough to fight the pirates in the Aegean Sea and off the coast of Lebanon.

Gershon wrote that the King is sending a detachment of soldiers to assist us and another detachment to Kedesh and Bar Am to protect the trade route.

71

Several spoke at once. "What does it mean to assist us?"

*Aba* answered with deliberate calm. "We will have to join the soldiers when they attack Anafa. Gershon has a plan to draw the bandits from Anafa and will participate in the attack."

A tall man with dried mud on his sandals stepped forward. "If soldiers come, why do we have to fight? We are farmers and artisans. We know nothing of warfare." Others murmured their agreement.

"Yes, that is true. We are not soldiers. Yet, a man, who saved one of our children, again will risk his life to protect us; he deserves our support. It is the least we can do. I, for one, volunteer to fight. I propose we listen to Gershon's plan and join the soldiers. Who will fight with me?"

Avner raised his fist. "I will join you. We must defend our families and our city."

Another pledged and finally a chorus shouted at once. "I too will fight to protect Dan."

*Ima* frowned when *Aba* volunteered to be one of the leaders. "Nadav, what if something happens to you?" What will happen to us, our children, me?"

*Aba* gently caressed her cheek. "Noa, Gershon has a good plan. There is far more danger to Gershon who will be the bait to draw the bandits from Anafa. Once they are in the open, we can defeat them once and for all."

I was afraid of the bandits. Now I realized the danger to *Aba* and all the men from Dan. I begged *Aba*. "Please do not go."

He kissed me and said, "I have to go."

Itai stood next to me. "I am going with you *Aba*. I am a man now and old enough to fight."

*Aba* frowned and put his arm around Itai. "Thank you, son. Yes, you are old enough. But I need you to stay here." He whispered, "This will be dangerous. If something happens to me, I need to know you will take care of our family."

Itai stood a little straighter, gripped Aba's arm, and said, "You can count on me."

Late that night, the force divided into four groups and left the safety of Dan. The bandits were vicious, and I worried that people I knew might be wounded or killed. I did not want to imagine what would happen to us if the bandits won. What if *Aba* was wounded?

The farmers and craftsmen from Dan were pious men. Killing would not be easy for them. True, it was not murder if they fought to protect family and home. I knew that was allowed by our law. The men showed a grim determination I found hard to reconcile with the family men I knew. Every man wanted to be brave and worried he might fail in battle. I shivered

73

uncontrollably as I remembered the man *Aba* killed lying on the ground with blood pulsing from his body.

***

Itai and I would not sleep until *Aba* returned. We talked about nothing. Neither of us wanted to repeat our worst fears. Itai assured me the soldiers were far superior fighters than the bandits. I wish he were more convincing. He seemed just as afraid of tomorrow as I was.

***

Avner's group left first and made their way to the Merom Lake. They walked along the shore, entered the cold water behind Anafa, and hid among the reeds. Next, four soldiers from Jerusalem with four men of Dan departed. Skirting the plateau, they took positions behind a rise to the south of Anafa. The men shivered in the night air. They were hungry, frightened, yet determined.

Twelve men, four archers, and eight soldiers armed with lances, commanded by Captain Gideon, moved to high ground on the Golan opposite, but out of sight of Anafa. *Aba* and twelve professional soldiers augmented by six men from Dan took positions north of Anafa. The trap was set. The critical role belonged to Gershon.

***

At dawn as the sun rose behind Gershon, he approached Anafa and yelled to Yosef. "Dog, I have come for you. If you are a man, come out and fight me."

With the sun in his eyes, Yosef squinted and yelled back, "Who is this squealing like a little girl?"

Gershon yelled back, "I saved the child from your gang in front of Dan last summer. I am sure you remember."

"Ah yes. The frightened rabbit."

"Two of your men were killed. I will have your head now unless you are too much of a coward to fight me. Leave your fortress and meet me like a man. If I win, your band will disarm and leave this area."

"And if I win?"

74

"You are a coward. You have no chance in a fair fight. Come out and face me if you dare."

"I do not fear you, rabbit. As soon as I finish eating, I will come out and kill you. Please do wait. And, since it will be your last meal, I will be happy to send you some delicious fresh-baked bread, sheep cheese, and vegetables picked a few minutes ago."

Gershon maintained the polite exchange. "Yosef you are most kind to think of my hunger. However, I am in a hurry to kill you and return to Dan. I will eat then. Please Yosef be quick; I am a bit hungry."

Yosef called his men together. He told them to wait until he starts to attack, then ride out. "I want this man dead."

Yosef stepped outside the compound with his sword drawn and walked straight toward Gershon. "Rabbit, you will die now."

Almost in slow motion, he moved right to force Gershon to parry movement from his weak side. Gershon, keeping his eyes on Yosef, moved back. Yosef lifted his sword and with surprising speed ran toward Gershon. Yosef's men swarmed out of Anafa riding at full speed. Gideon and Gershon expected the duplicity. Gershon turned and ran uphill toward the Golan.

Yosef laughed. "Cowards, all you farmers are cowards. Stand and fight, rabbit."

The riders and Yosef, concentrating on Gershon, missed the soldiers moving from cover on the right, others from the left, and Avner's group blocking their retreat to Anafa. As they neared Gershon, four archers stood and fired a volley of arrows. The arrows missed, and the archers turned and ran toward the Golan with twenty-five of Yosef's men after them.

Soldiers now converged on Yosef's band from the north and the south. The bandits could only move forward or retreat to Anafa. Yosef, still concentrating on Gershon and the archers, was oblivious to the trap about to close. Captain Gideon, watching the attack unfold, kept his force in check until Yosef committed his men. The soldiers covering Gershon's "retreat" stood and moved forward toward the horsemen with spears leveled. Yosef was surrounded.

Yosef gave the command to retreat as Captain Gideon's force charged forward at a run. Surrender would mean certain death. The bandits wheeled to the north attempting to break through Nadav's blocking force.

The men from Dan yelled, "Revenge." The battle was joined. Pulling men off their horses, the bandits were wrestled to the ground. The soldiers made quick work of the bandits. Many were thrown from their horses to be attacked by the farmers they so disdained. A fury born of years of fear and suffering provoked a frenzy of killing. Bandits were beaten to death with clubs and fists. One bled to death from a wound to his groin. Another was missing part of his nose, a man from Dan fell with a mortal wound, and four soldiers were wounded. They stopped the escape.

Captain Gideon's unit and the southern force closed on the bandits. Avner moving from the west ran forward with his unit. Halfway, he stumbled on a rock and broke his ankle. Avner yelled, "Do not stop. Close the trap." The farmers from Dan with the soldiers from Jerusalem fought bravely and did not stop until the last of the bandits surrendered.

Yosef, wounded by an arrow in the stomach, begged for death. It would come, but only after he watched his surviving men judged in the field by Captain Gideon. Eight of the young bandits were sentenced to labor in place of men injured or killed in previous raids; fifteen were sentenced to death and immediately executed.

Standing in a circle around Yosef, the soldiers laughed at the pitiful excuse of a man. The coward who brought all his gang to kill a single man, the man who kidnapped children, stole food from poor farmers, and preyed on women wanted mercy. One man said, "Let us tie him to a tree and let the crows eat his eyes while he is still alive."

Gershon spoke. "We are better than that. We are not like them. Leave him to die on the ground. Let us be thankful for our victory and return home to our families."

*Ima* took Yamima's hand. "Your husband is a good man and brave. We owe him a great debt of gratitude. It is the fight of Dan against the bandits and Gershon could have remained here."

"Thank you, Noa. Your words comfort me. I do fear for my husband."

"I know how you feel. We all fear for our men. I pray they will be safe."

"I knew my husband would not stay back. He does not see the Anafa bandits as a danger only to Dan, rather an attack on Israel that must be fought."

"And we are grateful for his help. In the north, we are on the front line."

"Gershon is an avid student of history; he knows we defended our country from enemies for thousands of years: Egyptians, Assyrians, Babylonians, Greeks, and tribes from the desert. Gershon says no matter the cost, we must defend our society and values. Even while in exile in Babylonia, we kept our religion and way of life. To Gershon, no other way is possible. It worries me that one day my sons will have to fight. I am proud they will protect us, stand up for our country, and keep our values. Maybe someday, it will be different."

*Ima* sent me to the market for vegetables needed for our evening meal. They continued to talk as I left. I wanted to stay and listen to their conversation. I wondered if they would discuss marriage for Ariel and me. I wanted to listen from outside the window. No, it would not be right. Still, I had to know so I listened for a few minutes before I went to the market.

I was right. They did talk about Ariel and me. Yamima told *Ima*, "I am grateful to you, Noa, for having us in your home. Everything Gershon told me about you and your family is true. Elisheva is truly a wonderful girl. I see why my son is so taken with her."

"My daughter is like a different person since she met Ariel. When your husband and sons shared our Shabbat evening meal with us, Elisheva and Ariel sat opposite each other. They looked at each other when they thought no one noticed. They were wrong. We all noticed. They do seem suited to one another."

"Between us, Gershon thinks the same."

"So does Nadav. Let us continue this discussion when the men are here. We should let the men start the conversation. It makes them feel good."

Yamima grinned. "Noa, you are so right. By the way, Ariel told me Elisheva helped you cook the Shabbat evening meal. He said the meal was the best he ever ate. Gershon also said it was wonderful, so I suppose it was not only Elisheva's magic touch."

"Elisheva will be an excellent cook."

"Noa, will you share your recipe with me?"

"Of course. I have several cook scrolls. I took that recipe from *Rachel's Galilee Recipes*. The scroll belonged to my Grandmother; I plan to give it to Elisheva when she marries."

"I have not seen that one in Jerusalem. I search the shops for new cook scrolls, in particular those with recipes from different parts of the country. May I see it?"

"Certainly. Someday I want to travel to Jerusalem and see the Temple. Perhaps I could see your library."

"Noa, I would like that a lot. Please do come. Jerusalem is always magical and even more so during the festivals."

As I left the market, the soldiers and men from Dan returned from Anafa. I ran home. "*Ima*, the soldiers are back."

"Did you see *Aba* and Gershon? Were there any casualties? Did they succeed?"

"The bandits were killed or captured; none escaped. We lost one man and Avner broke his ankle; others suffered minor injuries. They are inside the main gate. Everyone is coming to greet the soldiers. Captain Gideon will address the crowd. Hurry, *Ima*!"

Captain Gideon stood at the city entrance surrounded by his soldiers and the men of Dan who fought that day. They were tired, dirty, and elated. Captain Gideon brushed aside some dirt on his armor, cleared his throat, and spoke in a loud clear voice. "Citizens of Dan, in the name of King Alexander Yanai and Queen Shlomtsion, I have the honor to tell you we have defeated the bandits. We prevailed because of the outstanding bravery of your King's soldiers and the men of Dan led by Avner, Nadav, and Gershon. While we can never make up for the grievous losses you have suffered, several of the bandits will work in place of the men killed and injured over the years. My soldiers will ensure the work will be done and you will forever be safe. The people of Israel will always defeat evil. Long live our country. Long live our King."

The euphoria and celebration ended as each man found his family and silently hugged them. They would live in peace, but at a terrible cost. People died. They were evil, and the fight had to be made, but still, there was no joy in killing. I prayed this would be the last time. Subdued but satisfied, each man went home.

I felt a great weight had been lifted from me. The men of Dan and the soldiers ended the terror. I slept well that night and dreamed of Ariel.

Gershon and Nadav left to wash in the cool waters of the Dan stream while *Ima*, Yamima, and I prepared the evening meal. Usually, it would be a light meal. Except for a small piece of bread and cheese, the men had not eaten since they left for Anafa. While they claimed not to be hungry—I was sure they would be famished when the euphoria abated.

I made dough and with great care rolled it out into a thin sheet. Yamima, standing next to me, hummed softly while preparing a filling of mushrooms and green onions. I wrapped the filling in the dough. *Ima* prepared a mixture of eggs and cream. She added spinach leaves and baked the mixture in a shallow bowl to make a rich pie to accompany the baked mushroom wrap and fresh vegetables. Itai took a jug of mild chardonnay to chill in the stream and brought back one of the last ripe melons of the season.

I was happy; *Aba* and Gershon were safe, and I felt safe. *Ima* sang while she worked. I was nervous and concentrated on the dough. I wanted to make a good impression on Ariel's *Ima*. I hoped she was happy to cook with me.

*Aba* and Gershon were exhausted and raw from the emotions of the day. I sensed they were content having ended a reign of terror and happy to return to a warm home filled with delicious smells. They ate like starving men. Itai asked about the battle. Neither *Aba* nor Gershon wanted to talk about it except to say that Captain Gideon's plan to defeat Yosef was brilliant. The men of Dan fought well to protect the city.

My knees shook under the table. I did not look up from my plate or speak during the meal. I waited for Gershon and Yamima to discuss the marriage of Ariel and me. They said nothing. It must have been only to accompany the soldiers. Why come with the soldiers? Why did Yamima come too? Unless,

Gershon planned to join the soldiers and she worried about him. Yes, that must be the reason.

I could see the men savored the semi-sweet white wine and the relief it gave from the intense emotions of the last twenty-four hours. As *Ima* served the melon, Yamima said that she helped me prepare the mushroom roll. Gershon said, "This is the best I have ever eaten."

Everyone stared at me. I felt so proud, happy, and grateful that I blushed and could not even stammer a word to acknowledge the compliment. *Ima* added I would be a great cook. She said I even write recipes of the new dishes we invent in a special journal. Gershon said, "I am sure she will make someone a great wife."

There, in a second, it was clear why Gershon and Yamima were here. *Aba* and *Ima* smiled and tried to look calm. Itai looked up surprised. I blushed the color of cooked beets. As I ran from the room, my sisters, Ayala and Dikla, at the same time asked, "*Ima*, why did Elisheva leave? Is she not feeling well?"

***

The next morning I sat with *Ima* in the cooking area. She took my hand and told me how *Aba* and she went for a walk after dinner with Gershon and Noa.

"What did they say *Ima*?"

*Ima* said, "We walked along the city wall. The Merom Valley was beautiful in the setting sun, and with the clear sky, the stars sparkled against the deep blackness."

After walking in silence to the wall, Gershon stopped, turned, and said, "Our son is completely taken by your daughter. We would be honored if you agree to a marriage between Elisheva and Ariel."

As Yamima and *Ima* had discussed earlier in the day, the dance had started, and each according to protocol, bowed and spoke the correct words.

*Aba* seemed startled and protested. "Elisheva is too young to marry. She just turned eleven. It would be at least another three years before I could agree she marry."

Gershon replied, "We agree that now is too soon. I plan to bring Ariel into my business. It will take several years before he is ready to assume control."

*Aba* asked, "At what age do you think he will be ready for marriage?"

"Four years from now when he is sixteen."

"Will he be able to support my daughter?"

"My business provides well for my family. Ariel will be able to provide a good home for Elisheva. He is smart, respectful, keeps the commandments, and honorable. He loves her and would honor her his whole life."

"Are you thinking Elisheva would live in Jerusalem?"

"My plan is that Yoav, Ariel's older brother, will manage the trading business for the coastal plain and Jerusalem. Ariel will open a new branch in the Galilee and manage the trading from Dan. With operations in the north and the south, the business will grow. If you and Noa think this proposal has merit, we are prepared to discuss the dowry."

"We are impressed with Ariel. He is a fine young man. We are sure he will be a good husband. Elisheva is a special girl and needs a special man like Ariel to be happy. We welcome your proposal, as we are sure Elisheva will. We welcome uniting our families. As far as a dowry, I have to think about this. We want Elisheva to be secure should anything happen to Ariel."

"We agree. Our only task is to determine how much is necessary to ensure security. One thought I had was to give a share in my business to Elisheva's brother, Itai, with the provision that if anything happens to Ariel, Itai ensure Elisheva's security. Ariel's brother, Yoav, would also be responsible for her continued well-being.

"Nadav, I suggest tomorrow we work out the specifics of the dowry. I am positive there will be no problem to conclude a good and amicable agreement. Now, let us celebrate our good fortune, pray for the happiness of our children, and that they bless us with many grandchildren."

"Amen."

*Dear Ariel,*

*Everything I have long dreamt will happen. I have been soaring like the doves that delight in the sunshine as they rise and fall in a dance of love. Yesterday our parents agreed to our marriage. Since the day I first saw you, I have thought of little else. I knew deep inside we would be together forever. I knew it would be so.*

*Everything in Dan reminds me of you: the sweet smell of jasmine, the symphony of the market, the harmony of a thousand crickets at sunset, the rhythm of water rushing past stones, and the soft melody of the wind blowing through the trees. Sometimes I sit by quiet pools in the shade of the oaks and think of your poetry and the Song of Songs. I walk on the city walls and look over the Merom hoping to see you coming for me. It was not in vain; you will be coming.*

*I pray the time will pass quickly until we will start our life together. You are the one I will love all of my life. I see only joy and happiness being with you forever.*

*Elisheva*

# BOOK EIGHT—BLESSINGS

How long ago it seems I met Ariel. We were children and so young. Since then, I have dreamt of little else than a life with Ariel. How well do I know this boy now a man? Will I truly be happy? Do I want to share my life with Ariel? Will he decide I am not the woman he expected? And, what does it mean to be husband and wife?

*Ima* has been telling me about special times for a husband and wife. It scares me. *Ima* tells me that part of our life is sacred and from the love between a man and a woman, a family is born; and the bond between us will grow and become closer than we could imagine. Marriage is everything I want, but I am still frightened.

Last week my friends, whom I have known my entire life, Miriam and Micah, married. I asked Miriam what it is like to be married. All she did was smile and say you will soon know adding with a giggle, "It is wonderful."

Many people have come to Dan for the wedding. The start of a new family is a blessing to the community and to Israel to honor and celebrate with great joy. I met all of Ariel's family when they arrived from Jerusalem last week. Several traders from the Galilee and from Tyre came yesterday. The market is overcrowded with traders. Every day I feel the excitement increase.

Yamima and *Ima* arranged the wedding feast and invited everyone in Dan. Bakers prepared special sweet breads. Cooks roasted great quantities of sheep, goat, and veal. They prepared huge jugs of marinade comprising wine, apples, and persimmons for the veal, pomegranate juice and wine for the sheep, and figs with cardamom for the goat. Slow-roasted chickens brushed with olive oil and ground chili peppers from Pontus complemented the beef dishes.

Gershon arranged for fish caught in the Kinneret Sea to arrive in the morning. *Ima* will bake the fish with onions and then add ground sesame paste mixed with water and citron. All will be complemented with vegetables, fruits, hard-boiled eggs, and many varieties of red and white Galilee wines. Small cakes will end the meal so that our lives will be sweet. It will be the biggest wedding ever in Dan.

* * *

The noise of the crowd reduced to a low murmur. The wedding guests were silent, all looking at Ariel as he stood under a canopy of olive branches and flowers. He waited looking past the guests. Despite the cool air, beads of sweat glistened on his forehead and cheeks. Even though my face was veiled, I saw him look at me. I approached with a determined step. Time stood still. As I neared, I saw in his hand the ring he found at Dan years ago and promised to give his bride.

After an eternity, I was under the canopy, next to him, circling him, and he repeated the vows binding us together for all time: "with this ring, you are sanctified to me according to the laws of Moses and the religion of Israel." The seven blessings were sung. We were married. We would be together for a lifetime. People shouted mazel tov and with great gaiety sang songs of joy.

Ariel leaned over and whispered all his dreams had come true. I touched his arm for the first time. He jumped as if hit by lightning.

I whispered, "I knew you would come back. I will love you forever, Ariel."

He answered so only I could hear, "I will always carry your packages from the market."

The commander of the guard stationed at Dan interrupted the celebration. "I bring a message from Queen Shlomtsion."

There was complete silence. Everyone looked to the commander. Is there an imminent danger? Did something happen? What could be so important to interrupt a wedding party—why is a soldier reading a message? This could not be good news.

Ariel and I stood together as the commander read a proclamation from

Queen Shlomtsion: "I have the privilege to wish Ariel Ben Gershon and Elisheva Bat Nadav a long and prosperous life together. Marriage is a blessing to their parents and to Israel. They should bless their home and our country with many children. The spice box, the King and I send to you, should always be filled with aromatic spices to remind you of our Temple and the sweetness of our country. *Mazel tov*, Ariel and Elisheva."

*Aba* asked Gershon if he knew that the King and Queen would honor us.

"The Queen knew that my son was marrying a daughter of Dan and wanted to know about your family and Elisheva. I am as surprised as you. I am proud of the honor to our families, or now I should say, our family. Come Nadav, let us join our wives and drink to our future grandchildren."

All the guests congratulated Ariel and me. Our friends crowded around us celebrating the addition to the next generation of Dan families. Ariel introduced all the traders to me, and they half bowed honoring our marriage and me. The swirl of dancers, exuberant singing, feasting, and toasts to the newest family of Dan continued well into the night.

At some point, gifts were presented. None topped the King and Queen's gift and the honor everyone in Dan felt. Micah brought two wine cups he made in his workshop. They were exquisite. Micah engraved them with ornately detailed designs: Jerusalem on one and Dan on the other. Ariel hugged Micah. He promised to use these cups every Friday night.

I hugged Miriam, "Thank you, my best friend. You will be our first guests."

Moshe, the carpenter Ariel had befriended in Jerusalem, sent two unique chairs carved from selected Lebanese cedar. The wood had a beautiful grain and the curves of the wood flowed into a harmonious whole. The parts fit together perfectly. The careful match of the grains made it seem the chairs were carved from a single piece of wood. Unless you looked closely, it was hard to see how the parts were joined. The seats were padded with a fine cloth. Traders from Lebanon and the Galilee brought sets of pottery, cooking pots made from copper and iron, tools to pound, stir, mix, beat, turn over hot and cold food, an ornate mortar and pestle for crushing and grinding spices, and a fine set of sharp knives.

Gershon's long-time friend Hiram, and now Ariel's Lebanese trading partner, gave a special set of silver spoons and knives engraved with the images of lions that gave Dan its first name, Laish. My sisters, after working in secret for months, gave us a beautiful embroidered tablecloth. Gershon and Yamima brought down-filled pillows, a feather mattress, and a thick down-filled blanket to keep us warm on the coldest of nights.

Time seemed to stand still during the celebration as the evening changed to night. I brushed against Ariel and whispered, "Let us take our leave, my husband."

\*\*\*

Ariel had been building our house in Dan. It had three rooms built around a big courtyard. As our family grew, we could add more rooms from the courtyard area. There was more hard work in front of us, but the house was ready. Ariel had planned niches in the wall to hold candles and oil for light. He made small openings in the niches to vent the smoke. It was a small touch, but it made the rooms less smoky.

Ariel lit candles in all the rooms. I walked around looking at my new home. It seemed strange, and I was not sure what to do next. I entered the sleeping room and extinguished the light Ariel had just lit. Returning to the cooking area, I took Ariel's hand for the first time and with surprising calm, led him to the sleeping room. "My husband let us drink some wine."

He held me for the first time and whispered, "It is said that kisses with love are better than wine. I love you, Elisheva."

He kissed me; all of the sudden my knees felt weak; the room was suddenly hot. I could feel Ariel's heart beating. I kissed him back. His tongue touched mine; I held him tighter. He backed away and stared at me with a strange look. I could see love, urgency, fear, and a dozen other emotions in his eyes. I looked down not knowing what to do. He reached out and drew me to him holding me tight and kissing me harder. I held him tight. The kiss became gentle, and he held my face between his hands.

I pushed him away and started to loosen my gown. He stared, frozen, not moving. Turning to the right, I could see him remove his robe. He looked away while I turned from him and slipped off my robe. We were naked. We held each other joined by tender kisses.

He carried me to the bed. With his left hand under my head, his right hand gently touched my body. In an instant, all the images from the Song of Songs made sense as my body reacted to his touch and his to mine. He squeezed my breast too hard and it hurt. I took his hand. "Touch gently."

He did.

Wave after wave of new sensations flooded over me. His hands moved over my belly. He took my hand and guided it down. I shivered. Gently, he touched me too. I could feel we were both wet.

There was nothing else in this world, only the two of us in the still of the night. My beloved came to me and I to him. We were husband and wife for eternity.

The next morning, I woke early before my husband, as *Ima* did for her family, to make the morning meal. I set out berry jam, cheese, cucumbers sprinkled with dill, green onions, hard-boiled eggs, and a jug of pomegranate juice mixed with a little white wine.

I was in the cooking area as sunlight streamed through the window awakening Ariel. It was late. Luxuriating in the warm bed, he savored the memories, or were they dreams, of last night. He smelled the sweet aroma of bread and biscuits baking. It filled the house with the smell of home.

We sat opposite each other, both looking down as we ate. Ariel broke the silence, "How are you this morning, my wife?"

Smiling, I must have blushed a deep red. "I am well, my husband. Is the meal to your liking?"

"The meal is excellent. I knew you were a great cook from that Shabbat meal many years ago. Do you remember? It was the day I first saw you."

"Yes, I remember. You carried my packages from the market. I have always treasured that memory. Ariel, all my dreams came true yesterday." Smiling, I looked down and added, "And last night."

Now it was Ariel's turn to redden. "I love you, Elisheva."

"Ariel, did you know the King and Queen would send us congratulations?"

"No. I am still stunned by the honor accorded us."

"All my friends last night talked about how your *Aba* knows King Alexander Yanai and Queen Shlomtsion. They were excited that the Queen sent a message to Dan. Everyone says it was not only a great honor for us, but for all of Dan. Ariel, did you save that ring you found many years ago for me? I remember you promised to give it to your wife when you marry."

90

"Yes, I did. Then it was play, but deep inside, I knew I was saving it for you. I kept it safe all these years waiting for our wedding. I hope you do not mind an old ring."

"I love this ring. Not only is it beautiful, it ties us to people who came before us in Dan. We can pass it to our son to give to his bride."

"Elisheva, today let us walk around Dan. I have not yet seen the whole city. First, though, we should visit our parents. They made such a wonderful wedding party for us. Maybe we could also visit Micah and Miriam. I expect we will be good friends."

"Last night, I promised Miriam and Micah they would be the first of our friends we invite to our home. I should have asked you before inviting them. Do you agree?"

"We might invite our parents, brothers, and sisters first. Timing aside, I think it wonderful to invite them to our home. Let's walk along the river before we visit our family. My parents plan to return to Jerusalem in a few weeks. Tomorrow morning, *Aba* wants to meet with Yoav, Itai, and me to plan the future of our trading company. Come with me. I would like your opinion on the plans. I am not sure for how long we will meet, perhaps until mid-morning. Then we should plan how we want to build the rest of our home."

"I would like that."

"One idea I had is to add wooden cabinets and shelves in every room. We could use the cabinets to store kitchen tools, spices, scrolls, clothes, and sandals. What do you think?"

"I think you have wonderful ideas. It will be fun to make our home special."

"Also, I want to build a shelf to hold the spice box we received from the Queen."

"It is beautiful. I feel so honored the Queen sent us a gift."

"I will plan a special shelf for the wine cups Micah and Miriam gave us. The workmanship of the wine cups is superb. I have never seen anything like those cups in Jerusalem. Where does he get his ideas?"

"Micah looks at the world and sees it as no one else does. We see a tree; he recognizes an intricate living design of nature. Do you remember the day we hunted for old stuff near the wall? Micah found an old cup and stared at the design for some time. We all thought it was an old broken cup. He saw something different."

"I remember thinking that was strange."

"I once asked him why he looks so hard at the old things we find. He said that there is a timeless beauty in the designs. When he further develops the design, he links us to past generations that lived in Dan. He told me when he works in his shop, the metal, jewels, ceramics, and the wood he uses talk to him. I am glad you want to be friends with Micah."

Gershon started the meeting. It was time to pass the reins of his trading business to Ariel and Yoav. He welcomed my brother, Itai, as a new partner, and smiling at me said he was delighted that I was here and to please excuse him if I found the meeting boring.

Gershon said that ownership is to remain in our family. He and Itai will each have a twenty percent interest; Yoav and Ariel will each own thirty percent. In time, Gershon would transfer his share to Hillel, and at that time, each partner will have a twenty-five percent interest. The responsibility and scope of operations will determine the salary of each partner. Gershon would divide the year's profit according to ownership interest.

He said each of us would have an equal voice in all decisions and complete latitude and independence in our area—providing there is no conflict with the company's basic rules.

Gershon will keep the company's accounts and summarize the partner's reports into a company statement of expenses, sales, profit, and loss. The partners will meet twice a year: after the fall harvest and after the spring planting to chart plans for the coming half year. At that time, Gershon would allocate capital based on development plans and operational needs.

Yoav will manage the business in Jerusalem, the South, and the coastal plain as far north as Atlit, while Ariel will manage operations in the Galilee, Lebanon and Syria. Itai will be responsible for the transport of produce, wine, and manufactured goods between Dan and Jerusalem, Petra, Egypt, Dameseq and Lebanon.

Yoav will buy spices direct from the dealers in Petra. Ariel will increase the volume of Armenian, Roman, and Greek wines brought in from Tyre or

Syria. By handling the import and transport of wine and spices ourselves, we eliminate a layer of middlemen and gain a substantial competitive edge.

We should be aware that the combined operations might lead to new opportunities. A good example is Ariel's friendship with the Jerusalem cabinetmaker, Moshe. The gift boxes Moshe supplies have encouraged people to buy rare spices and fine wines as gifts during the holidays. Moshe has already hired more workers.

Gershon said the increased scale of business would require periodic investment. We must maintain sufficient inventory so if supply is interrupted we can continue to operate. Also, Itai's division will require investment and operating funds for continual care and replacement of pack animals as well as manpower to lead and escort our supply caravans. We have to include losses due to spoilage and theft as part of our cost basis; proper management should keep those losses to a minimum.

I was happy and relieved when Gershon told Itai he wanted to operate without regular transfers of cash between Ariel and Yoav. Gershon would ensure that Ariel and Itai would have enough operating capital from sales or credit to maintain sufficient inventory. Itai would not have to carry gold or silver between Dan and Jerusalem. He would balance the accounts and, if needed, transfer funds after their semi-annual meetings.

I listened to Gershon speak and marveled at the soundness of the business plan. He had thought about everything. I was sure my family would prosper. The next part convinced me. Gershon explained that since the company's success depends on many people, their customers—whether spice and wine shops, or people in the markets—they have to be respected and treated with fairness. The same is true for the dealers from whom we buy our wine and spices. He said the company's policy should be to participate in local affairs and charities. "It is a *mitzvah* and we should do more rather than less," he said.

Gershon had drafted a formal agreement and asked Yoav, Ariel, and Itai to read the document, sign, and place their seal at the end. They should make sure all the terms are clear. Gershon added that in the future it may be necessary to add amendments to cover new realities.

The meeting continued with my brother, Itai, reporting on his plans to transport goods between Dan and Jerusalem.

He and Ariel had developed a detailed plan to build a transport system. At the start, they would contract teamsters to deliver goods between Dan and Jerusalem. The advantage was an immediate capability that allowed time to acquire pack animals, build stables, contract for fodder, and engage permanent teamsters. They projected that it would take about three to four months to build an initial capability that could be expanded quickly. They also prepared an estimate of the costs.

I was proud of my brother. I had not realized Ariel and Itai had spent so much time working together. This new world of business interested me. A few ideas came to me as Itai presented his plan. Before I ventured a suggestion, I wanted to think a lot more. For now, I just listened.

Gershon took the estimate of costs and surprised Itai by asking if he had considered extending the transport capability to our buying centers in Petra or Tyre.

Itai said that so far he concentrated on moving supplies between Dan and Jerusalem; he had not thought beyond that. He promised to sketch a plan to include transport to our buying centers. Ariel added that if it was necessary to carry payment, they would need additional caravan security.

I was beginning to understand the scale of Gershon's plan. He meant to build a business that would cover Israel and extend the company's operations to neighboring countries. What a fantastic plan. In addition, Ariel and my brother were partners. The next part worried me greatly.

Gershon said he had something important to discuss that could not leave this room. He looked at me and I nodded my agreement. He said that Queen Shlomtsion wants us to begin trade in Dameseq. She provided a letter of introduction to the King of Armenia, Tigranes the Great, and asked that he grant us trading rights in Dameseq.

He explained that the Queen is concerned by the growing strength of King Tigranes since his alliance with King Mithridates of Pontus. His empire extends in the east to Mesopotamia, to the north as far as the Caspian Sea, and to Syria and our border. Queen Shlomtsion feels increased trade between our countries might improve relations with Armenia. We would be the catalyst and at the same time, close to news about Tigranes, his intentions, army strength, and defense spending. She asked that we report any information we gather.

Gershon leaned forward and almost in a whisper said, "There is an element of danger. As wine merchants, we will have access to people at the court, a perfect vantage to listen and observe."

There is risk, but he thought it minimal. He said we have an opportunity for a profitable expansion of our business. Gershon squeezed Ariel's shoulder with one hand and Yoav's with the other. "We have a duty to serve Israel. In the end, what we learn will help protect us from a potential invader."

Gershon said that Itai should accompany him and Ariel to Dameseq. If the trip was successful, Itai would have to include Dameseq in his transport plan. Ariel did not react. Itai was solemn as he accepted the new responsibility.

I did not know what to think. What exactly is the danger? Will my Ariel return to me safe and sound? Will he be imprisoned as a spy in Damaseq? Gershon does not seem too worried, so maybe I should not be worried. Maybe everything will be fine.

I never imagined how wonderful it is to be married. Life has been a whirlwind with Ariel. We work together to build our house and make it home. We started a small garden in the courtyard. Along the north wall, we planted lavender. I like the fresh smell that fills the courtyard and the house. On the western wall, outside our sleeping room, facing the afternoon sun, we planted jasmine. The sweet smell at night delights me. Ariel and I take pleasure sitting in our small garden at night. Ariel brought a rare plant that traders from the east gave him. He called it lemongrass and said it grows to about his height, and the plant keeps away flies and mosquitos. I suggested next to the cooking area was the ideal spot. Some of the plants, we will remove when we add additional rooms to our house.

In the center, we planted an olive tree. In a few years, there will be olives and shade. Ariel built a small table and chairs. Often after a day's work, we sit by our young tree, look at the stars, enjoy the fragrances of our garden, and drink lemongrass, spearmint, or mint tea.

We work on our home every day. I am not as strong as Ariel, but I can do a lot. He always worries I will lift something too heavy and hurt myself. I think, though, he is happy when we work together.

I set up the cooking area the same as my *Ima's*. Ariel built a shelf big enough to hold a large collection of spices. He sunk hooks into the wall to hang pots and cooking utensils. I have everything I need to prepare meals for my family.

I take great care to select the best vegetables, fruits, and meat for our meals. Even though Ariel is busy with his business, he makes time to go with me to the market. He is a wonderful man and a wonderful husband.

I enjoy cooking for Ariel. We have great meals together. He tells me about his day, the business, and the interesting people he meets. I tell him about the progress I made in our house, new recipes I have found, and the meals I plan to cook. We discuss everything—the latest stories, poems, business, current news, family, friends, and our plans for the future.

When we talked about the meeting with Gershon, Yoav, and Itai, I told Ariel I had an idea that might help settle accounts. Travelers between Dan and Jerusalem can deposit money with Ariel and in turn receive a letter that Yoav will give them the amount deposited minus a small fee. Travelers between Jerusalem and Dan can do the same, and Ariel would give them the money deposited minus a small fee. The travelers avoid carrying money. We earn a commission, and if accounts balance, there will be no need to transfer money at all. I thought enough travelers and merchants journey around the kingdom that it might be a good source of profits. Ariel took my face in his hands and kissed me. He thought it was a great idea and would propose it to his *Aba*.

Usually, we linger after our evening meal and have an extra cup of wine. We always have so much to say. Often we sit next to each other with no need for words. Sometimes he will touch my hand or I will touch his, and I feel as if a whole conversation took place.

The nights are best. We learn about each other, what pleases one another, and we explore a wonderful world. I do not talk about this with any of my friends; it would be an intrusion into our private world. We share a special contentment when late at night he puts his arms around me and whispers, "Sleep well, my love."

A day after the men left for Damaseq, Adah, my sister-in-law, knocked on my door.

"What a wonderful surprise. Please come in. I will make tea. How are you feeling, Adah?"

"I feel great."

"Adah, you look fantastic. How much longer before the baby comes and my brother will be an *Aba*?"

"Not long now. I think another one, maybe two months. How are you, my new sister?"

"I am well, thank you. Adah, that is a lovely necklace."

"It was a gift from Itai when I told him I was pregnant. He purchased it from Micah."

"I have never seen anything like it."

"Micah said he got the idea for this necklace after watching basket weavers' work with straw. The strands of gold represent the dried reeds used to make the baskets. Weren't you and Micah good friends?"

"Yes, since we were children. I always thought he had great talent, was extraordinarily creative, and would be successful in whatever he chose to do. Adah, do you find it lonely without Itai at home?"

"I do."

"Even though I work long hours on the house, I miss Ariel and wish he were home."

"Elisheva, the baby just kicked. Do you want to feel? It is moving now.

"Oh, that is wonderful. I can't wait until I am pregnant."

"To answer your question, yes, I miss Itai and worry about him going to Dameseq; it is a dangerous trip."

"I worry about the Syrian soldiers. Ariel tells me that soldiers are far more dangerous than bandits."

"I thought nothing could be worse than bandits."

"Soldiers are indeed worse. They are professional killers. Bandits are mostly thieves."

"Elisheva, now you have me more worried."

"I did not mean to worry you. I do not like it when Ariel is away. I always fear something will happen to him. I cannot imagine living without him."

"I know what you mean, Elisheva. I guess that is what love is: sometimes joy, sometimes completeness, and sometimes anxiety."

"When I first met Ariel, I knew I wanted to be with him. Then I did not understand why, and to tell you the truth, I still do not understand why. Sometimes I wonder why this man, and no other, makes me feel the way I do."

"This is excellent tea, Elisheva. What did you make it from?"

"Lemongrass. I enjoy its special flavor. I add it to vegetables when I sauté or even when I boil vegetables in water. I am glad you like it. I am sure Itai can take some too. We are lucky our husbands deal in spices and wines. We can get any spice we need, and we always have superb wine."

"Before I interrupted you, I was about to say Itai makes me feel complete. Now I understand why so much is written about love. Abraham loved Sara with all his heart. He was ready to sacrifice everything for her. The story of Ruth and Boaz is a beautiful tale of love and commitment. From their love, a king was born."

"And what about Yakov and Rachel? He worked seven years so he could marry Laban's daughter. Somehow, he marries Leah when he wanted to marry Rachel. He works another seven years so he can marry Rachel. He must have loved her."

"Maybe we should have asked Ariel and Itai to work seven years for us."

"I am sure they would—especially for you Adah, you are so beautiful."

"And so are you, Elisheva. I think we are both lucky to have such good men love us. We are blessed. But did you ever wonder what is love besides our good feelings?"

"When I was young and read the Psalms or any of our modern poets, I did not really understand what they meant. Now the poems make sense. I have a scroll on the lessons of Socrates and Plato. They questioned what love is. Before I met Ariel, I did not appreciate their wisdom. Now I understand love is everything they said: honor, sanctity, and willingness to sacrifice yourself for your beloved; feeling whole, and valuing your beloved's wisdom and intelligence. In short, love is the source of great happiness."

"Elisheva, you surprise me. Do you know Greek?"

"No, the scroll I have is a translation. Someday, I want to learn Greek. Our King and Queen are fluent in Greek as is Queen Cleopatra and many of the Kings around the Great Sea. There are so many plays, poems, epic stories, works of philosophy, and history in Greek. Ariel speaks Greek. He promised to teach me."

"Elisheva, I think the philosophers missed something important. Love is the basis of family, which is the strength of our society. Do they write about family, the love of a child for his parents, and the love of parents for a child?"

"Not that I read. They wrote more about love between boys than family. However, much of what they say about love is also true between men and women—at least I think so. Socrates did say that the greatest love is that of wisdom."

"I don't know about that, Elisheva. You cannot convince me to love wisdom more than I love Itai or more than I will love my child."

"You would agree though that wisdom is important and helps us value love."

"I don't know. I would love Itai with all my heart with or without wisdom. Would you not love Ariel the same?"

"Yes, I would. Adah, did you read the story about the Indian god Shiva and the goddess Saraswati? When Shiva bit her lower lip, she moaned in pleasure. In India, they believe that was the origin of language. I would like to believe that language started because of love. Do you not agree?"

"I must admit that until now I never thought about it. I know that when I am with Itai, everything is beautiful and sometimes we do not even need language to know what the other thinks. "

"Exactly. When I am with Ariel, the world is so much more alive, flowers are more colorful, grass is much greener, and the birds sing to us. I always thought sunsets were special, but when I am with Ariel and he holds my hand, I feel my heart will burst."

"And, the physical poetry between us will create our future."

We looked down, stared at our tea, and smiled.

Syria has never been a trusted friend or ally of Israel. Still, Ariel tells me I worry too much, and maybe I do exaggerate the danger. With a hug and a kiss, he said, "Gershon has traveled to foreign lands and nothing has ever happened to him. Has it?"

It would still be the longest two weeks of my life. I insisted Ariel tell me everything about his journey, the city of Dameseq, and the meeting with King Tigranes.

Ariel, Itai, and Gershon left early the next morning while the air still held some of the night's coolness. Itai explained they had a choice: either travel through the Beqaa Valley and cross the Anti-Lebanon Range to Dameseq or pass to the south of Mount Hermon and turn north to Dameseq. He said it was half a day shorter and easier to head east and around the Hermon. Also, there was less chance of being intercepted by bandits.

I was confident that Itai would guide them the safest way. Even so, when I saw Ariel leaving Israel for a foreign land, I worried. I wondered if Itai's wife, Adah, and Yamima also worried. I was determined not to show anyone that I feared for my husband.

It was a hot day when they left Dan and started the climb to the Golan Plateau. Mount Hermon loomed to their left silhouetted against a blue sky with puffs of white clouds hovering near the peak. In the morning sunlight, the brush covering the lower mountain stood out a brilliant green against the reddish-brown volcanic rocks and white-gray outcroppings of limestone. The air would cool as they left behind the sparse brush and lavender for the fragrant pine forests at the higher elevations. They found the climb tiring and stopped several times to rest and drink water.

Ariel said they would travel light carrying a few gifts and small quantities of local wines—gifts they thought appropriate to obtain a license to trade. King Alexander Yanai sent a silver menorah for King Tigranes.

I knew there was a long history of trade between Dameseq and Israel. I also knew that the Syrians carried a deep resentment of Jews and Israel. King Tigranes was Armenian. I hoped that would make a big difference. Gershon's reputation for selling fine Israeli wines should ensure a warm welcome in Dameseq.

Their path took them past an old Temple to the Greek god Pan. They rested near a fast-moving stream enjoying the cool water and a quick meal. Itai told them that the stream fed a spectacular waterfall of icy-cold water. The color of the water appeared to be painted in whites, blues, and black by the sunlight and the shadows of the leafy trees. Fish swam near the shore. "If you close your eyes, you could hear a magical symphony as the water cascades down the *wadi*, twisting and turning around rocks and fallen trees. A grand rhythm of nature," he said.

Gaining altitude, they reached the evergreen forests with soft carpets of pale-brown pine needles. They gathered pinecones to break open later for the tasty nuts inside the petals. Itai was in the lead when he stopped and with a slight movement of his hand motioned for Ariel and Gershon to stop. He pointed to two bear cubs on their left. A stone's throw away to their right, they saw the mother bear. In a low voice, Itai said, "Walk straight ahead. Be quiet; make no sudden movements. Do not run."

Ariel held his breath and tried not to show fear while they moved past the line between the mother and her cubs. Once they were out of sight of the bears, they stopped, relieved. If the bear sensed they were a threat to her cubs, she would have torn them apart.

Their position, high on the mountain far above Dan and the valley floor, gave them a panoramic view of the Merom Valley. Ariel could see the mountains of Lebanon to the north and to the south a bluish-white mist over the Kinneret Sea. As the Merom Valley fell into soft evening shadows, a thin yellowish-brown haze added an alluring tone to one of the most beautiful gardens of nature. Fed by streams that formed the Jordan River and protected by the Naphtali range to the west, the valley appeared to him a picture of Eden. Ahead of them lay the rocky plain leading to Dameseq.

They set out moving fast to reach a lake in the cone of a volcano at the upper reaches of the Hermon Mountain. They camped at the lake's edge near an outcropping of rock that offered perfect protection from the chill wind. Itai unpacked and fed the mule while Ariel gathered wood for a fire.

For their evening meal, I had baked small individual rolls and cut roast chicken into small pieces that they could eat with their fingers. Ariel described how I rubbed the chicken with olive oil and sprinkled it with *zatar* before roasting. The sweetness of the juicy chicken combined with the *zatar* flavored the whole with the taste of the earth. The balance of sensations was wonderful. I had added several salads: okra and red peppers, cucumbers and onions sprinkled with dill, and slices of green peppers. They completed the meal with a jug of a robust Armenian red wine. It was a feast. Gershon told Ariel that I am an excellent cook and that he was lucky.

After the meal, Ariel said they relaxed by the fire enjoying its warmth in the chill night air. Sipping wine, they talked about the day's journey and the encounter with the bears. Gershon asked, "So Ariel, how does it feel to be married?"

Itai looked from the fire to Ariel wondering what he would say.

"I have never been so happy and content in all my life. Elisheva is a wonderful wife. I look forward to being with her at the end of every day. I find her advice and opinions perceptive and interesting."

"I am happy for you son," his *Aba* replied. "A good wife and a good home are a source of great happiness. When will we see little ones?"

Content and pleased at the complement Ariel said, "Thank you, *Aba*. I hope Elisheva and I will be as happy as you and *Ima*."

Itai smiled as he thought about his little sister, now the master of her own household. "Ariel, how do you feel about living in Dan?" "Life here must be much different than in Jerusalem."

"It is different. I feel a certain tranquility in Dan that sometimes I miss in Jerusalem. The beauty of the Merom Valley is special. To me, tranquility and beauty are important. I was happy in Jerusalem—it is the heart and soul of our country. I enjoyed walking through the city and feeling the excitement of the capital. I always felt something special when I looked up to the Temple. I am happy in Dan with Elisheva. Life is good to me. And, I have a great brother-in-law."

"Yes, you do Ariel! I am glad you and Elisheva are happy. She deserves the best."

Gershon, pleased as he listened to their conversation said, "It is good you and Itai get along well. We will have to work hard to establish our business in Dameseq. No doubt, many merchants already offer a wide variety of wines."

Gershon said that by staying alert and aware of their surroundings, they could learn a lot about King Tigranes' plans. Rumors fly through cities. The market always knows what is about to happen. By observing the number of soldiers, the status of warehouses, the movement of diplomats, and work on the city's defenses, we can report valuable information to King Alexander Yanai. He can then determine if a threat to Israel exists.

Gershon told them, "Our mission is important. I caution both of you never ever to mention an interest in anything other than trade. Syria is a foreign country, and we are visitors. We must always be innocent merchants. I am sure I do not have to caution either of you to avoid strong drink and to beware of compromising situations. If anyone even suspects we are more than merchants, it will not end well for us, and no one will be able to help."

Ariel enjoyed relaxing and sipping wine by the warm fire although the discussion sobered him.

Gershon said, "We have a long day tomorrow. I suggest we sleep now. We will have plenty of time tomorrow to talk." Gershon told Itai and Ariel that they had to guard against dangerous predators and make sure the fire does not burn out. "Tonight, each of us will maintain the fire for three hours."

Gershon took the last watch and unpacked the morning meal. I had prepared a feast of smoked fish, goat cheese, carrots, sweet rolls, apples, and mint to make hot tea.

Their camp was a short climb to the plain leading to Dameseq. Just visible through a dusty haze were two small hills; like sentinels, they would guide them straight to the city.

On the high plain it was hot; they were hungry and would soon stop for their afternoon meal and rest for a while. As they looked for a shaded place, Syrian soldiers stopped them. Gershon explained they were probably the forward guard to prevent incursions from Israel.

"Travelers, identify yourselves."

"I am Gershon Ben Avraham, and this is my son, Ariel, and his brother-in-law, Itai. I am from Jerusalem, and my son lives in Dan. We bring a message from the King of Israel for King Tigranes the Great."

"It takes three people to carry one message? Let me see this message, Gershon Ben Avraham."

Itai started to reach for his knife, but a slight shake of Ariel's head stopped him. Ariel had seen professional soldiers in Jerusalem impose their will with ease. They would have made short work of them at the first sign of resistance. Gershon knew how to negotiate with soldiers.

"Captain, I am old. I sometimes mistake north for south and east for west. My sons make sure we keep heading toward Dameseq. After we deliver our King's message, they will make sure we take the correct route home. I am lucky to have sons—am I not Captain? I should add that as a matter of honor, I am obligated to present this message to King Tigranes in person. I can show you the container holding the message with the royal seal of King Alexander Yanai. I cannot open the container as that would break the seal."

"Well, Gershon Ben Avraham if you do not show me the message, you will not pass. Or maybe I will just take it from you, leave you here for the vultures, and bring it to the King myself."

"Captain, I understand I request a special favor to pass with the seal unbroken. Perhaps for your trouble, I can compensate you with some fine wine from the fields around Kedesh. The wine is renowned for its fruity flavors with a hint of berries and cinnamon."

"What if I take your wine and the message?"

"If King Tigranes does not respond, my King will send another message—this time with a guard of soldiers. He will inform King Tigranes he had sent a previous messenger who had left Dan, spoke with travelers near the Greek Temple to Pan, not even a day's journey from here, but did not arrive in Dameseq."

This stopped the guard, and he considered for a few minutes whether he could take what he wanted without being discovered. His men would betray him in an instant, and King Tigranes would show no mercy if he robbed and murdered an envoy. He decided to let Gershon pass.

In a commanding, rather than accommodating, voice he said, "Gershon Ben Avraham, I will try your wine. If I find it to my liking, I will escort you to the city entrance."

"I am sure, Captain, you will find this wine one of the best you have tasted. I would be most grateful for your escort. Thank you. It is a full day travel to Dameseq. We should rest here with the other travelers and continue in the morning. Will your offer of an escort still hold tomorrow?"

"Yes, Gershon Ben Avraham. Soldiers of King Tigranes the Great are honorable and always keep their word. We will leave at first light."

# BOOK NINE—PARTNERS IN CRIME

Doron was a big man, but he was lean and moved with the deliberate grace of a big cat. He wore a permanent scowl that inspired fear. Few trusted him, and none dared to cross him.

High on the mountain, he stood still in the cool night air and smoked a cigarette. He was exposed and an easy target for anyone following him. All night he sensed he was hunted and suspected it was the special police anti-smuggling unit. Several times, he stopped in the pine forest and listened. The wind in his face masked the sound of anyone trailing him. He turned around sure he could hear footsteps even if muffled by the pine straw.

He put out his cigarette and retraced his steps. There was no one. He was alone near the border and breathed easy. As he approached a bend in the road near the fence separating Israel and Lebanon, he spotted the camouflaged backpack. He picked it up, opened the flap to verify the contents, and then threw an identical backpack filled with Euros and Dollars over the fence. The anticipation of another successful drug transaction and a rich payday lightened his step as he walked to his car.

Phone taps had alerted police detectives that a delivery was imminent. Unaware that both the police and the border patrol observed him, Doron drove down the steep, winding mountain road careful to maintain the speed limit. He paid no attention to the nondescript car leaving the parking lot at Tel Hai College that followed as he turned to Kiryat Shemona and drove south on Route 90 towards Tiberius.

Money and drugs exchanged at the roundabout near Elifelet completed the night's work. Doron headed home, relieved and relishing the prospect of a good meal with his wife in one of the better restaurants in Migdal. With the money from this transaction in his pocket, he thought now a good time for a month long vacation in Las Vegas. He could return home, declare some of the money as winnings, and pay his taxes as a good citizen.

His cell phone rang. Aware of a police radar trap at the bottom of the hill, Doron pulled to the side and answered. "Hello, Ratib. How are you, my friend?"

"I am well, thank you. Doron, I have a matter of some urgency to discuss with you—it concerns what may be a golden opportunity."

"Tell me more. I do love golden opportunities."

"I think it best if we meet and discuss it in private. Where are you now?"

"I am on Route 90 just north of the exit for Tiberius. I could meet you in about thirty minutes in Kiryat Shemona. Does that suit you?"

"Good, let's meet at the café near the entrance to the industrial park."

Two men sat at the rear of the small café, eating croissants and sipping coffee when Ratib and Doron entered. They sat opposite the door on the other side of the room. It was a simple place decorated with several faded photos and framed magazine pictures: one showed a snow-covered Mount Hermon and the other a well-tanned girl smiling from a sailboat at Eilat. They looked at the menu and ordered espressos and poppy-seed pastries.

Ratib tasted his coffee. "Two days ago, a man came to see me. He said he possessed a rare scroll discovered at Tel Dan. He worked at the Tel and removed the scroll from the site forty years earlier. He has kept it hidden until now. I have not seen the scroll; he says it is long and maintains it is more than two-thousand-years old. He asked me to find a buyer."

Doron listened without interrupting. "This sounds interesting. Tell me what you know about this man? What is his name? Could he be working with the police? Do you think it may be a police sting?"

"I worried about the same thing. You never can be too careful these days. I checked. He is an honorable man and respected in his village. I think the theft was an indiscretion of youth and the fear of prosecution is the reason he kept it hidden."

"Ratib, why does he want to sell the scroll now?"

"He needs money to help his family in Syria. He is the patriarch of his family, and honor requires him to help even if it is at great risk to himself."

Doron thought about this for a few seconds and nodded. "Yes, I understand that as a good Muslim, honor demands he make every effort to assist. Tell me, Ratib, what do you think this scroll is about? Is it in good shape? Can it be dated?"

"Carbon dating established the layer above the scroll at 50 BC. Musa claims the scroll is in perfect condition. I told him the scroll's assessed value depends on its condition and subject. If it is simply an inventory or contract, the scroll might be worth a few hundred shekels. He believes it may rival the Dead Sea Scrolls in importance and is worth much more. Doron, would you be interested in being a partner in this transaction? Do you have contacts that could appraise the scroll and suggest buyers?"

"I will make inquiries. What sort of partnership do you have in mind?"

"I had not thought about it, but say forty-five percent for me, thirty-five percent for you, and twenty percent for the finder."

"That is reasonable, Ratib. However, I will be taking a great amount of risk; sixty-six percent of the net value is more realistic."

Ratib thought for a minute. This was a negotiation—nothing more. Yet, he had to be careful. Men like Doron were dangerous, and he did not want to lose control of this deal. "Doron, I think we can insulate ourselves from most of the risk; after all, we were not the ones who violated the antiquities law. If the seller is correct, we can make a lot of money. I could agree to forty-five percent for you, forty percent for me, and fifteen percent for the finder—and as a bonus, I will pay for the coffee."

Doron laughed. "You drive a hard bargain, Ratib. I agree. Let's go to the mall and buy two new cell phones to use for our new joint venture."

The two men on the other side of the café made a phone call, waited five minutes, and left.

# BOOK TEN—KINGS

I was relieved when Ariel told me that Gershon's diplomacy convinced the soldiers to escort them to Dameseq.

That night Gershon, Ariel, and my brother slept, along with other travelers to Dameseq, on the plain near the soldiers' outpost. It was a cool night, and the warmth of the fire after a good meal was a pleasant end to a long day. Staring at the flames, they listened to travelers from different countries speak about the never-ending wars around the Great Sea. Sometimes, Ariel was positive he had heard the same news years ago on the road to Jerusalem. Leaders and generals changed, locations were different, but the wars continued. It seemed a terrible storm approached closer and closer to Israel. Like the wind and the rain, they were powerless to stop or change its direction.

The future frightened me. I heard stories of women raped and people butchered by conquering armies. I knew the walls around Dan would protect us for a while. A long siege though would mean starvation, disease, and death. I did not want to think about what would happen if the enemy made it past our walls.

For the past several years, Rome pushed into Asia. Lucius Cornelius Sulla and his General Lucius Licinius Lucullus led their army against King Mithridates VI of Pontus. They were ruthless. King Tigranes of Armenia agreed to support King Mithridates and secure his flank against Rome. The alliance was ensured when Tigranes married King Mithridates' daughter, Cleopatra. The more I learned, the more I realized that many leaders did not marry for love, rather for advantage. I was lucky. I married the man I loved.

Tigranes was the son of a King. For him, love was a tool of ambition. He was a wise, clever man and avoided conflict with Rome. Free by alliance to send his armies east, he created an empire. King Tigranes—later known as "The Great"—ruled from the border with Israel in the south to the Caspian Sea in the north, and from Pontus and Phoenicia in the west to Mesopotamia in the east. People who had been to his court said King Tigranes believed that a magnificent comet announced his ascension to the throne. In recent years, in a show of power, he always had four kings attending him.

Ariel wondered, as did I, where his next conquest would be. A few travelers suggested he might follow Alexander the Great's path and attempt to conquer India. Others thought the obvious choice would be to move south and push into Israel and Egypt.

"Why," Ariel asked, "is Israel always threatened?"

He then told me what one particularly well-dressed traveler said. The group was silent showing unusual deference. "Israel is a rich land. The Jews' Torah defined it as a land flowing with milk and honey, and it does. Tribute has been paid to their Temple for hundreds of years, and the treasury is full. That alone guarantees invasions."

Now everyone paid close attention to his words.

"The land is productive, the people educated, and their cities beautiful. The Merom Valley, Jezreel Valley, and the lower Galilee region produce enough food for the population and still leave plenty for export. And, that is only the northern part of the country. Israel is a wealthy country with a high quality of life."

A man near the edge of the group interrupted, "and my friends, they have excellent wine and great food."

Many travelers murmured agreement.

A voice from the back shouted, "And beautiful women."

Ariel added, "Very beautiful women."

Itai grinned and put his arm around Ariel. "Well said, Ariel."

The travelers, a little drunk and knowing that Ariel was married to Itai's sister, laughed. Then a shout arose, "Ugly brother of a beautiful woman bring more of your wonderful wine."

A small man sitting near the back said in a quiet voice, "Brothers, the real threat today is Rome, not King Tigranes." That sobered the celebration. True, King Tigranes was close to Israel. In view of his ambitions to create a large empire, he had to be considered an immediate threat. For now, Rome, with inexhaustible armies and resources, pushed into Asia. How long would it be before Rome moved against King Tigranes? How long before advancing south to Israel and Egypt?

Now I understood the critical need for intelligence and why King Alexander Yanai and Queen Shlomtsion were anxious that Gershon trade in Dameseq. Intelligence would warn of a threat that could engulf and ruin us. I recognized our vulnerability. The lessons I had learned in school about the times we fought against invaders were now real to me. We have created a wonderful country and way of life. We will always have to fight to protect it.

Ariel, feeling the responsibility, enormity, and the danger of their mission slept uneasily that night. While it seemed noble and brave the day before, the discussion around the fire sobered him. He resolved to do anything and everything to protect his family and his country.

Anxious to reach Dameseq, Gershon, Itai and Ariel woke early. While they prepared to leave, they ate a cold meal with warm tea. The soldiers, true to their word, were ready at dawn to accompany them to the city gates.

Ariel looked forward to seeing Dameseq, the fabled city of jasmine. I had heard several travelers say that Dameseq was one of the oldest cities in the world—even older than Dan and maybe as old as Jericho.

Gershon, Itai, and Ariel were half a day's journey from the city when they first saw the outline of the walls. A faint haze of smoke and dust hovered over the city. The mountains of the Anti-Lebanon hugged the city to the west, and the Abana River bordered the walls to the north. It was a perfect location between the river valleys of Babylon to the east and the Great Sea two days journey to the west. Gershon told them that Dameseq had been and still was a central point in the spice trade between Arabia and the busy Lebanese ports on the Great Sea. For hundreds of years, there had been a robust trade between Israel and Dameseq—encouraged by alliances but interrupted, at times, by enmity and conflict.

They reached the city just before the gates closed for the night. Tired and dusty, they sought an inn. Itai and Ariel went to the market to shop for vegetables, fruit, and bread for a simple evening meal. Few stalls remained open. Ariel said the market was huge, much bigger than Dan's market and comparable to Jerusalem's. They would have to convince King Tigranes that they had something special to offer.

***

In the morning, they presented themselves at the gates of the palace. The soldiers that accompanied them introduced them to the palace guards and requested they notify the King's secretary that a courier had arrived from the Kingdom of Israel. After a short time, the King's secretary granted Gershon permission to enter. After a brief discussion, they permitted Ariel and Itai to accompany Gershon.

After waiting half a day, they entered a magnificent room—the floor covered with exquisite blood red carpets, the walls made from perfectly fitting sandstone blocks. Fruit trees and two citron trees in blossom in huge jars placed along the walls added contrast. The scent of jasmine mixed with the fragrance of the citron blossoms lent to the opulence of the room.

King Tigranes sat in a large cushioned chair receiving ministers and ambassadors. His personal secretary stood to his left and to his right the first minister. Four Kings from different provinces of his empire stood behind him. Gershon, Ariel, and Itai approached and bowed. The King looked at them for a short time and said, "I am told you have a message for me."

Gershon, replied, "Alexander Yanai, King of Israel has directed me, and it is my honor, to deliver this message to you. May I approach?"

"Yes. Tell me, how are you called?"

The King's secretary moved forward meeting Gershon halfway, taking the message from Gershon and handing it to the King.

"My name is Gershon Ben Avraham. I come with my son, Ariel, and son-in-law, Itai Ben Nadav from Dan."

"You have a noble name, Gershon Ben Avraham. I see King Alexander Yanai asks I grant you trading rights in Dameseq. Why should I do that?"

"My family and I are traders of fine wine and spices. I have the good fortune to supply wine to the King's court. My King felt you might also favor the wines from the Kedesh Valley vineyards. He asked me to relay warm greetings on his behalf and his desire for increased trade and closer relations with the Kingdom of Armenia. He also asked me to present a gift to you along with a sampling of Israel's wines."

"I will taste the wines your King is so proud of and recommends. I should warn you though that Armenian wines have been prized in the great cities of Mesopotamia as well as around the Great Sea for hundreds of years. It is written that wine was first given to Noah at Mount Ararat to alleviate all the suffering he endured during the Great Flood."

"Your majesty, because of the magnificent wines produced in Armenia and the sophisticated tastes for fine wines, we are confident that an additional variety also would be of interest. We hope that our wines will find favor as a complement to the excellent wines from Armenia."

"Return tomorrow. I will have a reply for King Alexander Yanai."

"It would be my honor to deliver your message to my King."

***

After leaving the palace, they spent the remainder of the day inspecting the market. They saw goods from the Lebanese ports, Mesopotamia, and all corners of the empire. There was an exciting hum of a thousand people haggling, hawking, and laughing. They could feel the tense rhythm of a great market. They understood the challenge to establish themselves as new merchants in a market where traders have done business for years.

Ariel thought they might have to forgo profit and might even lose capital to accomplish their main mission.

Gershon said, "Perhaps so. Let us see what tomorrow brings—we still do not have a license to trade. In the meantime, let us see more of Dameseq. I want to get a sense of the neighborhoods, in particular where the rich live, and also see the river to the north of the city wall."

They wandered through the different quarters of the city. The wealthy areas had well cared-for houses each shielded by an elaborate gate. The tree-lined streets portrayed elegance like the areas' inhabitants. In contrast, the poorer areas were noisy and colorful. Neighbors talked to each other through open windows across narrow streets filled with people, shops, and merchants announcing their products and services. Dameseq was a vibrant city built on a strength and resilience created after a millennium.

They woke the next morning before sunrise, ate a light meal of bread, olives, and cheese, and went to the palace entrance. Unsure when they would be summoned, they wanted to be at the gate early. They were the first ones there.

\*\*\*

They waited half the morning before a guard called Gershon's name and ushered them into an elaborate waiting room. The floor was strewn with beautiful carpets with light beige and pale blue designs of birds and flowers.

"Gershon Ben Avraham, your wine is truly excellent. Please tell your King I appreciate his gift and indeed agree Israel has fine wines. Please deliver my reply to King Alexander Yanai along with this prized Armenian Rose Wine. I grant you the right to trade Israeli wines in Dameseq. I asked my wife's nephew, Ciro, to become your partner, to assist, and to represent you in Dameseq. He will obtain a central location in the market and all necessary licenses. I assume this arrangement will be acceptable to you."

"You do us great honor, King Tigranes. We are most grateful."

King Tigranes beckoned one of the Kings in attendance and requested he escort them to meet Ciro.

\*\*\*

Ciro was an imposing figure: large-framed with a booming voice. He was a gracious, jolly man who quite openly relished the opportunity for profit. For him, this was perfect: Gershon, Ariel, and Itai would take all the risk, and he would share the profit.

Even so, it was a good business relationship. Ciro had something Gershon, Ariel, and Itai needed: he would obtain, by virtue of his position, a prime location in the market, and he had ready access to the noble families and merchants of Dameseq. As a member of the royal family—even if somewhat removed—Ciro would be knowledgeable about the latest news. They needed to establish more than a business relationship with Ciro. That might be the most important benefit of the partnership. The trip succeeded beyond all expectations.

\*\*\*

As soon as they left Dameseq, Gershon asked Itai and Ariel, "What did you learn while in Dameseq?"

Ariel responded, "We established a partnership with a member of the royal family that may provide us with relevant information."

Itai agreed saying, "We are off to a good start."

"But," Gershon again asked, "What did we learn? Who was at the court when we met the King? Who was not at the court?"

Ariel said, "There were no soldiers."

Gershon said, "Soldiers were there, but no high-ranking soldiers. What do we learn from that?"

Itai hesitated for a second and said that it meant no military operations were imminent.

"Maybe," said Gershon. "We need confirmation before we could be certain of that conclusion. Did we see anything we could use to confirm or deny a military operation? We approached Dameseq from the south and did not see any large encampments of soldiers. We walked around Dameseq all the way to the wall by the Abana River, again without seeing any soldiers or what looked like a group of senior commanders. Itai is correct. There are probably no plans for a military action—at this time.

"We have to remember that we can confirm only what we see. Chances are, we will never see the whole picture. It is important we be precise about what we see and what we do not see. The King and his military council will know how to understand what we report."

Ariel and Itai realized the task was far more complicated than they had thought. If anything, they were now more determined. It would be a great challenge—even if dangerous—to fit together the pieces of a complex international puzzle. They felt that the security of their families, Dan, and Israel depended on what they would learn.

I sat at the table by the olive tree when Ariel entered the courtyard. I ran to him, jumped into his hug, and we twirled round and round. "I missed you, husband."

"I missed you, wife."

"Kiss me, Ariel. Then tell me all about your trip."

"Only one kiss?"

"For now."

"Elisheva, show me what you have done in our home. I want to hear about everything you did last week."

"Every day I worked on our home. The cooking area is organized. I bought some decorations for our sleeping room, and I started to embroider pillows."

"Elisheva, I love the colorful decorations. It makes our home alive."

I blushed. I was happy Ariel was home. He was safe. I twirled around for no reason. "Thank you Ariel, I'm glad you like what I did. Now husband, tell about your trip. What is Dameseq like?"

"Dameseq is an interesting city. It is in a beautiful location. Mountains border the city to the west and a river lies to the north. Roads to Nineveh and Persia lead to the east. To the south, we can see the Golan plain, Bashan, and the Hermon Mountain. The city feels alive with an underlying pulse of life and vitality. Dameseq is a lot bigger than Dan although not as big as Jerusalem. I did not see all of the market. The part I saw had goods from all over the world."

"It was a good trip. *Aba* was granted an interview right away. *Aba* convinced the guards to let me and Itai accompany him. I was thrilled. The King is an imposing man. The palace is magnificent. I had never seen anything like it. *Aba* said it is nicer than the palace in Jerusalem. King Tigranes granted us a license to trade wine. He even arranged for his wife's nephew, Ciro, to be our business partner."

"Is that good? Won't you have to share your profit with the Queen's nephew?" I asked.

"Yes, but it is necessary. It will work to our advantage for several reasons."

"In what way is it to our advantage to share our profits with someone? Will he share in any losses that may incur? I do not understand the advantage."

"One of our objectives is to learn about Armenia's intentions. It is important to us, as we are close to the border; Dan would be the first city to confront an invasion. King Alexander Yanai wants to anticipate any action so he can act to prevent or defend against any attempt to invade Israel."

"It still makes no sense to me. Ciro assumes no risk and contributes no money to the business. Will he come to Dan to take delivery of the wine?"

"No. He will take delivery in Dameseq. However, as merchants selling fine wine, we will be in contact with rich and influential families in Dameseq. They usually know well in advance about planned actions. Not only should our business be profitable; we will be able to serve our country. Anyway, we could not refuse if the King wants Ciro to be our partner."

"Ariel, I am worried. What if someone suspects you provide information about King Tigranes' plans? Will you not be in danger? If you deal with the King's nephew, you might be suspected if their spies in Jerusalem hear of your reports."

"To be truthful, I am also concerned. I do not have a choice. Everything we have here at Dan, everything we believe in may be threatened. For a thousand years, we have had to fight to remain free in our country. Our ancestor's blood has soaked the soil. We have fought countless invaders to protect our country. I want my children to know peace, happiness, and safety. This has to be done."

"Well, I guess it is our lot to always be in danger. I am proud that you can do something to protect our country—even if no one will ever know. I understand now what Yamima felt whenever Gershon was on a mission for the King. Do always be careful, my love. Sit here a moment my husband; I will bring you something to eat and drink. You must be hungry."

"I am starving. And not only for food."

"Eat first, my love, and then go to the stream to wash. Afterwards, I will show you all the decorations I added to our sleeping room."

"And then?"

"Be patient, my husband—do you not want to see all that I added to our sleeping room?"

For the longest time, we held each other whispering in our special language. Soon I moved my hands over his back while Ariel responded by brushing my back from my waist up to my neck and then moving his fingers through my hair. He pushed me back and stroked my breasts while I traced his stomach with my right hand. It excited him, and I felt it immediately. The room seemed hot. Our kisses reached for a deeper connection. I moved my hand down at the same time he did, and we both felt a heat born of love and the need to be one. I moaned as we joined, and I felt love for this man that I would never ever feel with anyone else. I was his for eternity and as our rhythm quickened, I whispered, "I love you, Ariel. I never want to be without you."

We woke early the next morning. I went to the cooking area, started the day's bread, and prepared two cups of tea. I returned to the sleeping room, handed Ariel both cups before removing my robe, and lying down. We spoke about the house; we spoke about Dan; we spoke about vineyards and different types of wine; we spoke about the future.

Ariel said, "I am confident that our business in Dameseq will be profitable. I thought to build a secret place where we can keep our money safe. What do you think?"

"It is a good idea. Did I tell you that while you and Itai were gone, Adah came to visit? We had a wonderful time. We talked for what must have been hours. Itai had bought her a beautiful necklace. It might be a good idea to suggest to Itai that he also build a safe place to keep money and jewelry."

"I will talk to Itai. But we should not mention it to anyone—except of course our children when they are old enough."

"But, husband, we do not have any children yet."

"Yes, and I know exactly what we should do about that."

"Stop it, Ariel. You embarrass me."

124

"Anyway, I could build a double wall in our sleeping room. It would provide a layer of insulation that will keep us cooler in the summer and warmer in the winter along with a secret place to store what we consider too valuable to lose."

"Can you make it big enough so that I can keep my recipes and the scrolls I value in it?"

"I think so. I have to figure out how to seal the space so that it remains dry and well protected."

"Ariel, do you think we could add some shelves in our sleeping room so I can put some colorful ceramic plates or perhaps a ceramic pomegranate to remind us of the New Year and the good deeds we should do in the coming year?"

"I can do that. You have such wonderful ideas. Our home will be better than a palace."

"Come Ariel. Now we have to get up. The day must be half over, and I am hungry. I am sure we both have much to do."

"I will get up if you give me one more kiss... and one more hug."

"Only one more then up you go."

Ariel was away—this time to Tyre to negotiate with Hiram a new contract to export wine to Rome. Wines from the Kedesh Valley gained recognition and were prized in different capitals of the Roman Empire. Hiram told Ariel that the Romans, under the command of Publius Servilius and Julius Caesar, were in the midst of a naval campaign to rid the Aegean Sea of pirates. That would increase the safety of our exports.

Itai sent larger caravans and more wine to Tyre and Dameseq. This year, Ariel and Itai decided to sell a new wine aged for a short time. It was a light red wine that the aristocratic families in Rome prized. It added to the quantities we already shipped.

Ariel and I spent many nights developing a new approach to trading in wine. I thought that if we agreed to buy specific amounts and paid the growers in advance, we could then contract with the buyers who would pay us in advance for the guaranteed delivery. We had the capital to start the venture, and I was sure it would increase our dominance in the wine market.

The contracts were to everyone's advantage. The growers received money when they signed the contract. They used the advance payments in part to expand the vineyards. In return, they guaranteed Ariel a supply of wine. He then promised specific amounts to exporters like Hiram who advanced payment for guaranteed future delivery. Because the weather was similar year to year, Ariel thought the risk low. Nevertheless, Gershon insisted Ariel set aside some of the profit every year in case the weather was too wet, too cold, or there was a problem with the harvest.

Despite feeling sick, I started to plan my purchases in the market for a special meal to celebrate what I was sure would be another successful venture. Our business expanded, and profits increased every year.

I remembered the first meal I helped *Ima* cook for Gershon and his sons. Ariel and I were so young. We tried so hard not to look at each other. Or, maybe it was the other way around, and we tried hard to look at each other unobserved.

This time, I planned a red wine and pomegranate marinade. I would cook the chicken over a hot fire to seal in the juices and roast it over a low fire until golden brown, periodically brushing with pomegranate juice to produce a brilliant red glaze. I would add brown lentils cooked with chopped onion and stock made from the neck and back of the chicken. An onion cooked in olive oil and seasoned with salt, red pepper flakes, and golden turmeric completed the plate. I chose an exceptional white wine to chill in the stream and serve with the meal.

I always enjoyed the market—the colors, smells, and noise associated with the calls of merchants and the purchase of food. I started at the vegetable and fruit stands, breathed in deep to enjoy the fragrances of ripe fruit and the earthy smell of the vegetables. Before I left, I would purchase the chicken. I stopped at the cheese maker and bought sheep cheese to fry in olive oil and sprinkle with parsley and cilantro or perhaps a small amount of dill. Served with warm pita and salad, it makes a delicious light meal.

When I reached the meat section, I did not feel right. The smell of raw meat and chickens being slaughtered brought on an overwhelming wave of nausea. I felt faint and turned pale. Several people rushed to help me sit. A few of the women started fanning me all the while smiling. I was embarrassed and did not understand why they were smiling.

"What month are you in, dear?"

I looked up not understanding.

"Are you pregnant, my dear?"

All of a sudden, I understood. I was not sick. Everything Ariel and I prayed for would come true.

One of the women told me I would feel better if I ate a few bites of dry bread. Another brought a cup of fruit juice. I took a few sips, and the nausea passed.

I hugged the woman who helped me. I felt so many emotions I barely managed to thank her. I was so happy, I almost cried.

"Aren't you Noa's daughter, Elisheva, who married the trader from Jerusalem?"

"Yes. I am the daughter of Nadav and Noa; my husband, Ariel, is from Jerusalem."

"Now I remember. I was at your wedding. Even Queen Shlomtsion sent you and your husband greetings. We were honored the Queen recognized a daughter of Dan. My name is Ya'arah. Please give my best regards to your *Ima*."

"I will and thank you so much, Ya'arah, for helping me."

"Take care of yourself, Elisheva. You have a new life growing in you."

I ran home—being careful not to slip and fall. Tonight would indeed be a special meal.

Ariel came home at midday. I prepared cheese, vegetables with pita, and a cup of pear juice. Ariel said he had much to tell me. Now, he had to eat and leave to meet Itai. He said it would not take long and that we would talk when he got home. Smiling, he added perhaps we could even whisper secrets to each other.

"I want to hear all about what you did while I was gone. I have a lot of good news to tell you," he said.

"I accomplished a lot while you were away, my husband. I will tell you everything later. Meanwhile, I planned a special meal for tonight to celebrate the good news of what I assume—or rather—am sure was a successful trip. Would you mind purchasing a few of the scented candles I like?"

I decided to cook one of Ariel's favorite appetizers. After sautéing onions in olive oil flavored with sage leaves, I added chicken livers to the sauté, poured in a small amount of red wine, increased the fire to burn off the alcohol, and finished the dish with several spoons of date paste. Warm bread and a new red wine complemented the sauté. The main course would be chicken paired with a chilled white wine. For desert, I planned a plain yellow cake covered with warmed crushed persimmon—just as *Ima* made when we sat opposite each other that first Shabbat evening meal.

Ariel came home before sunset after reviewing the contract negotiations concluded with Hiram. If all went as expected, Itai needed to expand his part of the business. They considered adding either a senior manager or perhaps another partner. They would discuss it at the next semi-annual meeting with Gershon and Yoav. Meanwhile, they would need to work overtime to carry the expanding business. I was not happy that Ariel would spend more time on business. At the same time, I was pleased our family prospered. Itai and Ariel became close friends in addition to brothers-in-law and business partners. They felt and acted like brothers.

We sat in the garden by our olive tree. I brought a small plate with cut vegetables, a spicy eggplant spread, and toasted pieces of bread to go with a small cup of wine. "Tell me, husband, how was your trip?"

"It was a good trip. The path was easy, and it was good to see Hiram. He is a fine man; our business went well. We will supply more wine for export to Rome. It has become a favorite among the wealthy in the capital. I see our business being even more profitable in the future. Itai will be busy; he needs to add employees. Business in the south also increases; Yoav already proposed that our brother, Hillel, work with him. Your brother, Allon, might be just the right man to work with Itai. I need to speak with *Aba* and Yoav. I doubt there will be a problem. To be safe, we should not say anything yet to Itai."

"Of course. I do not discuss what we talk about with anyone."

"Most of all, my wife, I missed you."

"I missed you, my husband. I did manage to do something important."

"Tell me, Elisheva."

"First, I should tell you that I almost fainted in the market this morning."

"What happened? Are you all right? You do look different. I think you have never looked prettier. What might this be? Did you ask your *Ima* what to do? Maybe you should take some medicine? Maybe you need some lemongrass or ginger tea. I'll make some for you now."

"Wait, Ariel. I will have tea later. No, I did not tell *Ima*. I wanted to tell you first."

"Why didn't you tell your *Ima* you don't feel well?"

"Because I never felt better in my life."

"I don't understand. If you fainted, I think you should talk to your *Ima*. We can go over now."

"Ariel, I am pregnant."

For a long moment, Ariel sat not saying a word. He just stared at me. His mouth opened, but he said nothing. As the realization sunk in, he looked at me and shouted, "You are pregnant," so loud I was sure all the neighbors heard.

"Yes, Ariel." He hugged me and kept saying how much he loved me.

"Did you tell your *Ima*?"

"No. I wanted to tell you first."

"Here I tell you all about my business deal with Hiram and plans with Itai while you are growing a life and our future. I feel so foolish boring you with trivial and unimportant business dealings."

"Ariel, everything about our family is important." I sat in his lap. "Kiss me, Ariel." He put his arms around me, kissed me, put his head on my breast, and held me tight. He then lifted my robe and kissed my belly. We were so happy.

I worried about the safety of our Kingdom and my family. Many invaders sought the riches of our land and tried to impose their way of life and religion on us. I felt an ache in my heart when I thought of the generations that fought, and those who died to keep us free. My King, Alexander Yanai, like other Kings of Israel before him, worked to increase the size of the kingdom to provide strategic depth. The wars were a constant reminder that we were never completely safe.

I try not to think about the enemies around us. I want my family to have a normal life. I worry about Ariel when he travels. My imagination runs wild when I think of all the things that can happen. I have heard stories about traders leaving home and never returning.

I know it is a dangerous world. I think the principle danger is in the north—too close to Dan and my family. I am frightened by Armenia. After everything I have heard about the brutality of Rome, their expanding power, and steady approach to Israel scares me even more.

Ariel suspects that King Tigranes cannot avoid a clash with Rome. While King Mithridates challenged Rome for control of Pontus and Greece, King Tigranes expanded his empire to the east. He gained time to build strength for the inevitable war with Rome for control of the Levant.

Ariel and I wondered if the child growing in my belly would be safe and what we could do to protect our family. While I worried Ariel would be in danger because of his real mission in Dameseq, I knew it was necessary. I was proud of Ariel. He risked everything for Israel and our family's safety. I hoped it would not be this way forever. Maybe someday, there will be peace, maybe someday we could prosper together with our neighbors, and maybe someday I would not have to worry about my children's safety. I wish that someday could be now.

I trust our King will protect us. He recognizes the growing threats in the North and moves to strengthen our position. He recruited a new army enhanced with foreign recruits. Because of the long-standing enmity and downright hatred of Jews, none of the recruited soldiers were from Syria. That was good, as the campaign centered in Bashan, not far from the border with Syria.

Today a personal representative of Queen Shlomtsion came to Dan. People gathered near the city gates to hear his message.

He told us the army laid siege to Ragaba—one of the walled towns of Bashan originally settled by the Israelite tribe of Menashe. It was a pastoral land fed by springs. Ragaba was strategically located to attack the flank of any army approaching Israel from the north as well as to interrupt trade between Mesopotamia and Dameseq.

The operation made sense to me and would keep us safe.

The messenger told us that Queen Shlomtsion accompanied the King. She was highly educated, an excellent strategist, and often led the army in battle. The soldiers respected her.

I so much admired her.

The next part frightened everyone listening. Disease ravaged the army, and our King suffered from an intense fever that recurred every four days. Each time the fever struck, it seemed harder for him to tolerate the bouts of high temperature. The healers feared it was quartan ague, made worse by years of excessive drinking and campaigning in primitive conditions. As far as I know, people living near swamps suffered from this disease. After prolonged suffering, they died.

Queen Shlomtsion tried to comfort the King telling him that he must be strong and fight the sickness. She said they have a greater responsibility than themselves. You cannot die now that we face so many threats.

But Alexander was dying and he wanted to make amends. He asked Shlomtsion to forgive him that he was always busy with affairs of state and often away protecting or expanding the borders of the kingdom. He said that he tried to be a good King like David and Solomon, but he knew that he failed and it was only because of Shlomtsion, that civil war did not divide the country. He wanted her to correct his mistakes.

He told her that he was jealous when she married his brother, Aristobulus. He said, he had always been in love with her, and fears now it is too late to make up for all the time spent away. He told her he wished he had been a wiser and a better husband.

The Queen tried to comfort him. She assured him he will recover—even though she probably did not truly believe it. Alexander, you are a good man. It was ordained at the creation of the world that I would be your wife. Even though affairs of state always pressed, I never doubted you loved me. I understood your commitment to be a good king. It is not yet your time, Alexander; stay with me.

But it was too late. King Alexander Yanai knew he would not recover. He wanted her to know that he regretted having supported the Sadducees against the Pharisees. You were right. The new way of life that the Greeks imposed on us and we embraced for a time has not produced the balances needed for a healthy society. In our tradition, all members of society—men, women, rich, poor—have dignity and are honored. Our society will stand the test of time. Despite the remarkable achievements in art, literature, and science, the contradictions in Greek society will doom their way of life.

The King admitted that he should have insisted that we return to a pious path. He should have supported the Pharisees as Queen Shlomtsion advised. He told the Queen to make that right now. "Return the Kingdom to the correct path." He said, "When I die, which will not be long now, I want you to rule. Our people need you. Neither of our children is ready to assume the throne, and neither would be a good King now."

His final instruction to Queen Shlomtsion was that if he dies before the battle for Ragaba is finished, she should complete the fight and return to Jerusalem before word of his death reaches the capital. Take the reins of government. Make sure that no one threatens her ascension to the throne as the sole ruler of Israel.

Now his strength was failing, but he continued to instruct Queen Shlomtsion. He said to her, "Enemies surround us. It seems that every day a new threat arises.

Keep our country strong. Your friendship with Cleopatra in Egypt and neighboring Kings will help you navigate a dangerous world. Our people have always loved you and valued your piousness. I know you will be a good and wise Queen. Under your rule, I am sure the Kingdom will be safe and our people will prosper."

He begged Queen Shlomtsion to bury him in Jerusalem and mourn him not as Alexander Yanai but by his Hebrew name, Jonathon. "Do not forget me, Shlomtsion."

Shlomtsion's husband, known to the world as Alexander Yanai and to the people of Israel as Jonathon, one of the last of the Hasmonean Kings that had ruled since the time of the Maccabees, died two days later. As he wished, she kept his death secret and led the final attack that captured Ragaba. She secretly brought Jonathon's body back to Jerusalem for burial. At her urging, and despite suffering at his hands, the Pharisees honored his grave together with the Sadducees, thus paving the way to unite the government and the people once again.

We were frightened. What would happen to us in Dan? I listened with my head lowered. My tears fell on the ground by my feet. All my life, he had been my King. I remembered the night Gershon said Queen Shlomtsion would make an excellent ruler. I prayed he was right.

Queen Shlomtsion now ruled Israel. In Jerusalem, the Pharisees said she was determined to rule wisely and be a good Queen. She promised to protect Israel in a world ever more dangerous, reform the legal system, expand the rights of women, strengthen the Kingdom's defenses, increase the size of the army, form new alliances, reinforce old ones, introduce economic reforms, and most important, lead the country back to a path of piety and righteousness as established by our forefathers at Mount Sinai. She said, "Our covenant with God is the strength of our people; its laws are the strength of our society."

I mourned our King. I looked at the sky, bright with sunshine and towering white clouds. A gentle wind blew from the south carrying the scents of my paradise. In my heart, I knew Queen Shlomtsion would be a good and wise ruler. I trusted in our future.

The day started like every other one. I lingered in bed listening to the birds welcome the sun. It gave me pleasure to hear the morning music and the discussions I imagined taking place. After several minutes, I arose to prepare our morning meal. I found it harder and harder to get up from our bed. I was sure I carried the world's biggest baby in my belly.

*Ima* is so happy that she will have another grandchild. She visits me every day and insists that I come to her house to eat when Ariel is away. Her friends look at my belly and predict whether I will have a boy or girl. Half say boy, and half say girl. Ariel laughs. "We can be sure we will have either a son or daughter."

I feel so huge. "Maybe there is one of each," I replied.

This morning was different. Before I baked the rolls, I felt a sharp pain in my back. I grabbed the table and closed my eyes. I was about to call for Ariel. A few seconds later, the pain faded. Maybe I got up from the bed too fast. I put the rolls into the oven and prepared cheeses and vegetables for Ariel's morning meal. I boiled water for tea and brought it to Ariel. We sat in bed drinking tea and talked about the coming day.

Ariel planned to meet with Itai. They needed a larger stable for the caravan mules. They transported ever-greater supplies of wine and produce to Jerusalem, to towns and villages in the Galilee, to the Lebanese coast for export to Rome and Greece, and to Dameseq. Business was good, and both worked hard.

Ariel said that we should be cautious. The good times might not last. "You never know what might happen—war, drought, a disease in the vineyards." He said it is prudent to save for a time when business might slow down. We discussed whether to use the reserves we saved in our hidden section of the double wall for a new stable. We both agreed it was a good risk. Even with this new investment, we had enough to carry our family—soon to be larger— through tough times. Itai had followed Ariel's advice. He and Adah also prepared for anything that might reduce their income in the future.

I had a long list of tasks for the day. Most important was to continue knitting blankets, sweaters, and little shoes for the baby. I prayed the baby would come soon. If it did not, I was positive my stomach would burst. I found it hard to maintain the house and cook the meals that Ariel so loved. *Ima* helped as much as she could, but in the end, it was my house and my responsibility—even if I moved slower than usual and tired faster.

Adah came over for lunch. I grilled the fresh fish she brought from the market with onions and green peppers. Earlier I had squeezed pomegranates. The juice was a wonderful complement to the grilled fish. *Ima* had told me not to drink wine while I was pregnant; although she said, occasionally, a little is permissible.

Adah and I talked for a long time. We both looked forward to the time when our children would play together. Her first-born is three years old; he is such a sweet boy.

I took a few bites of the fish enjoying the fresh taste when I felt a sharp pain. Sweat formed on my forehead. My face must have turned red as I tried to smile through the pain. Water ran down my leg and I was greatly embarrassed and did not know what to do. "Adah, please excuse me. I lost control of my bladder. I am so embarrassed."

"Elisheva, this is the start of your labor. By this time tomorrow, your baby will be born. Sit still. I will clean the floor, and we will resume eating. Expect more pains. They will hurt a lot. Just remember, at the end of all the pain, there will be a new life, and you will be an *Ima*. I will tell Noa that the labor has started. She will want to be with you."

After a while, the pains started coming at regular intervals. I had never felt such intense pain before and wondered if every woman suffered like this. Each time the pain came, I found I could manage if I took short fast, breaths.

I was determined not to give in to the pain. I would be brave and have my baby as *Ima* and countless other women in Israel have done before me.

*Ima* told me she admired how I continued my daily routine despite having to stop every time I felt pain. She told me that for the first baby, the pains continue for a whole day and night. If they became too hard for me to tolerate, she could give me something.

"*Ima*, I want to remember everything about the birth of my child. I will manage no matter how intense the pain."

"Very good, Elisheva. I did the same when Itai was born. After the first baby, the birth of additional children is quicker. I will stay with you until the birth. I am anxious to see my new grandchild."

"Thank you, *Ima*. Do you think I should send a message to Ariel? He is at Itai's house discussing business."

"Good idea. I will let him know that your pains have started, and by tomorrow, he will be an *Aba*. He does not have to come right away; if it looks like the baby will be born before he comes home, I will send for him. As soon as I return, I will prepare everything we will need."

The day passed slowly. I tried to continue my daily routine, but it was all I could do to tolerate the pain. Each successive pain was sharper. I would lean against the wall and hold my belly trying not to cry out. Towards the end of the day, the pains came close together. I had to lie down. Ariel was so worried I had to calm him and assure him everything was as it should be. I hoped I sounded confident.

I made a light meal for Ariel. I did not feel like eating although I sipped some hot tea. *Ima* said I should rest and try to sleep. I did not see how it would be possible. She said rest would help me later. I asked Ariel to come to bed with me and apologized in advance if I woke him during the night.

I did manage to sleep although fitfully. Ariel slept well. Before the birds began their morning songs, I felt a series of sharp pains coming closer and closer together. I woke Ariel and told him to get *Ima*. It was time.

My screams frightened Ariel. I knew he would worry about me. As hard as I tried not to scream, the pain was excruciating, and I screamed. Men did not understand the pain women could and would suffer to bring a new life into the world. He thought something was wrong. He was frantic.

*Ima* held my hand until each pain subsided. She wiped my forehead and said, "You are doing well. It won't be long now."

I reached for Ariel and whispered, "Go my husband. Leave me now."

*Ima* smiled at him. "Do not worry. All will be well. I will call you when your child arrives."

The pains continued. Every time I hoped it was the last one, a few minutes later, another followed. *Ima* kept telling me I was almost there. Then she said, "Push. Push, Elisheva. Push now." I did. Sweat ran down my face. The pain became more intense. "Push, Elisheva. I see your baby's head. Push Elisheva." Suddenly, the pain stopped, and it was quiet. Then I heard a soft cry.

Our baby came with the morning sun, and the birds announced his birth to the world. When *Ima* put the baby in my arms and I saw his face, I never imagined that such a powerful love was possible.

I held my baby. Nothing in my life prepared me for this moment. I have known great joy. I have known great happiness. Nothing compared to the love I now felt.

*Ima* brought Ariel to me. I held our son and kissed his face all the while crying with joy.

"Ariel, isn't he beautiful?"

"Oh yes, he looks like you. He has such beautiful blue eyes."

"Ariel, *Ima* says the eyes will change color in a few days."

"How do you feel, Elisheva? I was sure something was wrong. I prayed you would be well. I prayed we would have a healthy baby."

"I have never felt better. The pain was not so bad."

"Can I hold our son? He is so little."

"Yes, let *Ima* show you how."

"Here Ariel, and then we will give him back to Elisheva. Now that he is out in the world, I am sure, like all men, he wants to eat. Then, Elisheva should rest."

"My son, you are so beautiful, and you are so lucky to have such a brave and wonderful *Ima*. Elisheva, I will send a message by a fast rider to my parents telling them they have a new grandson. I will start planning the circumcision ceremony. I will be back soon."

\*\*\*

Later that night, Ariel, exhausted but elated, sat with *Aba,* and they toasted the next generation. Ariel asked *Ima* if she would help him organize the ceremony and party that we would have in eight days to welcome my son into our religion and the community.

I wanted Ariel to invite everyone in Dan. Big events in life must be celebrated. I wanted to introduce our son to his world.

While Ariel and I would not tell anyone his name until the ceremony, we decided to call our first-born Eitan. Like his namesake, the grandson of Judah, we prayed he would be strong, optimistic, and part of this land forever.

# BOOK ELEVEN—MUSA

The message from Ratib was worrisome and encouraging. He told Musa to prepare the scroll for appraisal. Now it was time. If he decided not to sell the scroll, he risked Ratib's anger. That worried him. This was not a man you crossed. He heard stories of people beaten, of children threatened, and of 'accidents' that happened. Of late, Musa felt shadowy figures observing him. He suspected that someone followed Aisha and him while shopping at the Mall in Kiryat Shemona.

If he took the scroll from its hiding place, he was sure he risked arrest and prison. He feared the Israeli police would know the minute he gave the scroll to Ratib for appraisal.

Since Ratib's phone call, he hadn't been able to sleep an entire night. He had a nervous feeling in his stomach.

Why did I take this scroll? In the end, it may turn out to be worthless—was it worth the risk if the scroll only brings a few hundred shekels? That would not be enough to save anyone. Why did not I listen to Aisha? What will happen to my family if the police arrest me and I go to prison? What will happen if I tell Ratib I do not have a scroll? Will he beat me? Cripple and shame me to my family? Why was I so stupid?

Yet, family honor is important. Everyone in the village will know I did the only honorable thing. I will be able to hold my head high. Better men have gone to prison upholding honor. Young Abdullah took his sister's life after she lay with a man before marriage to preserve his family's honor. He returned home after twenty years in an Israeli prison with honors befitting a hero. Yes, I must do this. I will meet Ratib and insist on thousands of shekels for this valuable scroll.

Musa went to the kitchen and started to remove the special cabinet that held an electric mixer. It had a shelf that when pushed down swung out to counter height raising the mixer for use. It was a narrow cabinet and impossible to see that it was not as deep as the others.

After he pulled out the cabinet, a plastered block wall was visible. Musa, using a small sledge and chisel, with great patience, chipped away the center of the wall. Reaching his hand through the opening, he grasped the container and slowly pulled out the scroll with the six Hebrew characters written on it.

Despite the cool morning, he sweated profusely. He swept up the broken blocks and plaster. He added them to the center of a rubble pile in the back of his house. No one could detect the fresh plaster. He repaired the opening in the wall with fresh cinder blocks and plaster and moved the cabinet back into place.

Musa called the special number Ratib gave him, and feeling a sudden relief, he said, "Ratib, I need to see you as soon as possible concerning our business deal. The scroll I promised you is ready."

"Musa, that is good. Let us meet at the Banias Waterfall Nature Reserve parking lot in four hours. Is that convenient for you, Musa?"

"Yes. Will your buyer be there?"

"Yes, he will come with his appraiser. If all goes well, we can successfully close this transaction today."

"*Inshallah.*"

***

As they ended the less than cryptic call, the police team monitoring the phone line called the anti-smuggling unit. They, in turn, contacted the Archeology Department at Tel Aviv University mobilizing an expert in ancient scrolls. He joined the team, and they drove to the Banias parking lot.

# BOOK TWELVE—LIFE

Ariel returned from Dameseq and sat under our olive tree tightly gripping his wine cup. He stared at nothing. I had never seen him so tense. I walked over, sat opposite him, and for a long time did not speak.

I waited. As he drank the wine, I saw the tension drain from him little by little.

"I am sorry, Elisheva."

I took his hand and asked, "What is it Ariel? What happened?"

He rubbed his forehead and frowned as if the weight of events shook him to his core. "This was a hard trip."

"Tell me, Ariel. What happened?"

He stared at me for a second as if debating whether to talk or not. I tried to be patient. After a long pause, he told me about his meeting with Ciro.

At first, he spoke slowly and deliberately. Once started though, his tale streamed out in a torrent.

He and Itai arrived in Dameseq after a hard trip. The cold and rain made the caravan difficult to manage.

Ciro's warm, effusive greeting raised Ariel and Itai's suspicions. It was not his usual manner. Most times, he grumbled about how he did most of the work and did not receive enough of the profit. They were sure that whatever came next would not be welcome.

It was not. Ciro decided to cheat them. Neither Ariel nor Itai were surprised. But they were shocked at the scale of the fraud. Ciro told them that most of the wine they brought last time had spoiled and that he could only sell it as vinegar. He then demanded that he be paid in full since it was not his fault.

Ariel and Itai decided that even if they had to forego all profit, they had to deal with Ciro. The information they were reporting was far too valuable to Israel. They told Ciro he would receive his full share. In the future, they would check the wine on delivery to ensure it had not spoiled.

I was glad Ariel did not hide anything from me. Ciro is a dangerous man. Dameseq is far away, and there is a threat to my family. I could never again be at ease while Ariel traveled. "I wish you did not have to go."

Ariel looked down at his wine cup and said, "There is something else." He told me that Ciro had a dinner party and seated Itai and me next to two beautiful women. They were introduced as Tomiri's friends. The women's husbands were away on business; both proposed a later rendezvous.

I felt like someone hit me in the stomach. I let go of Ariel's hand and gripped the edge of the table. I felt the blood drain from my face. I did not say a word.

He hesitated before continuing. "I love you, Elisheva. I would never ever betray you. I do not want anyone else but you. Please do not be angry with me. I did not want to tell you that an impropriety had been proposed. Long ago, I decided I would never keep a secret from you. You are my life."

I had stopped breathing. For a minute, I thought my world had ended. "I am glad you told me. And, I am glad you are still my husband."

I could see the relief on his face. He sat a little taller as if I had lifted a great burden from his shoulders. I took both his hands and squeezed them as hard as I could. I sat in his lap, and he held me tight. I leaned my head against his chest and listened to the steady beat of his heart. I felt safe.

Since the twins, Talitha and Levi were born three years ago, Ariel and I have not spent a restful evening together. We are always busy. We hardly have time to talk to each other. Pressures from Ariel's responsibilities weigh on him, and business is always on his mind. I am exhausted after a day with the children and constantly think about what meals to cook for my family.

At the end of the day, we still sit in the courtyard by our olive tree. I look at Ariel and want him to take me in his arms, to kiss me as he did after we married. I sit next to him and do not say anything. Many times, I want to go to him, but I am tired.

Ariel is away from home a lot. He travels to Lebanon, Dameseq, or towns in the Galilee. He is active in the growing communities around the Kinneret Sea. When he is away, I manage the house, shop, check on the warehouse, and continue our charity work. I love my life; I am glad my family is healthy and prospers. I do wish there was more time to rest, experiment cooking new dishes, and hug my husband.

Ariel's last visit to Dameseq haunts me. He is now a player in a world he cannot control. I know little about that world except it is a threat to my family. I trust him. He is a good man. I see he also worries when he goes to Dameseq. Even if he does not talk about it, I sense his hesitation to leave the house before a trip. He tenses and tries to look determined and confident, but I know, like me, he worries.

I decided we had to change our routine. I want our life to be good. One morning, after Ariel left for work and Eitan for school, *Ima* took the twins to her house; I sat in the cooking area with a cup of tea. The usual tasks of the day waited. I held the cup with both hands and stared out the window. I did not look at anything in particular and did not see anything. I started to tap the table with a steady beat—more the rhythm of a nervous tic than a determined beat of life. I had to walk.

Outside, the crisp air and the medley of colors in the Merom Valley appeared to me like a rainbow of life. I walked by the stream and heard the chorus of water hurrying over big and small stones in its path.

I must have walked a long time before the answer came to me. We had limited our spectrum. Our life too should be a rainbow of different colors, a chorus of sound. I knew what to do.

Once a week, after the children went to sleep, I would make a special meal for Ariel and me. It would be a time for us. I would wear a special perfume, light scented candles, and make a few small dishes to eat while we sip wine and talk to each other. I would cook a dish we both relished, and for dessert—well I know for sure Ariel will love the dessert.

Ariel and I have marvelous friends. We know many interesting people and take pleasure in listening and talking to them. Several of our friends are like family to us, and of late, we do not see them near enough. No matter how busy or how tired we are, I plan to invite our friends over for dinner more often.

A long time had passed since we had spent a quiet evening with Miriam and Micah. I invited them for dinner. Ariel, at first, hesitated. He had too much on his mind, and he had to plan his next trip Dameseq. I looked up at him. "Ariel, it would make me happy."

He stopped, thought for a moment, and said, "Yes, let's invite them."

***

The next evening, Miriam and Micah came. We looked forward to the evening with them. We wanted to be good hosts, but all the things we had to do weighed on us. We felt the tension drain as soon as they entered. I hugged Miriam and Micah. Ariel took Micah's arm and said, "It has been far too long since we have talked." He told Micah about a new wine from Kedesh that he discovered. He wanted to hear what Micah did in his workshop.

He filled a big glass for Micah and a smaller one for Miriam and me. He said, "It is a light refreshing wine grown in rocky soil at the western edge of Kedesh. The winemakers tell me that they discovered, by accident, that the area is just perfect for producing wines that ferment in just two months. Sometimes accidents are wonderful. I had thought that without a thick layer of topsoil, the grapes would be of poor quality. Clearly, it is not so."

Micah, staring at the wine, moved the cup to catch the light from different directions. "Ariel, this wine is delicious. I like the purple-pink coloration. Miriam, taste this wine. I think you will enjoy it."

I felt like it was old times. It was good being with my best friends again. I smiled and took Miriam's arm. "I am so happy you could come. The days fly by; we have so little time to see the people we like most. What is the latest news from your home?"

"We are fine. The children grow like weeds. Micah is always busy in his workshop. He makes beautiful jewelry and has developed a devoted clientele. He has been experimenting with a new technique for making decorative glass vials and cups. I do not understand how he does it; he will have to explain it to you. We brought you a piece he made yesterday."

"Ariel, come look at what Miriam and Micah have brought us. A perfume vial like none I have ever seen before. It is so beautiful and so delicate. I love the purple color. You will have to buy me a perfume that is equal to this vial."

"I will be happy to buy you whatever you wish—in exchange for a kiss—or perhaps two kisses." Ariel held the vial up to the light and said, "Micah, this is indeed exquisite. How did you create something so beautiful?"

"It's a new technique of shaping glass. I blow air through a long tube into the glass all the while twisting, swinging, and moving the tube. It took me a long time to get the proper material mixtures, furnace temperatures, and above all the motions needed to shape the glass. The key to making delicate shapes is to cool the piece slowly. I add different soils and metals to the basic glass to create color. If I add a tiny amount of gold flakes, the glass takes on a rich ruby color; silver particles sometimes produce yellow and sometimes orange. A small amount of copper produces a beautiful turquoise color.

Miriam has been working with me the whole time and we learn together.

She stretches the glass and cuts the molten glass to make different shapes. She has a talent for the work and instinctively knows how much to work the glass. We make a good team. I could not create such unique and beautiful pieces without her. Forgive me if I bore you with too many details."

"Not at all Micah. This is fascinating. I would like to come to your workshop to see how you create such wonderful glass pieces."

"Ariel, you are more than welcome anytime."

"Have you made any decorative pieces?"

"Yes, I have made a calf of red glass, a giraffe of yellow glass, a baby turtle, and a small challah from brownish-yellow glass. Our kids love them. They are not to play with, as they are easily broken. I am also getting better at making elegant wine glasses with delicate twisted stems. This new glass blowing technique offers unlimited possibilities and opportunities."

"Micah, this is exciting. Perhaps I could visit tomorrow morning? I have an idea to discuss with you."

"I look forward to it, Ariel."

Miriam said to Micah, "Elisheva has wonderful news."

I smiled. "Yes, I do. We have not told anyone yet, but I have to tell my best friends. We are expecting a baby in the spring."

"That is wonderful news. Congratulations. I hope our children will be close, and I pray that they will not have the worries we had. Remember the time we had to run for our lives when the bandits attacked Dan?"

"I will always remember that day. I was scared and worried about you. Thankfully, Gershon was there. It was because of Gershon and *Aba's* bravery that I met Ariel. It is strange how unexpected events change your life. I believe what they say is true: 'everything that was or will be was planned in the beginning.' Come; let us continue our conversation while we eat. I have made a special meal in honor of Ariel's successful trip to Dameseq and the visit of our two dearest friends."

"What is this dish, Elisheva? Miriam asked."

"I found the last of the summer peaches in the market. I warmed them together with crushed persimmons, a little white wine, a dash of vanilla, and a pinch of nutmeg. I thought it would be an excellent dish to start the meal—especially with the young Kedesh Valley wine that Ariel brought. There is even a hint of peaches in the wine."

I followed with a vegetable soup made with white beans, summer squash, zucchini, cabbage, onions, and carrots. Ariel matched the soup to a chilled dry white wine.

"This is delicious, Elisheva. Is this from the cookbook your *Ima* gave you—what was it called?"

"*Rachel's Galilee Recipes.* No, this is my creation."

"Something gives this soup an excellent flavor."

"I added chicken bones to the mix of vegetables, a little vinegar to contrast the sweetness of the squash, and a small amount of zatar to emphasize the earthy taste of the vegetables. I am glad you like the soup. The preparation time is a bit more than usual, but we think it is well worth the effort on cool nights."

The main course was a tough old chicken that had neared the end of her egg-producing days. I found it a great challenge to create an excellent meal fit for our best friends. I started by marinating the chicken overnight in a mixture of diced apples, persimmons, and sweet white wine. The wine softened the meat while the fruit added a hint of fall. I first cooked the chicken over high heat turning it every few minutes to brown the skin. I then let it cook over a low fire while basting it with the marinade. I was apprehensive and not sure how it would taste. Ariel said it was the best chicken he ever ate. Miriam and Micah agreed.

The dessert was the perfect end to the meal. I had mashed pears and added sugar and a touch of citron juice. I placed the mixture in the icy waters of the stream earlier that afternoon. It had gelled to a sweet and tasty dessert. It was the first time I had tried to make a dessert of that sort. The taste was just as I had imagined. I reminded myself to add the recipe to my cooking scroll. After dessert, I served lemongrass tea with a small bowl of nuts. Micah and Miriam said it was one of the best meals they ever ate. I wanted the meal to come out well. I was happy they enjoyed the dishes.

None of us wanted to get up from the table. We delighted in being together, the conversation, the food, and we drank too much wine. We had lost track of time.

Miriam said, "We so much enjoyed the evening. Thank you for a wonderful meal. Next time you must come to our home, although I am sure my cooking is not equal to yours, Elisheva."

"I doubt that Miriam. You are an excellent and creative cook. I use several of your recipes. I have written them down in a special scroll that I keep so that I will always have them. I am glad we share recipes. Good night, my dear friends."

After Miriam and Micah left, Ariel helped me clean the dishes. We talked as we worked. Ariel said, "Micah has extraordinary talent."

I always thought Micah was special. He always looked at the world around him and saw what no one else did. He saw a smiling face in passing clouds. He also imagined shapes such as menorahs, books, and soldiers fighting the devil. Dew on a simple patch of grass seemed to him like pearls decorating a necklace of the earth. He saw beauty in old broken pottery when all we saw was a broken jug.

"I think you noticed it when as kids we dug by the wall. He found an old cup and just kept touching the design to 'feel' the thoughts of the artist who made it."

Ariel rubbed his chin. "I remember that day. I am sure Micah could sell his glass creations in Tyre and Dameseq. I will talk to him and see if he is interested. After his success with jewelry, I have no doubt he will be successful with his special glass cups and figurines. Elisheva, what would you think if I propose a partnership with Micah and Miriam? We could finance a workshop to produce glass products for export. If I convince him to make a flask with a broad, flat bottom to aerate wine, it would be a great product to accompany our wine sales."

"My husband, you have wonderful ideas However, I do not want to jeopardize our friendship with them. That, to me, is more valuable than money."

"I agree. After I see his workshop and better understand the possibilities, we can discuss whether to propose a partnership. Elisheva, it was a fantastic meal. I am glad you invited them. I enjoyed the evening. Now we should sleep or perhaps think of the Song of Songs."

"An excellent idea, my husband."

I dreamt my whole life of visiting Jerusalem. I was so excited. We stayed with Ariel's family. They had a huge house. From their salon, I could see the Temple. I had to pinch myself every day.

One evening, as I crossed the courtyard, Gershon called me over and introduced me to Eli, Queen Shlomtsion's personal secretary. For a moment, I was too startled to answer and looked at the ground. Gershon explained that he and Eli have been friends since the time many years ago when he brought Eli a jug of fine Armenian wine.

Eli said he was pleased to meet the woman that so captivated Gershon and his son. While I sat there, he and Gershon continued their conversation about a typical day at the palace. Maybe I should not hear all this. I got up to leave, but Gershon said, "Please stay, Elisheva. If you don't mind the ramblings of two old men, I would be happy if you sat with us."

Eli told Gershon he planned to invite Ariel to the palace tomorrow to discuss events in Dameseq with the Queen. He told me that Ariel was well-regarded and that the information he forwarded about Dameseq was of extraordinary value. Gershon nodded in agreement and said, "It is our honor to serve Israel." I looked at the ground and tried not to smile from pride. I was proud of my Ariel. The Queen's personal secretary complimented my husband.

\*\*\*

True to his word, when Eli saw the Queen after morning prayers, and she asked, "Eli, what is on my schedule today?" He outlined the day's agenda.

"My Queen, several seek appointments with you. I asked Ariel Ben Gershon to come to the palace, an Ambassador from Rome wishes to see you this evening, and I arranged your visit to several workshops of carpenters, glassmakers, ceramics, and stone masons in the crafts district."

"Thank you, Eli. You serve me as well as you served my late husband. I am pleased you schedule my appointments and manage my correspondence; I trust your judgment."

"Thank you, my Queen."

"Sometime today, I want to meet with Shimon Ben Shetah. Relations between the Pharisees and Sadducees are again problematic and require my attention; as leader of the Pharisees, he can help. No matter how hard and how often I try to convince them to respect one another, after a few days, another controversy occurs. This is not good. For the country to advance, we must work together. It might be a good idea for my sons to provide leadership here. In the meantime, please invite Shimon to the palace for the mid-day meal. I will talk to him while we eat. Again, we will try to find a formula to satisfy everyone."

"I will see to it. Ariel Ben Gershon is here for an audience with you."

"Remind me, who is Ariel Ben Gershon?"

"He is Gershon Ben Avraham's son. Many years ago, when he married a young woman from Dan, Elisheva Bat Nadav, you sent greetings to them on their wedding day."

"Yes, I recall."

"He forwards intelligence about King Tigranes through Gershon. He has developed good connections with King Tigranes' family and is privy to intentions before they become obvious. So far, his intelligence has been excellent. Now that Armenia may be an immediate threat to Israel, his connections in Dameseq might be of great relevance. He is in Jerusalem now with his wife and family."

"Thank you, Eli. That is good. Please ask his wife to attend. I should like to hear her reaction to my plan to increase legal protections for women. After I hear the latest assessment from Dameseq, I want to meet with the commander of the army. Please arrange for him to come to the palace tomorrow."

"Should I also ask your advisors for foreign affairs and the treasury to attend?"

"Not for this meeting. I want to review the current strength of our defenses and capabilities before including them. First, let us hear what Ariel Ben Gershon has to report."

"My Queen, what shall I tell the Ambassador from the Roman Commander, Lucius Licinius Lucullus?"

"I will meet with him after evening prayers. I want you to attend that meeting. Either later tonight or tomorrow morning I wish to compose a letter to Queen Cleopatra. Is anything else scheduled for today?"

"The Governor from Tsipori is here to report on your plan for developing more schools."

"Again a long day. Eli, please ask Shimon Ben Shetah to return for the meeting with the Governor. I want Shimon to continue the lead in building schools for all children."

"If you desire, I can postpone the visit to the crafts district."

"No. It is important I meet and talk to people so that I know what they think. They should also see their Queen. I spend most days talking to officials who all too often worry more about themselves than the people they serve."

"If you have nothing else for me, my Queen, should I summon Ariel Ben Gershon?

"Please wait a short time, and then show him in."

***

"Ariel Ben Gershon, please approach and sit here."

"Thank you, my Queen."

"I receive your reports from Dameseq, and I find your information timely and accurate. Tell me, how are you able to find out so much before my Ambassador in Dameseq?"

"King Alexander Yanai, of blessed memory, tasked my *Aba* to trade in Dameseq and report on Armenian plans. King Tigranes gave us permission to trade fine Israeli wines on the condition that his wife's nephew, Ciro, become a partner.

"We have had problems with this arrangement. Ciro cheats us. However, he is well connected at court. At every opportunity, he tells us how important he is and how much he knows about affairs of state.

"We try to verify what he tells us. It is not always possible. Some of his information relates to internal debates among King Tigranes advisors rather than actual decisions or policy. I report the internal debates since they emphasize issues the court feels are important. In all our reports, we identify what we have verified, what we think is Ciro's drunken boasting, and King Tigranes' actual views or decisions. I am honored you think our service of value. I consider it a privilege to serve my country."

"Ariel, when were you last in Dameseq?"

"I was there last month. The nobility and wealthy families have developed a taste for our wines. The Kedesh vineyards and the wineries produce excellent wines. We send a caravan with wine every month. We may even increase the amount we ship.

"Ciro told us Rome's intentions are of great concern at court. King Mithridates VI considered the inclusion of Bithynia, on the coast of the Black Sea, into the Roman Empire three years ago a strategic threat to his kingdom. He renewed his war against Rome. The Roman Commander, Lucius Licinius Lucullus, in a series of battles beginning with his victory at Cyzicus two years ago has destroyed King Mithridates' army. The King has fled to Armenia.

"Commander Lucullus demanded the surrender of King Mithridates. King Tigranes refused. The consequence is Rome will move against Armenia.

"According to Ciro, Rome's growing strength concerns his uncle. Three years ago, Rome faced a rebellion in Hispania, a slave revolt, and rampant piracy from Cilicia that threatened food supplies to the capital. Pompey defeated and killed Sertorius in Hispania; Marcus Crassus and Pompey ended the slave revolt led by Spartacus, and Lucullus reestablished command of the sea. Ciro said that Crassus had six thousand captured slaves crucified along the Via Appia."

Queen Shlomtsion looked up in shock. "That is barbaric. King Tigranes is correct to fear Rome. Ariel Ben Gershon, I thank you for your report. Your information is important and will influence how we proceed.

"I am pleased we have met face to face. I have known your *Aba* for a long time, and we greatly valued his service. I find myself fortunate you

157

continue in his footsteps and serve our country. Before you return to Dan, I should like to speak to you again. Eli will let you know when to return."

"Thank you, my Queen."

"Now Ariel, I should like to speak to your wife."

\*\*\*

"Elisheva, please sit next to me."

"Yes, my Queen."

"Tell me Elisheva, what is Dan like?"

"It is nice."

"Do not be nervous. Please tell me what life is like in Dan."

"I do not know what to say. I was born there. I have not been to many places. This is my first trip away from Dan. I find Jerusalem overwhelming."

"How so?"

"The city is so big. I have never seen so many people. The Temple leaves me speechless. Now I meet the Queen. I do not know what to say."

"How many children do you and Ariel have?"

I trembled. The Queen reached over and covered my hand with hers. Her warm smile put me at ease. My voice was steadier, and I said, "We have three children. Our son Eitan was born five years ago. Our twins, Levi and Talitha are now two years old."

"What lovely names you chose. Do you think your children will have a good childhood like you did?"

My words came out before I realized I was answering her. "Oh, I hope so. I pray even better. We were always worried about bandits from Anafa until King Alexander Yanai sent soldiers to help us defeat them.

"Ariel and I have a good life. We find peace and contentment in Dan that I wish everyone would feel. We are simple people, pious, and live according to our Torah. When we see pomegranates ripen, we know that the New Year is near; we celebrate Succoth after the harvest; we prepare for the spring planting on the fourteenth day of the month of *Shvat*; seven weeks after we celebrate Passover, the wheat ripens. We govern the cycle of our lives as written in the Torah. We are so happy you are our Queen."

"Elisheva, are the people in Dan satisfied with their lives? Do they have any worries?"

"We always worry. The rains may come late, or it may rain too much. We worry about powerful forces that threaten Israel and what would happen to our children and us. But, we are happy. The past few years have been good. We trust in God. We trust that you will always protect us."

"Thank you, Elisheva. I want to ask you a few more questions. Do you know how to read?"

"Yes, my Queen. I went to school, and *Aba* always made sure we had scrolls to read. He taught us Torah. I keep a diary and even write all my recipes in a separate scroll."

"Do you think all children—girls and boys should go to school?"

I answered as if Queen Shlomtsion was my best friend. "I do. I definitely do. Reading is one of my greatest pleasures. Learning about our history, culture, and philosophy has fascinated me since I was a little girl. I know my friends feel the same. I wish I had learned Greek. I do read translations of plays and the writings of the philosophers, Socrates, Plato, and Aristotle. I am sure I would understand more if I could read the original Greek. Ariel promised to teach me."

"Elisheva, I ask you these questions because I plan to make sure all children in Israel attend school and learn to read. I also want to correct an inequality in the law by improving certain protections for women."

"I do not understand. *Aba* taught me the Torah gives women a special place in our society. I do not feel that men have more rights or protection under the law than me. We are different, but equal. At least that is what I understand."

"You are a wise woman, Elisheva."

The compliment surprised and embarrassed me. I must have blushed because she, again, took my hand. She looked at me and continued.

"I refer to the status of divorced women; they have few protections. I want to require a written marriage contract specifying the property a woman would receive should divorce occur. The contract would be enforced by the Sanhedrin courts."

"Ariel's *Aba* made such an agreement with my parents although it was not written. I know that Ariel and I will never divorce. One of my friends in Dan did divorce. She and her children were left destitute. I think a contract could have prevented her living in poverty. I am sure your law will be welcomed by all women."

"What happened to your friend—how does she survive?"

"Ariel and I help her. Ariel employed her to keep track of inventory for his trading business. Rather than giving money, we give her work. That way she keeps her dignity and pride."

"Elisheva, I am glad we met. You are a fine woman and a credit to Israel. I pray we will meet again. Gershon has told me that you—like your *Ima*—are an excellent cook and you prepare dishes suitable for a King. Well, I am a Queen, and if I am in the North, perhaps I can visit you for one of your special meals."

"Oh, my Queen, it would be such an honor."

"The honor would be mine, Elisheva. I have enjoyed talking to you. Now, I have other meetings and must bid you *shalom*. Be well, Elisheva."

***

Later that night, she received the ambassador sent by Lucius Licinius Lucullus. It had been a long day, but she could not ignore the growing storm in the north.

"Ambassador, please approach."

"Queen Shlomtsion, Commander Lucius Licinius Lucullus on behalf of the Roman Senate and the Consuls sends greetings. He regrets that he cannot be here to speak to you himself. I will deliver his message according to his instructions and will try to express his thoughts as best I can."

"Thank you, Ambassador."

"Commander Lucullus requested I present his most earnest desire to assure you that he has no hostile intentions toward Israel. On the contrary, he believes we share a common interest. King Tigranes is a threat to both Israel and Rome. After Rome defeated the Pontic King, Mithridates VI, my Commander sent an ambassador to King Tigranes asking that he surrender

King Mithridates to him, as is right and proper. King Tigranes refused. Commander Lucullus takes that as a hostile act. He considers that a state of war now exists with Armenia."

"Ambassador, I welcome Commander Lucullus' comments. I agree that our interests are aligned in this matter. What does Commander Lucullus propose?"

"Commander Lucullus wishes that we pledge to respect the actions of the other without fear or suspicion of hostile intent and, moreover, that we agree to consult with each other before any misunderstanding of intentions may result. To this end, Commander Lucullus would immediately receive your ambassador at any time and requests you do the same. Should you be agreeable to such an arrangement, Commander Lucullus has instructed me to deliver his personal letter stating his position."

"Ambassador, please inform Commander Lucullus that Israel has no intention of interfering in the conflict between Rome and Armenia. We desire peace on our northern border. Our interests are indeed aligned. We welcome Commander Lucullus' proposal. Please return to the palace tomorrow evening for my response."

CHAPTER FORTY-FIVE—FRIENDS—3689 (71 BC)

Ariel seemed at ease when he talked to the Queen. I am proud of him, especially when Queen Shlomtsion said his information is of great value and helps Israel. I am ashamed to have worried about myself while he was in Dameseq. He does our family great honor.

Ariel said he was nervous at first. He had never been to the palace and did not know what to expect. He said she makes you feel comfortable and listens closely to everything. She wants to see him again before he returns to Dan.

Ariel wanted to know what we spoke about for so long.

"Oh Ariel, it was a great privilege to accompany you to the palace, to be in the same room as the Queen of Israel, and to see the Queen speak to you. I was surprised when she asked me to sit near her. I only remember shaking and being too nervous to speak. She smiled at me and made me feel that what I had to say was very important. I hope she did not think me a fool. She asked about our family, about life in Dan, and if I knew how to read and write. She wants to build schools in the whole country so that everyone will learn to read and write. She wants to make laws to protect women.

"She is such a wonderful Queen. At the end, she told me that she heard I was a good cook, and when in the north, she will come to our home for a meal. I almost cried. It feels like I dreamt talking to Queen Shlomtsion. I will never forget this day."

"While you were with the Queen, Eli said we are not to tell anyone about meeting the Queen; the conversations were for her ears only. It does not matter why our Queen does not want it known we were there; we must obey her wish. Tonight we are invited to Boaz and Rachel's home. I did hear that a year or so after I moved to Dan, they married."

"If you had known, would you have gone?"

"Absolutely. I was sorry not to be at their wedding. Boaz is like a brother to me. I have known Boaz and Rachel since we were little. Anyway, if they do ask us what we did today, we can tell them we walked around the palace area."

That night, Boaz hugged Ariel, and like two kids, they patted each other on the back saying it has been too long my brother. At the same time, they both said, "You have not changed at all."

Rachel told me she heard so much about the woman Ariel married and was glad we finally met. She put her arm through mine and said, "Let us leave the men to discuss whatever men talk about. Would you help me finish preparing the appetizer? Yamima told me you are a fantastic cook."

"Thank you, Rachel. That is a big compliment. Yamima is an exceptional cook. She and *Ima* made all the meals when they visited Dan. Every dish they prepared was sublime. I try but have not reached their level."

Rachel's recipe sounded delicious. She would sauté mushrooms with onions and black olives, season with a pinch of hot pepper and wrap it all in thin dough. She asked me to clean and slice the mushrooms, dice a small onion, and roughly dice a few black olives.

"Do you mind if I copy the recipe, and prepare it when I get back to Dan? Ariel will love it."

"Not at all, Elisheva. I am happy to share my recipe with you."

"Rachel, I am glad we finally meet. Ariel has told me so much about you. You and Boaz have been a big part of his life—one that he will never forget."

For a brief moment, Rachel looked down and seemed sad. I must have said something to upset her. She asked, "What do you think of Jerusalem?"

"I am just speechless. Jerusalem is magnificent. The buildings are beautiful. Jerusalem is so big with so many people. People from places I did not know existed, and I hear so many different languages in the streets. Everything anyone could want or dream about is here. I must have stopped at every shop selling scrolls. The Temple leaves me speechless. There is so much that I want to see and do. It must be exciting to live here."

"Yes, I suppose it is. I have lived here all my life and never think about it. I have never known anything else. Do you think Ariel misses Jerusalem?"

"He does. I mean, who would not miss Jerusalem? The Merom Valley is spectacular. Ariel enjoys living in Dan. We have a beautiful house and good friends. My parents live close, and Ariel's business is centered in Dan. We have a good life. I am sure though that Ariel would like to be nearer to his family. Maybe you and Boaz will come to the north and visit us in Dan. You are always welcome in our home."

"Thank you, Elisheva. It would be wonderful to visit you and see the Galilee."

"Rachel, what do you think the men are talking about?"

"If I know Boaz, they are talking about everything they did together growing up. I am glad you and Ariel are here. I wish we lived closer. We would be great friends."

"Oh, thank you, Rachel." I put my hand on her shoulder. "Yes, we would be great friends."

I liked Rachel. I may be wrong, but every time she looked at Ariel, I sensed a touch of regret.

We sat at the table a long time. Ariel brought a jug of a delightful wine that we finished over the course of an excellent meal. Rachel is a great cook. We talked about our children; the men talked about the gathering storm in the north. We talked about the laws of Moses and how strangers should be welcomed when visiting a town. We talked about life in the Galilee and our friends in Dan. Toward the end of the evening, Rachel asked how Ariel and I met.

"I met Ariel when he carried my packages home from the market. *Aba* invited him and his sons to join us for our Shabbat evening meal. I knew then that I wanted to marry Ariel."

"Are you still friends with Micah?"

"Yes, we consider Micah and his wife Miriam our best friends. If you do visit Dan, we will have a big party and you could meet our friends. We could also cook together."

"I would like that, Elisheva. I would like that very much."

Late that night, Queen Shlomtsion, tired from a long day, dictated to Eli a message for Queen Cleopatra. She told him to send it by special courier.

*Your Majesty, My Dear Queen Cleopatra,*

*I write to you with a sense of urgency in view of events occurring in Pontus and Syria, as well as my desire to maintain our close relationship and share information that may prove vital to our mutual as well as separate interests.*

*The Roman Commander in Pontus, Lucius Licinius Lucullus, has defeated King Mithridates VI who has fled to Armenia. Commander Lucullus prepares to move against King Tigranes. I suspect within a year he will attack Armenia. Commander Lucullus believes Armenia poses a mutual threat to Rome and Israel.*

*If King Tigranes moves his army south before Commander Lucullus engages the Armenian army, I believe his objective will be to subjugate Israel and Egypt. If an invasion does materialize, I hope, with your cooperation, to reinforce my army with recruits from Egypt.*

*Commander Lucullus assures me Rome has no designs on Israel. He pledges not to undertake any action against Israel and proposes an arrangement to prevent misunderstandings that might trigger conflict between our countries. I assume his objective is to secure his flank while he prepares to act against King Tigranes.*

*I view this agreement with Rome as in the best interests of my Kingdom at this time. At present, though, I am concerned by the concentration of powerful armies—friend as well as foe—on my northern border. King Tigranes may move south with a powerful army that greatly outnumbers my forces. I anticipate my agreement with Lucullus will yield me enough time to prepare to defend my Kingdom.*

*In the meantime, I plan to strengthen the defenses of my cities and increase the size of the army. These plans are defensive and represent no intent to infringe on the sovereignty of neighboring countries.*

*I believe our countries may face difficult days ahead. The power of Rome grows daily. They have overcome a number of rebellions. Most important, Sulla, Crassus, Pompey, and Lucullus are excellent leaders. They are dangerous men. We should not underestimate them.*

*I have prepared a summary of events in a separate scroll that my sources have reported to me. The information I receive has, in the past, been reliable. Sharing information, communication, and cooperation between us is, I believe, in our best interest.*

*At this time, I can only view the threats facing our countries as serious. I desire and pray we shall, as in the past, remain in close contact.*

*Faithfully,*

*Shlomtsion, Queen of Israel*

Ariel and Yoav stood at the side of the courtyard watching me dance with the children. They had not seen each other in months. Yoav put his arm around Ariel and said, "Little brother, I am so happy you are here. It has been far too long since we last met. Our children hardly know their cousins nor their Uncle Ariel and Aunt Elisheva."

"Yes, big brother, far too long. I am glad our children get on so well. It is as if they have always been together."

"No doubt, Ariel, because we talk about each other so much."

I was happy. I stood in a circle with my children, nephews, and nieces. We held hands and danced in a circle singing:

*"We are Maccabees.*
*In a circle, we dance.*
*We love our Queen.*
*In a circle, we dance,*
*Round and round we go,*
*Faster and faster,*
*In a circle, we dance."*

The little ones sang as loud as they could; the older ones laughed. I was caught up in the dance and threw my head back and forth, as I felt the rhythm, joy, and happiness of the children.

After the dance, I walked over to Ariel and heard Yoav tell him that he was a lucky man. "Your wife is wonderful. I am happy for you Ariel. I now understand why you are so content in Dan.

"Elisheva, that was a beautiful dance. The children really like you."

"Thank you, Yoav. They are so sweet. I wished we lived closer to each other. It would be fantastic if you and Rivka could visit us in Dan. The children can see their cousins. Perhaps the children could stay longer and return to Jerusalem after a few weeks with Itai's caravan. Similarly, Eitan and the twins could spend some extra time in Jerusalem."

"I like that idea. Let's talk about this when Rivka can join us. Ariel, while you are here, we should review our business plans. Later today, *Ima* wants to cook with Elisheva and Rivka. If *Aba* does not take a nap, we might meet then."

"That would be good," Ariel replied. "With three excellent cooks preparing the food, I have no doubt it will be the finest meal of the year. Let's go to the warehouse and select a great wine."

***

Ariel and Yoav left for the warehouse and an afternoon of meetings. Ariel asked Yoav if he had been able to hire good workers.

Yoav told him he had been lucky so far. "Still, the business grows, and we need new partners."

Ariel agreed saying that he had the same problem in the North. "It is our good fortune to have such problems. Bringing more family into the business is wonderful. Speaking of which, Itai needs more people to handle the transport of goods." Ariel proposed that my younger brother, Allon, become a partner at the same time as their brother, Hillel.

Yoav agreed and added that the money transfer part of our business had been successful and Gershon said "we owe a special thanks to Elisheva for suggesting it."

I was thrilled that my idea worked out so well. At first, I thought it would be a safe way to transfer money without using the caravans. People trust Ariel and Yoav. It worked out that the transfer service itself generated a large profit. The demand for the service far exceeded all expectations.

Yoav said, "*Aba* proposes that Hillel take charge of finance, keep the records, and manage the accounting. *Aba* is still in command, but he tires easily and is happy spending more time with *Ima*." Yoav agreed it is a good idea, but he still needed help. He agreed that my brother, Allon, should join the transport division and suggested that Allon and Hillel be junior partners for five years before becoming full partners.

Ariel suggested that one of his sisters help Gershon and become a partner. Both Shulamite and Tamar could handle the work.

Yoav thought a better idea might be for Shulamite to take over the money transfer business and work with *Aba* on the accounting while Hillel joins him in the field. "After Shulamite marries, managing the financial side of the business might be a better arrangement—either she would continue or perhaps her husband might assume some of the burden. She would remain the partner."

They decided to propose all this to Gershon—both Hillel and Shulamite would probably agree with this arrangement. Another possibility was to split the financial job between Shulamite and Tamar. One could focus on money transfers and the other on accounting.

So far, the business issues made sense to me, but then came the bad news. Ariel told Yoav, "We have a problem in Dameseq. Ciro is a big concern."

***

Rivka and I set the table as if for a big festival. Three families would be together for the Sabbath meal. It would be special. Gershon and Yamima sat at opposite ends of a long table. They were happy to see the family all together, healthy, and doing well. The older grandchildren—Eitan and Itamar—sat together to the right of Gershon while Levi, Asher, Talitha, and Karen sat opposite them near Yamima. Yoav and Rivka sat opposite their parents with Hillel and Shulamite. Tamar sat next to Elisheva and Ariel.

Blessings were recited with the children all joining the blessing for the wine at the end. Rivka and I brought dish after dish to the table beginning with chicken soup, rich with root vegetables and flavored with copious amounts of parsley, dill, salt, pepper, turmeric, and a little cilantro. Appetizers consisted of mushrooms and onions sautéed in olive oil, red wine, and sprinkled with thyme; liver pate accompanied by half a pear soaked in brandy; bowls of celery, radishes cut to resemble flowers, and black and green olives. Two main courses were prepared: roasted chicken with an apricot-persimmon sauce and meat roasted in a rich red wine-celery root sauce. Spectacular white and red wines accompanied each dish. Sweet wines, made from the last harvested grapes, were reserved for the children. The conclusion was a nut cake made with dates, cinnamon, cardamom, walnuts, almonds, and honey. I made a special dessert from crushed persimmons, sugar, and water that I had set on the rooftop to chill and solidify under the cloudless night sky.

The meal over, all the children helped clear the table and clean. They sang while they worked. The children were happy and content in the warm family.

Gershon, Yoav, and Ariel sat in the courtyard each with a cup of wine. After a contented silence lasting several minutes, Gershon asked Ariel about his meeting at the palace.

Ariel was not sure what to think. He did not meet with Queen Shlomtsion. However, her secretary, Eli, asked if he would agree to deliver confidential messages to King Tigranes should the need arise.

Ariel agreed, of course. If our Queen thought it important, he would do whatever she wishes. It seemed to me though that this introduced a new set of risks and may compromise their position in Dameseq.

Ariel is right to worry. No one knows how Ciro will react if he delivers a message to the King.

It is a worrisome problem. None of us trust Ciro. So far, Ariel and Itai have made every effort not to see his cheating and not to hear his lies. They feel obligated to maintain the business relationship that so well serves our country's interests.

Ariel fears Ciro's reaction if he goes to the court and meets the King without him. Ciro would, no doubt, consider it a blow to his pride, even though he could not arrange an appointment or attend even if he wanted to. He likes to be thought of as an important person. Chances are he would consider it a betrayal and be furious.

Yoav and Gershon agreed that Ariel should worry about a jealous reaction—whether rational or not. He should always beware of Ciro and remember that he is a product of a court life filled with betrayal, lies, and mistrust.

Gershon had no suggestions. They could not even guess as to what Ciro would do. They did agree that Ciro was capable of great evil.

All Gershon and Yoav could advise was to "try your best to avoid making an enemy of him." That left Ariel a difficult problem to solve. If he carried a message from Queen Shlomtsion to King Tigranes, he could not tell anyone nor ask for assistance. The correspondence was meant to be private; otherwise, she would ask the Ambassador in Dameseq to deliver the message. Ariel should assume that King Tigranes' wife, Queen Cleopatra, will see him at the palace and tell Ciro.

Ariel had no choice. If asked to deliver a message in secret, then that was what he must do. If Ciro did find out, he would have to manage his reaction as best he can. No matter what, Ariel had to recognize that our relation with Ciro could change, and that was dangerous. Although Ciro has no influence with the King, he could cause great trouble.

The discussion and late hour tired Gershon, and he bid them a good night.

Ariel and Yoav joined Rivka and me, and we walked around Jerusalem. The men agreed a walk was necessary as they ate far too much and had to walk before they could sleep. I guessed they also had to relieve the tension.

"The trip was wonderful, Adah. I now understand why Itai is happy to accompany the caravans to Jerusalem. We crossed mountains sheltering beautiful valleys and passed through fields covered with red poppies. There were yellow, orange and deep purple flowers as far as I could see. We walked by fields of wheat, barley, oats, and sunflowers. We followed well-worn paths leading through thick forests dotted with violets. Along the way, we met travelers from all over the world—especially as we neared Jerusalem.

"I was so excited when I saw the walls of Jerusalem. They seemed to glow a soft yellow as if they were made of gold. I thought my heart would burst from joy when I saw the Temple towering above the city, gleaming in the sunshine. Tears came to my eyes. I was speechless. For almost a thousand years it has held our conscience, our soul, our being."

"Tell me more, Elisheva. Don't leave out anything."

"Jerusalem is stunning. I saw so many buildings—all built with the same type of stone. The city has several huge markets with goods from all over the world—far more than we have in Dan. Along the streets, I saw shops that sold or made everything you could desire. I saw a whole street of glass workshops, a jewelry district, pottery workshops, weavers, cabinet shops, offices with scribes, and metal shops. None of the jewelry or glass shops had goods like Micah's.

"Jerusalem is much bigger than Dan. Sometimes I worried that I might not find my way home. Ariel told me I could never be lost as long as I realized the Temple was a short distance to the east of his parent's house."

"I pray someday I will see Jerusalem too."

"Adah, I am sure you will one day visit and will also love Jerusalem. It is a magical city.

"Ariel's little brother, Hillel, is a man already. Shulamite and Tamar both look like Ariel's *Ima*; they are adorable. We had so much fun together. I liked Ariel's best friend Boaz and his wife Rachel. At one time, I think she might have been in love with Ariel. She reacted strangely when I told her about meeting Ariel. I pretended not to notice. I asked her how she and Boaz knew they were meant for each other. She told me how he helped carry her packages from the market. I am convinced markets have a special magic.

"It was a great privilege to be in Jerusalem. Still, I missed Dan and the beauty of the Galilee and the Merom Valley. I missed the rich smell of the earth, the hills covered with lavender, and the scent of rosemary, thyme, and zatar in the fields. Dan will always be my home. I feel great contentment here."

"I am so happy to hear that Elisheva. For a minute, I thought I was about to lose a friend whom I love like a sister."

"I will never leave. Adah, I too do not want to lose my good friend. Tell me all the news of Dan, my sister."

"Nothing exciting happened. Itai worked long days to manage all the deliveries while you and Ariel were in Jerusalem. I suppose we should be happy business is so good."

"Ariel, Yoav, and Gershon talked about adding more partners. Ariel's brother, Hillel, and possibly one or both of his sisters, Shulamite, and Tamar will become new partners. They plan to ask my brother, Allon, to become a partner and work with Itai."

"That is wonderful. Maybe with additional help, our men will be home more."

"Oh, I hope so. I do want to be with Ariel. The children miss Ariel and wish he was home more."

"And I wish Itai was home more. Let us pray their plans and our wishes come true. You look well, Elisheva. How do you feel—you are in your fifth month now?"

"I feel great. This has to be my easiest pregnancy yet. I am so happy we will have another child."

"Are you hoping for a boy or girl?"

"As Ariel says, I will be happy with a boy if it is not a girl, and a girl if it is not a boy. All children are a blessing."

"You are so wise, Elisheva. I think the same. Have you picked out names yet?"

"Yes, but please do not say anything. If a boy, it will be Avshalom—the father of peace, and if a girl, Bilha—the mother of Dan."

"Those are beautiful names."

Ariel wanted to stay and be here when our baby is born. I bit my lower lip rather than say that he could go to Dameseq another time. He read my mind and said, "I have neglected business in Dameseq for too long. I must go."

"I will be fine Ariel. *Ima* and Adah are close by, and chances are, you will be back before the baby is born."

It was cold in Dan when Ariel left and even colder on the Golan. Several times, Ariel and Itai were caught in rainstorms that left them wet and miserable. Bundling up against the cold, they pushed on thinking only of a warm fire with a hot meal at the end of the day's travel.

They had a lot to discuss. Ariel had to catch up on developments since his last visit. Their discussion centered on Ciro. He asked Itai, "How are relations with Ciro?"

"Not much has changed. Ciro is Ciro. He still cheats us; he is still insufferable. I keep reminding myself that this is only business and we have broader interests."

"Have you noticed any changes in Dameseq of late?"

Itai said there was a different atmosphere that he could not quite define. He suggested they make a few trips around the city, or perhaps approach Dameseq from the north.

Ariel said, "It might be better if we make it a day trip while we are there. We can invite Ciro and suggest we might plant vineyards if the land is suitable."

The cold sapped their strength, and they decided they should not push the animals or themselves any harder. They stopped for the night. Itai unloaded the animals. There was enough new grass for them to graze after the recent rain. Ariel took the ax and gathered enough branches to build a shelter. He cut enough to shelter the animals too.

Itai said, "A great pity we are not in the desert. At least, we would be warm and not have to worry about rain."

"True, Itai, it is warmer, but you still feel the cold at night. And when it rains, the desert is dangerous."

"If it doesn't rain often, how can it be dangerous?"

"I asked the same question. Once I was with Yoav on our way to Avdat to buy spices from the caravans. The sky darkened, and it looked like rain. Yoav said we should immediately leave the *wadi* and camp for the night on higher ground. 'Why?' I asked. 'Because of floods.' Yoav said. I thought he made fun of me. Yoav insisted we construct a shelter much stronger than usual. After we made our camp, it rained. We were pelted with giant raindrops mixed with hail. I sat under the shelter amazed.

"Soon the *wadi* filled with a raging torrent. If I had not seen it, no one could have convinced me it was possible. Later Yoav explained that since the ground is hard, the rain runs off and flows to the low areas. Floods are not only possible; they are dangerous. After the storm passed, the sky returned to its normal brilliance. We saw thousands of stars against a black nothing. Shooting stars streaked across the sky. The air had a different smell. Yoav explained that it was due to the lightning."

Ariel told Itai they were lucky that floods do not occur in the north. All they had to worry about is the cold.

Later that night, following their meal, they sipped tea by the fire—warm and content—well, at least as much as possible in miserable weather under an inadequate shelter. Itai, staring at the fire asked Ariel what he thought would happen.

"What do you mean?" Ariel asked.

"Enemies surround us. They all want to conquer us. Dan would be one of the first cities attacked."

Ariel said, "I think we live in a dangerous time. Although I am not sure there was ever a time without some peril."

I was surprised as Ariel told me about this part of their conversation. He had my full attention. He must have seen the worried look on my face because he added, "So far, our Queen, by negotiation, treaty, or alliance has kept our enemies at bay. I trust she will keep us safe."

I trust her too. In the past year, Queen Shlomtsion had the walls and gates strengthened—not only at Dan but in other cities as well. Dan could withstand a short siege. I think she is concerned. Why else strengthen city defenses in the Galilee? After all, improving our defenses and increasing the size of the army requires a huge budget.

Itai also worried. He suggested that they think about how they could move both families to the safety of Jerusalem should an invasion be imminent.

Ariel said, "For my part, I will stay and fight. I will not run." But, he agreed that it was a good idea to have an evacuation plan should it be necessary.

Itai also said, "I too will stay and fight. Still, I would feel better if I knew my family was safe. Would Yoav or your parents take my family in should it be necessary?"

Ariel said, "Of course, Itai. Your family is part of our family. I am sure they would be welcome. In any event, let us bring it up the next time we see Yoav and Gershon. Perhaps it would be a good idea for us to acquire a house in Jerusalem for our families. At the same time, we can add one or two new wagons that we can adapt to carry our families to Jerusalem. We can prepare provisions in advance so that everything is ready should the need arise. We have both put away enough money to see us through bad times—we could transfer some to Yoav to hold for us. We could also build a secret place for money in the wagons."

Itai agreed that this was a good plan. "Do you think our wives will leave? We want them to be safe, but if I know Adah and my sister, they will stay. They will say that this is their home, and they too will fight to protect their family. Anyway, let us prepare in the event we will be able to convince them to leave if necessary."

They were correct. Adah and I would not leave without our husbands. We would defend our homes too. Still, we had to think of our children. I hope we never have to face an invasion. I knew generations before us had the same dilemma. I wish I knew what to do.

Ariel and Itai resolved to make plans when they returned from Dameseq.

177

# BOOK THIRTEEN—CAUGHT

"Musa, please do not do this. I am afraid that you will not return home. Ratib is a dangerous man. Please do not go. Give the scroll to the police—maybe if you voluntarily return it, there will be no criminal charges. I do not know what I will do if something happens to you."

"Aisha, we talked about this. I have to do it. We must help our family escape from Syria. I am their only chance to survive. I have to see this through. I promise to be careful."

I sat in the taxi holding, close to my chest, the box with the ancient scroll. I told the driver to take me to the Banias Nature Reserve—the side with the waterfall.

"Are you sure that is where you want to go? What do you have in the box? Are you going to make sketches of the waterfall?'"

"Yes, that is what I am going to do. I am going to make sketches."

The taxi driver shrugged. He drove slowly as he started to climb the winding road to the Golan and the Nature Reserve.

Fifteen minutes later, the taxi pulled into the parking lot driving almost to the ticket booth. Ratib waited. He casually walked over smiling.

"My good friend, Musa. I am so glad you came. I see you brought the book you promised me. It is such a beautiful day to hike. Come; let us have coffee and cake at the kiosk before we start. We should see the new sky-bridge. My friends tell me the views of the waterfall are extraordinary. The trail is a little steep in places, but it is not a long hike. I am sure we can manage. Everyone says the effort is worthwhile. I invited two of my friends to join us."

It was all I could do to keep my legs from shaking. I was afraid. This is all wrong. Why did not I listen to Aisha and go to the police? Yigal trusted me, gave me a good job, promoted me, and considered me part of the archeology team. I should have brought the scroll back the next day. I could have arrived at the site before anyone came to work and replaced the scroll; nobody would have known. Even if Yigal was already there, he might have been mad at me; however, I am sure he would have accepted my apology, especially since I was careful with the scroll.

But, here I am with Ratib, his friend Doron, and a small man with glasses whom I guess will verify the value of the scroll. I do not trust any of them. Ratib scares me, and so does Doron. Aisha was right from the beginning. They will cheat me. Why did I try to sell the scroll? I wish I had never taken it. However, if I rescue my family, it will have been worthwhile. How much longer will they be safe in Syria? No, I cannot change the past; I have to continue no matter what happens to me.

Ratib introduced me to Doron who would arrange for a buyer, and Shlomo, a Professor of Ancient Literature, who came to appraise the scroll.

Doron looked at me and asked, "Did you bring the book?"

I started to open the box. Ratib quickly put his hand on mine. "Of course he did; Musa is an honorable man. He always does what he promises."

Shlomo said, "I cannot do an appraisal here with people around. We need a private area where I can examine our friend's book."

Doron smiled and said, "Do not worry, I have arranged everything. I found a place where no one will see us. After we complete our business, I want to see the waterfall. After all, we are just four good friends out for an afternoon hike. Meanwhile, let us have a light snack before we get down to business."

There were many people in the kiosk area: families with children and several couples having coffee and pastry or ice cream. At a table, near the rear, a middle-aged man and woman sat holding hands. They appeared oblivious to everyone but themselves—except they noticed the four men sitting at one of the tables in the middle. Three other couples paid close attention to the four men. One couple stood at a flimsy table selling olives and jams to the right of the kiosk. Another sat at a table next to an old woman making Druze pita on a *tabun*. Two police officers, wearing jeans and sweatshirts, parked near the entrance to the parking lot, were eating sunflower seeds. Two athletic female police officers, also dressed in jeans and casual shirts, studied a map of the nature reserve at a fork in the trail. A focused listening device, operated from a parked car, augmented the surveillance.

After ordering cappuccino with an extra shot of espresso, Doron walked over to a row of tour buses at the back of the parking lot. He spoke to the driver for a few minutes before returning to the table. "We have about forty minutes to use the tour bus. The driver will stand outside and smoke. He will prevent anyone from entering."

Ratib looked at Doron and nodded. "Very good, Doron. We are in a public area yet have complete privacy. Perfect."

"Thank you, Ratib. I thought you would appreciate my arrangements."

"Come, Musa. Let's see just how valuable is your scroll."

***

**Provenance**

Once inside the bus, Shlomo took charge. "Tell me, Musa; how did this scroll come into your possession?"

"In 1968, I worked at Tel Dan. I unearthed some broken pottery. It was photographed as protocol required. Later the fragments were dated to 50 BC. I continued to work and uncovered a jug holding this scroll. I took it home with me and did not return to work."

Shlomo turned on a tape recorder, took out a high-resolution camera, photographed the box, and removed the top. He then photographed the scroll from several different angles.

Doron curtly told Shlomo, "We don't have all day. Move this along."

"An appraisal cannot be rushed. At first glance, this is an old scroll. I think it may be quite valuable."

Ratib and Doron looked at each other. In their wildest dreams, they did not expect this. They could barely contain their excitement at the prospect of riches.

Before proceeding, Shlomo set up a high-intensity light and put on magnifying eyeglasses. He opened a package containing a new pair of white gloves as if he was a surgeon fearing contamination. He put the gloves on being careful not to touch anything. He gently lifted the scroll from the box.

"The writing on the outside of the scroll is similar to the script used at the time of the Second Temple before the birth of Jesus Christ. It says, *Elisheva's Diary.*"

There was silence in the bus. Hopes soared that this might be a discovery on par with the Dead Sea Scrolls, a glimpse into the life of a simple citizen, not royalty, not a prophet, not a priest, but a common person.

With great care, Shlomo unrolled a part of the diary and started to read. "This is written by a woman who grew up and lived in Dan. I believe it is the story of her life in the Galilee. The writing is a mixture of Hebrew and Aramaic. Both were commonly used at the time of the Second Temple."

Doron looked at his watch and said, "We do not have much time. We will have to leave the bus in a few minutes. Tell me, Professor, how much do you think the scroll is worth?"

"I need to examine it in far more detail to give you an exact figure. It appears authentic—the scroll, the script, the ink, the style of writing. The lack of an exact provenance is a problem; although I have no doubt the scroll is genuine. Carbon dating can determine the exact age."

"So, tell me your best estimate of what you think it is worth?"

"This is a major find. I think it is priceless."

Doron and Ratib smiled as if they had discovered the key to immortality and happiness. Had they not been rushed, they would have hugged each other, danced, and sung to the heavens above for blessing them with such good fortune.

Musa was sad. Riches were in his grasp. All he felt was an overwhelming sense of sadness. He stole what might be an intimate glance of life into ancient Israel, a national treasure—stole it from people who trusted him—stole it from a country that fought to survive for thousands of years—stole it from people and a country that treated him with dignity, compassion, and insured his rights in law. No, this was not right.

The time was up. They had to leave before the tour group returned to the bus. Shlomo reluctantly replaced the scroll, closed the box, and returned it to Musa.

Outside the bus, Ratib and Doron stood to the side and argued.

At the edge of the parking lot, the observer team alerted the force that the suspects had left the bus. "Has the exchange been made?"

"No, Musa is still holding the package."

"No one move until the exchange takes place."

Ratib and Doron finally walked over to Musa. "My friend, this is a great day. Why are you so sad?"

"I am simply overwhelmed by Professor Shlomo's appraisal."

"Well, you should be. Doron tells me he may have a private buyer willing to pay as much as 100,000 shekels. This is far more than we originally thought. He has agreed to pay you 50,000 shekels. He is prepared to pay you now in cash. What do you say, Musa?"

"He will pay me in cash now?"

"Yes. I too am surprised he has that much money with him—I think he routinely keeps large sums in his car."

"The Professor said that the scroll is priceless. It should be worth more."

"You may be right, Musa, except it cannot be sold in a public auction. We need to find a buyer who will secretly keep it in a private collection. That limits the amount it can be sold for. I think Doron's offer is a good one; as your friend, I advise you to accept it. Of course, you can choose not to and try to find another buyer. Before you decide, I will ask Doron if he will make a better offer."

After a few minutes, Doron approached Musa. He stood before him for a long second before speaking, "Musa, you have persuasive friends. Ratib has convinced me to offer you another 5,000 shekels. We may lose money after all our costs are considered. I should not agree to pay more, but to close the deal now, I will. What do you say?"

Musa thought for what seemed like an eternity. Looking down at the ground, he replied, "Okay, I accept your offer."

Doron walked over to a blue BMW. He opened the boot, and after a few minutes, he returned with a backpack that he handed to Musa. At the same time, Musa handed the box with the scroll to Doron. "Congratulations, Musa.

You have done a noble deed. I will pray Allah keeps your family safe."

The deal was done. The exchange made. The police moved in and arrested all four men.

Ratib and Doron immediately protested, declaring they "hadn't done nothing."

"And what is in this backpack?

"A loan to my friend, Musa."

"And what is in the box?"

"A present Musa brought for me."

"Musa, did you bring Doron a present?"

It was finally over. All the long nights he lay awake thinking of the shameful thing he had done to people he respected and who had trusted him. The worry about the danger to his family by dealing with Ratib was over. Finally, the scroll would be returned. He could admit his sin and suffer the shame. The agony of deceit was over. At last, he will be at peace. He hoped at the end of days, Allah would forgive him.

He hung his head low like a beaten dog. "No, this is a scroll I found at Tel Dan. I hid it until today. I was too ashamed to return it. I only now tried to sell it to raise money to save my family."

"And you, Sir, what are you doing here?"

"My name is Shlomo. I am an internationally known Professor. My good friend, Doron, asked me to appraise an ancient manuscript. I know nothing more."

"Well Sir, we will have to find you a prison cell that is suitable for a distinguished professor."

A Senior Researcher from Tel Aviv University's Department of Archeology and Ancient Near Eastern Cultures took the box from Doron. He walked over to the kiosk, selected a clean table near the rear of the dining area, and opened the box. He gasped. It was an ancient diary, written in gall ink, apparently from the time of the Second Temple. He immediately closed the box. He told the commander the scroll was extraordinarily valuable; it should have a police escort to guarantee its safety until it could be locked in a temperature-controlled vault.

The commander called everyone together. "You have done great work today. We have broken a ring trafficking in drugs and antiquities. I was not sure what we would find today, but it appears that we have recovered a manuscript of immense value and importance to Israel. I am imposing a news blackout. No one is to talk to the press. I repeat. No one is to talk to the press or say anything of today's arrests. The top leadership will make all necessary announcements. I will keep you appraised as to any progress in this case. Does everyone understand what I just said?"

Each officer nodded his assent.

"I will require a signed statement from each of you acknowledging that our job here today is confidential. Under no circumstance should anything be discussed outside this group except with the state prosecutor. I also require a written report from each of you on your role and actions today. Again, I commend you for an excellent job. I thank you all."

The prison authority transferred the prisoners to the jail in Tsfat and isolated them from each other. Doron, Ratib, and the Professor were indignant, loudly proclaimed their innocence, protested their arrest, and demanded to see lawyers. Ratib shouted that his arrest was motivated by racism. "I done nothing wrong."

The police commander briefed the investigative-interrogation teams on the surveillance, arrests, and the discovery of the diary. He recommended indictments for theft, attempted sale of antiquities, smuggling, drug dealing, conspiracy, and money laundering.

Musa was brought to a bare room with pale green concrete walls, a small barred window, and a single light bulb hanging over a rickety well-worn table with two metal chairs. A simple black telephone, left over from the days when phones were connected with wires to the wall, was the only equipment in the room. Recording equipment, while present, was not visible.

A slim, attractive, middle-aged female police detective conducted the questioning on the first day. She arranged her note pad and for a long moment stared at Musa.

"Good morning. My name is Mali. Do you know why you are here, Musa?"

He looked down avoiding her stare. "Yes, I know."

"Where do you live, Musa?"

"I am from the village of Ghajar."

"Is this your Israeli identity card number?"

"Yes, that is my number."

"Are you married, Musa?"

"Yes, my wife's name is Aisha; we have three sons and a daughter."

"Aisha is a pretty name."

Musa nodded acknowledging the compliment. "Thank you. My wife is very beautiful."

"How long have you been married?"

"We married in 1969 after I built our house with the money I earned at Tel Dan."

"Tell me, Musa, what did you do at Tel Dan?"

"At first, I moved soil to a disposal site outside the Tel. Later, Yigal promoted me, and I became one of the excavators. I was a careful worker. With the extra pay, I was able to build my house."

"Were you happy with your treatment at the Tel?"

"Oh yes. Yigal was good to me as were the other workers. They treated me the same as everyone else."

"Tell me about the day you found the diary."

"It was late in the day. Everyone had left and I wanted to uncover what I thought was the cornerstone of a building. It turned out to be a jar containing a scroll."

"Why did you take the scroll from the site?"

"I wanted to show it to Aisha."

"Musa, this is important; tell me why you did not return the scroll."

"I wanted to. I wanted to arrive at the Tel before anyone came to work and put it back—then I could discover it as if for the first time."

"Why didn't you?"

"I worried someone might already be there and see me. I wish I had brought it back. I am so sorry."

"You know that you violated the law. Theft of an antiquity is a serious crime. You will have to go to prison."

"Yes, I know."

"You could have left it hidden; why now did you decide to sell the scroll?"

"My relatives in Syria are starving, their village destroyed, they have no home, and they have nowhere to go. I needed money to help them escape and come to live in Israel. They would be safe here."

"Are you related to Ratib?"

"No. I did not know him before asking his help to sell the diary. He is known to have contacts with dishonest people and even criminals. Once I told him about the scroll, I was afraid to tell him I did not want to sell it. He is a dangerous man. I was worried he might hurt me or my family."

"This is enough for today, Musa. We will talk again tomorrow."

"Madam Investigator, could I ask you to call my Aisha? I am sure she is worried. Please tell her I am okay. She wanted me to bring the scroll to the police; she begged me not to sell it. Will she be allowed to visit me?"

"Yes. I will call Aisha for you."

\*\*\*

**Second Day of Interrogation**

"Musa, please sit down. We have a lot to cover today. Yesterday, we talked about Ratib. It was not clear to me how you knew Ratib could help you sell a stolen antiquity. Would you explain that please?"

"In my village, smuggling of drugs across the border near Ghajar is common. Money crosses the border—some counterfeit, some moved out of the country to avoid taxes, and some to help relatives in Syria. Ratib has many contacts with the smugglers. I assumed he would know who could help me."

"Musa, I have talked to my superiors. I told them you are cooperating in our investigation. I want to ask you something, and you should think about it. Are you prepared to testify in court to everything you told me?"

"Yes."

"Musa, will you testify against Ratib and Doron at their trials?"

"Will I or my family be in danger?"

"We will protect you, but I cannot guarantee there will not be repercussions. I assume you will be honored in Ghajar and safe from any harm in your village."

"Yes, I will testify. It is the only right thing to do at this point."

"In return, Musa, I will recommend that you receive a light sentence. The prosecutor and the court will make the final decision. Generally, though, they accept an investigator's recommendation."

"I am most grateful. Thank you so much, Madam Investigator."

"Musa, tell me exactly—to the best of your memory—what you told Ratib and what he promised you."

"I told him about the scroll. He told me that for a share of the sale he would inquire if a friend of his knows anyone interested in purchasing an ancient scroll."

"Did you know Doron, or did he mention Doron was his friend?"

"No."

"Had you met the Professor before the exchange?"

"No. I knew only Ratib. I was afraid of Ratib. I wish I had never taken the scroll. I was just a stupid kid too ashamed to correct a horrible mistake."

"Musa, I have no further questions. If I do have additional questions, we will meet again. I am sorry that you did not return the scroll. I wish you luck, Musa."

***

## Indictments

The prosecutor's office informed the media that a press conference announcing major indictments would be held at the criminal court in Tsfat.

Reporters from the major newspapers, radio, and TV news agencies converged on Tsfat. All the hotels were filled. The morning of the conference, reporters gathered at the courthouse. Despite the serious business, there was an air of excitement and tension in the courthouse. As they waited for the state prosecutor, rumors swept back and forth across the room. One loud reporter assured the crowd that this was nothing more than an effort by a government official to make himself important. Another shouted he heard something substantial had happened. No one knew, which was unusual in a small country where secrets were notoriously hard to keep.

The Chief Prosecutor together with the Senior Police Commander and a man in an old ill-fitting suit entered. The reporters were quiet—this promised to be more than the usual arrest of a minor criminal or even a politician. It must be something important to have a Senior Police Commander come to Tsfat for a press conference.

"Ladies and Gentlemen, I have a short statement to read. Then I will accept questions.

"Indictments were entered this morning against three men. The charges include drug smuggling, money laundering, theft, and the proposed sale of an antiquity."

The reporters yawned. One stood up and asked, "What antiquity was offered for sale?"

The low murmur circled the room as reporters asked their neighbor if they knew of a stolen antiquity.

The prosecutor introduced the man in the ill-fitting suit, a Professor from the Hebrew University in Jerusalem, Department of Archeology.

He approached the podium. His hand shook as he started to speak. He took a sip of water spilling some on the floor. The reporters were patient. As a professor at a prestigious university, they accorded him respect and listened.

"This past week I had the privilege of examining one of the most important ancient scrolls discovered since the Dead Sea Scrolls."

The reporters sat straight up. For a long moment, there was absolute silence. Then like water bursting from a dam, a reporter's hand flew up and a thousand questions were yelled.

Not rattled by the flurry of questions, the Professor continued. "Forty-five years ago, a young worker discovered a jar containing an ancient scroll at Tel Dan. He recently attempted to sell the scroll. He was arrested after a long police investigation.

"The scroll is the diary of a woman from the city of Dan. The story starts when she is a young girl during the reign of King Alexander Yanai. The diary is the most complete picture of life we have of that period—especially life in the Hula Valley then known as the Merom Valley. This diary predates the chronicles written by Josephus by more than one hundred years. It also tells us more than we had previously known about Queen Shlomtsion. As a historical document, it is priceless. As a window to life in Israel during the Second Temple, it is priceless."

The barrage of questions continued, "When will the diary be released to the public? Who is in charge of the research? Who were the people arrested? Who is in charge of the investigation? When do the trials start? What is the condition of the diary? Where did the arrests take place? What units were involved? How long did the investigation take?"

For a moment, the avalanche of questions startled the Professor. Slowly he responded, "The diary is in excellent shape. It is written in a mixture of Hebrew, Aramaic, and Greek. A team of scholars is preparing a copy of the text for access by qualified scholars in Israel, Europe, China, and the Americas. We will need years to digest all the information in the diary. I have no idea when it will be released to the public.

"I can only add at this time that the diary is a rare and significant archeological find. Personal diaries are one of the best sources for historians. I expect, or I should say I hope, this is only the first of similar discoveries as the archeological program in Israel continues."

The Police Commander took the microphone. "The criminal investigative unit has been following the principals in this case for some time. When we learned an antiquity was offered for sale, we reinforced the investigative team and started 24/7 surveillance. We made the arrests two weeks ago at the Banias Nature Reserve when a former employee at Tel Dan, Musa, attempted to sell the scroll he discovered in 1968 and kept hidden until now."

"Who were the others arrested?"

"One man is a known drug dealer. He is charged with smuggling, selling drugs, money laundering, and the attempted illegal sale of antiquities. He has been under surveillance for several months. The second man is from a village in the Golan. He has been long under investigation for money laundering, shylocking, extortion, and various other illegal activities.

"During our questioning of the suspects, two maintained they are innocent and victims of police harassment, racism, and entrapment.

"Musa admitted his guilt. He expresses remorse and great regret for his actions as a young man."

A reporter stood and asked, "Did he not try to sell the scroll now? Does he not regret his actions as an old man?"

Looking uncomfortable, Commander Nimrod thought for a moment before replying, "During the interrogation we asked exactly that—perhaps you should be a police interrogator."

The Commander waited for the laughter to subside before continuing.

"Musa responded that he needed to sell the scroll. His family in Syria is desperate. He felt, as the patriarch of his family, he had no choice even if he went to prison."

At this point, the prosecutor took the microphone and thanked everyone for coming. There would be additional press conferences when and if there were significant developments.

# BOOK FOURTEEN—CRISIS

Ariel entered the Palace in a great hurry. He moved with a quickness that betrayed the nervousness he felt. His senses were all sharp. He had to tell Queen Shlomtsion about the danger so she could save the kingdom. "My Queen, I bring an urgent report of observations I made in Dameseq."

Queen Shlomtsion in a calm voice said, "Please approach, Ariel."

In a nervous stream of words, Ariel told of his visit to Dameseq. How he arrived in Dameseq two weeks ago bringing a shipment of wine cups made in Dan's workshops. To the east, he saw a large encampment of soldiers and in the city; he observed a great number of army commanders. He circled the city and saw several large encampments of soldiers to the north. King Tigranes is preparing for war.

Queen Shlomtsion listened and to calm him, she said, "This is interesting news. Please continue Ariel."

"I met King Tigranes' nephew, Ciro, later in the day. He demanded I return to Dan and bring another shipment of wine. Ciro said there was double and even triple demand for our wine.

"That night, Ciro invited me to his home. He talked about the situation in the world. He told me, in strict confidence, that his uncle mobilizes an army of 500,000 men for a major operation. Ciro promised he could supply the army with wine.

"I told Ciro this was indeed excellent news. Ciro said he needed at least three to four times the amount we now sell.

"I told him we could not supply that much unless we shorten the aging of some wine and arrange to bring wine from Jerusalem. All that, though, will take some time. I also said our warehouse is not large enough to hold more wine and

194

asked if we could deliver the wine to a different location. I would also require immediate payment to acquire two to three times as much wine.

"Ciro's response was telling. He said not to worry about payment and we could deliver the wine about a day's journey south of Dameseq.

"It was not clear to me whether the army would march north to engage Lucullus or south toward Israel and Egypt. I counted enough warehouses to stockpile supplies for a protracted campaign. Many warehouses are south of the city; his objective may be to invade Israel. Ciro did not say. He may not know."

Queen Shlomtsion bit her lower lip and for a second appeared deep in thought. "I appreciate your bringing this intelligence to me. This is the first indication we have about Tigranes' mobilization. I thank you. Have you learned anything else?"

"Yes, my Queen. That evening, Ciro hosted us. He was jubilant. I guessed in anticipation of enormous profits by not paying us for the wine. He may also believe the King will reward him with a position in a conquered land. In any event, he related to me—in strict confidence—discussions at court concerning Rome.

"Pompey and Crassus have formed an alliance, and both have become consuls of Rome. On one hand, the alliance is strange as both are vain, pompous, ambitious, and self-confident. On the other hand, they recognize shared power is better than no power. Both are focused, ruthless, and talented. Crassus has taken Julius Caesar, himself an excellent military commander, as his protégé. Rome has a group of excellent leaders that have clear objectives and know how to mobilize and use their power to great effect.

"Rome has annexed Pontus even while Lucullus still consolidates his victory over King Mithridates VI. King Tigranes has given his father-in-law sanctuary in Armenia. Ciro claims King Tigranes expects a clash with Rome soon.

"My Queen, I stayed another day in Dameseq to verify my suspicions as much as possible without raising suspicion. I come direct from Dameseq. I thought it important to bring you this report without delay."

I was surprised when Ariel told me what the Queen said next. I felt goose bumps.

She said, "I am grateful to you Ariel. This is important information. Please stay in Jerusalem another day or two while I consider your report. I may ask you to deliver a message to King Tigranes. Eli will send for you. Before we finish, tell me, how is Elisheva? She is a most impressive woman."

"Thank you, my Queen. Elisheva is well. She feels safe knowing you protect Israel. That feeling is widespread in the Galilee."

"Go in peace, Ariel. Thank you for your report."

I learned that later, Queen Shlomtsion summoned her advisors, military commanders, and finance secretary. She outlined two options: prepare to fight or attempt to pay Tigranes not to invade. The military commanders said they needed more time to prepare defenses and increase the size of the army. It was impossible to fight an army that large at this time. In the minimum, the northern cities and large tracts of the north would be lost leaving the approach to Jerusalem vulnerable. If a clash was to come, the more time we had to prepare, the better chance we had of holding back or even defeating Tigranes' army.

The finance secretary proposed a solution. The treasury, despite the past year's expense in strengthening walls and city defenses, could support a large tribute, as long as it was not too large. This could allow time to prepare for the invasion that would inevitably come.

In the face of catastrophe, she was calm and instilled confidence in her commanders. She said, "I thank you all for your thoughts and advice. We face a difficult time. I want this meeting to remain secret. I do not want to alarm the people. If it does become necessary to prepare openly for an invasion, I will then announce our plans. Meanwhile, continue preparations to defend the Kingdom in secret. Thank you all for coming."

She then asked Eli to stay to prepare two letters: the first to Commander Lucullus; the second to Queen Cleopatra.

***

Letter to Lucius Licinius Lucullus

*Most Honorable Consul and Commander Lucius Licinius Lucullus, Greetings,*

*I again have the honor to address a correspondence to you. With regret, I do not send glad tidings. My sources report the mobilization of a large army in Syria by King Tigranes. One estimate puts the mobilization at 500,000 soldiers supported by heavy cavalry.*

*I have no confirmed information as to his objective. Construction of large warehouses south of Dameseq shows a large move is imminent. Moreover, plans to stockpile a great amount of supplies indicate a prolonged operation. My advisors think King Tigranes intends to move his army far from his base. The movement may be south toward Israel and Egypt. Caution dictates that I prepare for an invasion. Should this be King Tigranes' plan of action, I need to ask your plans to appreciate whether Israel will bear the full force of King Tigranes' army?*

*I want to assure you that any mobilization in Israel will be only to defend against invasion. I will attempt to arrive at a diplomatic understanding with King Tigranes. Any accommodation will in no way involve violating any or part of our agreement.*

*I congratulate you on your victories in Pontus against King Mithridates VI. The annexation of Pontus is to the glory of Rome.*

*Shlomtsion, Queen of Israel*

***

Letter to Queen Cleopatra

*Your Majesty, My Dear Queen Cleopatra,*

*I feel compelled to pass on intelligence that has come to my attention. I have received solid and credible evidence that King Tigranes is mobilizing a large army. While his objective is not known, his deployment suggests he will attack south toward Israel, and I assume thereafter to Egypt.*

*As he is preparing his army now, I suspect the onslaught will come soon. I am preparing two possible solutions: defending against an invasion, or arranging a diplomatic solution to appease King Tigranes.*

*The first option has been ongoing for several years. I have strengthened the walls of my northern cities. My commanders tell me that despite my long-standing commitment to increase the size and strength of the army, it is not yet strong enough to counter an invasion force of the size arrayed against us.*

*My preference is to pursue a diplomatic course. Should this not prove successful, I believe it is our mutual interest to develop a joint strategic defense plan. To this end, I am sending a special ambassador and a trusted senior army commander to provide any information or clarification that you may require.*

*Amid a threatening environment, good news reached me concerning the birth of your daughter, Cleopatra VII. Please accept my warmest regards and heartfelt best wishes. I am told that she has your beauty, and I have no doubt your wisdom.*

*Shlomtsion, Queen of Israel*

"Ariel, I am so happy you are home." I hugged him and did not let go. He held me tight, and a thousand emotions flooded over me. My husband was home and safe. "I was worried when Itai told me you went straight to Jerusalem from Dameseq. He did not say why except you had important business. Kiss me, Ariel."

"I missed you Elisheva, especially this time. Before we talk, I must see our new baby. Did we have a boy or girl? When was he born?" I picked up Bilha, kissed her twice, and handed her to Ariel. He looked at her with total joy and smiled. He kissed her and said, "She is so beautiful—just like her *Ima*."

"Bilha was born two days after you left for Dameseq. *Ima* and Adah were with me the whole time. I wish you had been here."

"Are Eitan, Levi, and Talitha excited about their new sister?"

"Yes. They are a great help. They hold Bilha and sing songs to her. Bilha looks up at them and smiles."

"I wanted to come home from Dameseq. I so much wanted to be here when Bilha was born. I agonized whether to put off reporting to our Queen. I know it was selfish of me. How many times do we add to our family? I was sure, though, you would have said for the safety of our children, first go to Jerusalem. We have a lifetime to hug and kiss Bilha."

"Did you see Queen Shlomtsion?"

"Yes. She asked me to relay her best regards to you."

For a brief moment, I could not say a word. "I cannot believe she remembered me. Why, all of the sudden, did you go to Jerusalem?"

"I will tell you, but you must promise to not ever repeat a word of what I will say. Do you promise?"

199

"You scare me, Ariel. Yes, I promise."

"While in Dameseq, I saw a large army encamped around the city. I thought it should be reported to Queen Shlomtsion right away, rather than sending a message with Itai. It turns out I was right."

"Does that mean Dan will be attacked?" In my mind, I visualized hordes of soldiers running through Dan and killing everyone in their path. I shivered. "Oh, this is terrible. What will become of us? What will become of our children? When do you think the invasion will come?"

"Elisheva, be calm. I am not certain there will be an invasion. The intention may be to attack the Roman army in Pontus. At this point, no one knows. Queen Shlomtsion has directed me to deliver a message to King Tigranes and wait for a response. I leave early tomorrow morning.

"Do not worry, Elisheva. We will have plenty of warning; if necessary, we can go to Jerusalem. I talked to Itai about us buying a house in Jerusalem together. He will discuss it with Adah, and when I return from Dameseq, we should decide together whether to buy a house in Jerusalem or not."

"Ariel, all this makes me nervous. I want you here with me. Our Queen does so much for us. I know you cannot refuse to serve. Be careful, Ariel. Come back to me soon."

"I will be careful. Since everyone is sleeping, let us listen to the music of the wind in the trees and the song in our hearts. Come, my beautiful bride."

Ariel traveled with Itai to Dameseq and told him that Queen Shlomtsion directed him to deliver a message to King Tigranes. Our Queen preferred a diplomatic solution that convinces King Tigranes not to invade Israel. She empowered Ariel to negotiate the terms of an agreement.

Itai asked if he felt competent to negotiate with King Tigranes. Ariel said he told Queen Shlomtsion that he does not have any negotiating experience, especially with a King.

She did not agree. "Ariel, you are a successful merchant with the ability to negotiate better than any of my ambassadors. You are more than competent to negotiate with a King."

I hoped she was right. I also worried about how they would deal with Ciro. I feared he would do great harm to my Ariel although I could not imagine what it might be.

Ariel said, "The wine we bring should show Ciro our good faith and keep him happy."

While Itai went with him to the warehouse to register the delivery, Ariel would go to the palace to see King Tigranes.

While Ariel told me his plan, I rubbed my head. I hoped he is right. Would it really be that easy?

***

Early the next morning, Ariel was at the palace gate. The guard informed the King's secretary a message from Queen Shlomtsion had arrived. Ariel was shown in immediately. The Palace was far busier than the first time he had been there. Military commanders, in ostentatious armor befitting their rank, were everywhere. Ariel was sure a major operation was imminent.

201

After a short wait, Ariel was brought before the King.

King Tigranes appeared distracted. He stared at Ariel before saying, "Approach."

Ariel handed the message to one of King Tigranes' attending kings and said, "Your majesty, my Queen directed me to remain in Dameseq and await your response."

King Tigranes found it curious that she chose a merchant to deliver her message.

Ariel said he was humbled by her request and was sure that her ambassador would be far abler than him. However, she felt that by sending a simple merchant, the discussions could be managed in secret without the usual court cross currents.

King Tigranes smiled and said, "Your Queen is a wise woman. I see that her Greek is excellent. She writes that you are empowered to respond on her behalf should I choose to accept her proposal of a treaty. Why should I reach a treaty with Israel, Ariel Ben Gershon?"

Ariel took a deep breath before answering, "Your Majesty, my Queen is convinced that friendship is a great prize that benefits us both. The trade between our countries grows. More important, though, our mutual border is peaceful and requires little expense for defense, an ideal environment for prosperity. Moreover, both our countries can devote resources to defend against other threats."

"Your Queen makes a persuasive argument. Peace is indeed to be valued. However, I have confidence in my army. If I control both sides of the border, then I have no need for a treaty and no expense."

"Occupation, however, is expensive. Israel values its freedom, will vigorously defend against an invasion, and resist any occupation. Such defense though is expensive. My Queen feels friendship between our countries is a far better solution. We both save ourselves considerable expense."

"Ariel Ben Gershon, you are a credit to your Queen."

King Tigranes studied the letter and then responded to Ariel saying, "I do not consider the amount she pledges to me in friendship sufficient."

"Your Majesty, my Queen asked me to underscore the difficulty of putting a price on friendship. She asked that I request your estimate of the value of friendship between our countries."

"Philosophers have written volumes on friendship. I appreciate Queen Shlomtsion's approach. Return to the Palace tomorrow for my response. Go in peace, Ariel Ben Gershon."

Ariel came home earlier than I expected. When he stumbled into the house, I nearly dropped Bilha. His face was covered with bruises. One eye was swollen shut. "Ariel, what happened?"

"I was arrested in Damaseq."

"What? Why in the world were you arrested? What did you do?"

"Ciro accused me of raping his wife."

"Please tell me you did not rape Tomiri."

"Of course not. The guards beat me and threw me in a dungeon. The rats, the rats..." His voice trailed off.

I shook my head. I could not have heard what I heard. I had to sit down. All of the sudden, I was covered with a cold sweat, and my leg shook under the table as he told me what happened. I knew Ariel feared Ciro, but I never expected something like this.

Ariel took my hands. His eyes reflected a deep pain. "I am okay. Everything will be fine."

"Tell me what happened, Ariel.""

"I was kept me in prison for two days. It was the worst place imaginable."

"Oh my poor husband, I just knew something bad would happen. For some reason, this time, I was afraid for your safety. I never thought that as Queen Shlomtsion's Ambassador, even if in secret, they would harm you. How could they accuse you of rape? That is outrageous; it is worse than despicable."

"I met with King Tigranes and delivered our Queen's message. He is an impressive man and appeared to welcome Queen Shlomtsion's offer of friendship. He told me to return to the palace the next day for his response. When I did not show up, the Captain of the Guards told him I was arrested on Ciro's orders.

"I am not sure what happened next, but two days later, I was released, and Ciro was put in that same prison cell. It was not my destiny to remain in that prison. My destiny is to be with you."

"Hold me, Ariel. Let me kiss you to make all your wounds better."

"I love you, Elisheva. I must go to each of our children and kiss them a hundred times. I want so much to stay with you. First though, I must deliver a message from King Tigranes to Jerusalem."

"What kind of message? What is so important that you cannot stay a few days to recuperate?"

"Based on the negotiation, I am sure it concerns a treaty of friendship between Israel and Armenia. If I am correct, Queen Shlomtsion's diplomacy will keep our country safe. We will be safe."

I cried. I cried and could not stop.

*** 

Ariel pieced together what happened while he was in prison. One of the guards told him some of King Tigranes' reaction when he did arrive at the Palace the next morning. Later, Ciro's wife, Tomiri, told Ariel about her meeting with the King.

She said that Ciro, as usual, fumed about the supposed injustice he suffered at the hands of Ariel and Itai. He ranted, "That miserable Jew went behind my back to meet with my Uncle, the King. He did not even have the courtesy to tell me he planned to go or ask me to arrange an appointment for him. Ariel had the nerve to complain to the King to force me out of the business. In spite of everything I have done for him, the little weasel. I will have to teach him a lesson he will never forget. No one betrays me. No one betrays Ciro." Ciro called his Guards and told them to arrest Ariel for raping his wife that morning. "Take him to the prison."

The guards found Ariel at the Inn where he usually stays. He and Itai were having their evening meal. Ariel looked up when the soldiers came to the table.

"Are you Ariel Ben Gershon?"

"Yes, I am. How may I help you, Captain?"

"I have an order for your arrest."

"What? On what charge? I have not broken any laws."

205

"Come with us. You cannot rape a woman and not be punished. Maybe rape is acceptable in Israel, but not here."

"That is absurd. I raped no one. I am married and love my wife."

"This morning you raped Ciro's wife. Come with us now."

"That is not true. I would never rape anyone."

"Seize him."

\*\*\*

As the soldiers took Ariel from the Inn, he turned to Itai, "get word to *Aba*."

Itai panicked. Remarkably, Ariel stayed calm. The room was deathly quiet. As soon as the soldiers left, a low murmur circled the room. Several diners, afraid the soldiers might return, left. They patted Itai's shoulder as they passed his table.

At first, Itai was not sure what to do. A man from the next table leaned over and whispered, "You should leave immediately. Do not go to your room. Leave the Inn. Find a safe place where no one knows you."

Ariel told Itai to contact Gershon. Itai hoped all this was a mistake, and Ariel would be released tomorrow. At first he thought to ask Tomiri to tell the Queen no rape occurred, that Ciro wanted to discredit Ariel. He decided that would never work; she would not dare to speak against her husband.

Itai wondered whether he should leave Dameseq, and if he did, how could he tell me that he left without Ariel? He considered going to the palace. He could tell King Tigranes that Ariel was with him. Or, maybe he could tell his secretary or one of his attending kings. Even if granted access to the king, why would they believe him over the Queen's nephew? Still, King Tigranes expected Ariel at the palace tomorrow to receive the official response to Queen Shlomtsion.

Itai decided to stay another day. Worried that Ciro may decide that he is also a threat, he left the city and made sure the guards remembered him passing through the gate. He circled around the city to the west and went to an Inn near the northern wall pretending to be a trader from Smyrna. Somehow, he would get word to Ariel not to despair.

\*\*\*

**Prison**

An hour later, Ariel found himself in almost total darkness. It was bone-chilling cold; he instinctively drew his robe tighter. The stench was awful, a mixture of urine, feces, and the smell of men who had not bathed in a long time; overlaying all was a pervading smell of rot. He sensed there were others nearby.

The little light that came into the cell was high above him—a small slit near the ceiling. Fear gripped him. Despite being a sunny day, the walls were wet, cold, and slimy. He felt engulfed by a malignant force that would rot his body and destroy his sanity. He sat with his back against the wall on a cold stone floor covered with filthy straw. It seemed to be alive. Maybe this was hell. Surely, Job never suffered anything like this.

A deep sense of despair gripped him. In the morning, he talked to the King of an empire. Now, imprisoned, he was cut off from any help. He would die in this cell without ever seeing his family. He would never see his new child. We were right to worry about Ciro.

Ariel told himself not to think this way. If he ever wanted to see his family, he must survive. He repeated the psalms and never gave up hope. Itai was still free so there was hope that Queen Shlomtsion would learn that he was arrested. He would not be forgotten and left to rot.

*She will rescue me,* he thought. *I just pray Itai manages to get out of Dameseq and reports to Gershon. Queen Shlomtsion would rescue him. Help will come. After all, it is against all convention to arrest a Queen's envoy.*

Ariel paused as he stood with his back to the cooking area wall. For the first time since he returned, he looked directly into my eyes and told me about the prison cell. In his eyes, I could see him reliving the nightmare.

***

I heard a voice from the dark. "Friend, what is your name?"

There was someone to my right. I turned but could not see anyone. I took a deep breath and said, "I am called Ariel Ben Gershon. I come from Dan to sell wine in Dameseq. Where are you? I cannot see anything."

The man replied saying, "It will take time before your eyes adjust to the dim light. Tell me, why are you here?"

"I am falsely accused of rape."

"Was she worth it at least?"

"I have done nothing."

"My friend, it doesn't matter. Once here, truth is unimportant, just existence. Who did you rape?"

"I am accused of raping Ciro's wife."

"That is not good, my friend. Ciro is related to the King and a powerful man. I am sorry to say, you have no chance of ever leaving this hell hole."

I asked him, "What is your name, and why are you here?"

"I am called Ishmael. I was accused of stealing bread."

"Did you?"

"Yes, I was hungry; my family was hungry. I worry about them now. They have no one to care for them. Although I was not a good provider, we did get by. I tried. I tried as best I could, but nothing ever went my way."

"Something just bit me. I itch all over."

"It could have been a rat, or simply the lice. Try to ignore the itching. You will get used to it soon enough. Fight against the rats or they will keep at you."

A low mournful moan came from the corner opposite me. "What is that, Ishmael?"

"A prisoner. We do not even know his name. He was brought here two days ago unconscious—he was beaten and tortured. No one knows his crime. He never regained consciousness; he is dying."

At some point, I slept. Morning came. Either I was used to the gloom or it was brighter in the cell. There were five prisoners in addition to the dying man. All were in rags. They looked at him, and one asked, "What is your name, friend?"

"I am called Ariel Ben Gershon from the Kingdom of Israel."

"What did a nobleman like you do that landed you in this wonderful place?"

"I am a simple merchant, not a nobleman. I have not done anything wrong."

"No matter, nobleman. Here you are and here you will stay until the end of your days. Maybe you want to share your fine clothes with us, Sir Nobleman?"

Ishmael spoke. "Brothers, he is a prisoner like us. His fate is our fate. Let us not make it worse. I say let him be."

\*\*\*

**Tomiri**

King Tigranes beckoned one his attending Kings. "Has my response to Queen Shlomtsion been prepared?"

"Yes, Great King. It awaits your seal."

"Has the messenger from Queen Shlomtsion, arrived at the palace? Why has he not been brought before me?"

"Great King, Ariel Ben Gershon has not come to the palace today. The Captain of the Guard said he has been arrested. He is in prison."

"What? On whose authority was an ambassador to me arrested?"

"Great King, Ciro ordered his arrest for raping his wife."

"If true, this crime will not go unpunished. I will send Ariel Ben Gershon back to Shlomtsion in pieces."

"Tell the Captain of the Guard to invite Ciro and Tomiri to the palace. I wish to speak to them."

\*\*\*

Later that day, Ciro and Tomiri waited in a private room for their appointment with King Tigranes. Tomiri asked Ciro if he knew why the King wanted to see them.

Ciro looked at Tomiri. "Listen to me, Tomiri. I had Ariel Ben Gershon arrested for raping you."

"He did not rape me. He is a good man and would never do such a thing. Why did you do this, Ciro?"

"He went behind my back to the King to complain about me. I could not let him get away with malicious slander."

"What have you done? Do you not remember when he first came to Dameseq? His *Aba* was a representative of King Alexander Yanai? Only the gods can help us if your Uncle suspects the truth."

"You say what I tell you to say. Ariel raped you yesterday morning. Do not dare to contradict me."

"I am afraid, Ciro."

"Stupid woman, you just do as I tell you." A guard entered to escort them to the King. Ciro warned Tomiri, "Remember what I told you."

King Tigranes rose from the throne to greet Tomiri and Ciro. "Tomiri, I am so sorry. I trust you are recovering. This crime against my family will not go unpunished. You did right, Ciro, to have Ariel Ben Gershon arrested."

Ciro was smug and confident. "Those Jews think they can do whatever they want. He should be flayed alive for daring to touch my wife."

"Do not worry, Ciro. Justice will prevail. You will have your revenge. Tomiri, when did this happen. Why did you not come to me or Cleopatra?"

Looking away, Tomiri replied, "Ciro said he would handle everything, and I shouldn't bother you or the Queen."

"When were you attacked, dear Tomiri?"

Ciro responded, "She was attacked mid-morning. I was at the warehouse to check on supplies. When I came home, Tomiri was hysterical. Her robe was torn. After I calmed her, she told me Ariel Ben Gershon forced himself on her. I called the guards to have him arrested."

"You say it was mid-morning when you were attacked?"

Tomiri looked at Ciro who nodded. "Yes, it was mid-morning."

"Tomiri, you know if someone lies to a King, their tongue, and their children's tongues will be cut out." Tigranes again asked Tomiri, "When were you attacked?"

"I am sure it was mid-morning."

"Tomiri, do not lie to me."

"Ciro said it was mid-morning. It was while he was at the warehouse that I was attacked."

"And my nephew, why are you so sure of the time? Did not Tomiri tell you when the rape occurred?"

"That is what she told me. I always thought Ariel had designs on Tomiri. I feared this would happen someday; we even invited him to our home many times."

"Tell me, Ciro, what would you do to someone who lies to you or accuses someone of a crime they did not commit—especially one as heinous as rape?"

"I would prescribe a severe punishment for the accuser. I would let them rot in the worst prison in Dameseq or I would skin them alive."

"Tomiri, my nephew thinks a false accuser should receive a severe punishment. Did you lie to your husband? Did Ariel Ben Gershon rape you?"

She started to cry. "No, my King. Ariel never raped me. Ciro told me to say that. He thought Ariel complained to you about Ciro cheating him. Please do not hurt my children. I only did what my husband commanded me to do. I am so sorry. I did not want to lie to you. Ariel Ben Gershon has always been proper and respectful to me and everyone else."

"She lies. The stupid woman told me she was raped."

"Enough, you worm. Because you are my wife's nephew, I made you a partner with traders from Israel. You weasel, you cheated your partners; you lied to me. You force this good woman to lie to her King. And, you have the audacity to arrest a Special Ambassador to me. Guards, seize this poor excuse for a man. Free Ariel Ben Gershon from prison, and put this cockroach in his place. Make sure you tell all the prisoners who he is."

"Uncle, I would never lie to you. It was all Tomiri. She is the liar."

"My dear Ciro you will rot in prison until I decide what to do with you. I would have you killed in the slowest and most painful manner if you were not the Queen's nephew. Take him away. Have Ariel Ben Gershon cleaned up, fitted with new clothes, and brought to the palace. Tomiri, I hold you blameless. It was proper you obeyed your husband. But, never, ever lie to me again. You are dismissed."

Despite the beatings and imprisonment, Ariel claimed his mission in Dameseq a success. The information he provided led to an accommodation with King Tigranes the Great, and war was averted. Our Queen kept us safe. I was proud of my husband for his contribution, even if only our family knows about it. Queen Shlomtsion's secretary told Ariel that after his negotiation, Rome and Armenia did clash. He showed Ariel a letter from the Roman Commander Lucullus that acknowledged Ariel's intelligence.

*Queen Shlomtsion Greetings,*

*I was pleased to receive your correspondence in which you confirmed the mobilization of a large army around Dameseq by King Tigranes. Your accommodation with King Tigranes, while you build the strength of your army to withstand an invasion should it come, bespeaks your wisdom.*

*My legions have completed their occupation of Pontus. I have laid siege to the new Armenian capital, Tigranocerta. King Tigranes reacted as I expected by bringing his army from Syria to engage me. Despite his powerful cavalry, and being greatly outnumbered, my legions were victorious. His entire army was destroyed. King Tigranes has fled to northern Armenia; I intend to pursue.*

*I have the pleasure to inform you that Gnaeus Pompeius Magnus has been systematically and vigorously attacking the pirates that have plagued commerce on the Great Sea for far too long. Close to Rome, he destroyed the pirate fleets threatening grain supplies from Sicily, Sardinia and North Africa. He garrisoned the areas to prevent their return. Commerce is unimpeded in the west. He now engages the pirates and their fleets based in Cilicia.*

*Because of his success in the west, many surrender to him without a fight.*

*I have no doubt he will be successful. Rome and all the kingdoms around the Great Sea welcome the news.*

*I desire, and I have the distinct privilege on behalf of the Senate, to extol the virtues of our alliance, and your efforts to respect its terms with honor and dignity.*

*Lucius Licinius Lucullus*
*Commander of the Roman Army of the East*

The past two years have been peaceful free from worries about an attack. Content to let the new young partners in their trading company assume more responsibility, Ariel has been spending less time away from Dan. After the frantic pace of building our home and business, at last, we have more time to spend with our children, our friends, and each other. It is a good time. My family is whole, and we are happy.

It took Ariel a year to recover from his imprisonment in Dameseq. Many nights he awoke in a sweat or kicked at an unseen terror. I fear the nightmares will haunt him forever. I hug him and gently stroke his back until he calms and breathes normally. I cannot even imagine the horrors he suffered in that prison.

In spite of much trepidation, he trusted in fate and returned to Dameseq. Several of their old customers sought him out to assure themselves a supply of Kedesh wines, especially now that Rome has interrupted the supply of Armenian wine. Only a trickle breaches the Roman lines and reaches Dameseq.

May God forgive me, but I was happy to hear that when King Tigranes withdrew his army to confront Lucullus, Ciro was left in prison. I heard a rumor that he later escaped and fled to Pontus where he tried to ingratiate himself with the Romans. He abandoned his wife and children without a second thought. What kind of man abandons his family?

Ariel and Itai decided to help Tomiri, despite her being party to the false accusation that imprisoned Ariel. They suspected and later learned that Ciro forced her to lie to his Uncle, King Tigranes. Fortunately for her, the King recognized that it was Ciro. She escaped punishment but lost everything except for some money she found hidden in the house.

They decided to help her because she too suffered at the hand of Ciro.

She was paid a salary to manage the storage and delivery of wine. Ariel and Itai decided to offer her a bonus at the end of the year, providing the business prospered. Tomiri was left speechless. The Jews that Ciro despised and regularly cheated were honorable and showed compassion.

Tearfully, Tomiri apologized to Ariel and Itai for the party where her supposed friends, Dorilla, and Nysa tried to seduce them. She said it was Ciro's idea to blackmail them so they would not say anything about his cheating.

"Neither Dorilla nor Nysa were my friends," she said. "They were 'ladies of the night' that Ciro hired." She was ashamed to be part of such a hideous scheme and was glad neither of them were unfaithful to their wives. She said, "I envy your wives."

I applauded Ariel and Itai's charitable actions. Yet I resent that they help someone who was complicit in my Ariel's imprisonment. He still bears the scars.

The agreement Ariel negotiated at Queen Shlomtsion's direction worked well. The fighting moved far to the north as Lucullus continued the war against King Tigranes. His legions reached the Aratsani River and Tigranes' ancestral capital of Araxata. Tigranes mobilized a large army to engage Lucullus, who suffered a humiliating defeat. The Romans retreated to the south. Still, all the armies were far enough to the north of our border that a significant buffer remained. We were safe. My family was safe.

Ariel goes with me to the market almost every day. As he did long ago, he carries my packages. I still glance over at him when I think he is not looking. He is heavier now with sprinkles of gray in his hair. While the packages are heavy, he refuses to admit the years and carries them as if they are light; trying not to show it is an effort. I suppose I too have changed. Four children have taken a toll. They have also given me a joy and contentment I never imagined possible. Now that I am with Ariel more, I have never been happier. My life, our life is good.

The Galilee flourishes. We have had rich harvests for several years. Queen Shlomtsion has ensured our safety. She has built strong defenses to protect against any challenge that may arise. Her foreign policy has led to peaceful relations and trade with all our neighbors. We are prosperous; we live in peace.

215

Now that Ariel is home more, I spend more time on dance. I feel a freedom in the poetic movements of dance, a special language that allows me to bare my soul in motion rather than words. Sometimes when I dance, I think of my children and express a sublime joy; sometimes I am just at peace with the beauty of Dan, the Merom Valley, and the Galilee.

Often, I lose myself in the expression of emotions. At times, my dance tells Ariel how much I love him. I start slow and dance in a wide circle while swaying to a rhythm I hear in my head. As I quicken the pace, the circle becomes smaller and smaller until I twirl on one leg with my arms crossed as if I were hugging Ariel. I sense he knows what I am expressing without completely understanding all the 'words.' Often after a dance, he hugs me and whispers he loves me.

I work with children teaching them to express themselves through dance. Their imagination is boundless. They are creative in their use of this new language to communicate complicated emotions. Adah and Miriam send their children to join mine once a week to dance. They enjoy the time. We find it a delight to observe their creativity.

Last week, I had them choose and imitate an animal from Noah's ark. The boys selected aggressive beasts such as lions, bears, and apes and acted out frightening motions—some succeeding quite well. The girls chose docile animals: graceful cats, gazelles, soaring birds, and in a burst of creativity, one picked a porcupine. It was a delight to watch our little porcupine. She arched her back as if to shoot her quills at an enemy or rolled up into a ball to protect her soft parts.

Another time, I asked each child to imagine that he was a tree in a forest. In unison, they swayed in a gentle breeze, bent in a strong wind, and stood completely still when the wind stopped. They used their hands to depict the leaves falling in winter or the start of growth in the spring and the beginning of a new cycle.

Once, after observing the interactions of individuals in a herd of goats, I asked the children to imitate the goats. They grazed and moved in quick movements—each on its own path, yet together as a unit. Some children were

216

shepherds guiding the herd. They swirled around the outer edges of the herd in sweeping graceful motions. It became a beautiful multi-rhythm dance.

Once, before we began, I asked them to imitate in dance the market before Shabbat. The girls all moved from place to place and mimicked putting fruits and vegetables in their baskets. The boys moved with the girls to carry their baskets and occasionally, in fluid motions, circled the girls offering the baskets as if to accept produce. Maybe all this was closer to theater than dance, but I thought the motions of life were in themselves a dance—and perhaps also theater.

While still winter and a thick blanket of snow covered the Hermon as well as some peaks in the Golan, there were clear, sunny days. The rivers in the Merom Valley flowed with fast moving streams that tossed white sprays of water and created a seducing symphony of peaceful sounds.

Ariel said we should pack a picnic and take the children to the river Snir. We could invite Itai and Adah to join us.

"Ariel, let's go this time just with our children. It has been so long since we have been on a picnic; I do not want to share you with anyone. Please, say yes."

"I will if you promise me a kiss when the children are not looking."

"I promise you many, even if they are looking."

"What do you think if we all make the picnic together? You and I will cook with the children—everyone, even the twins—can help. It will be a special picnic."

It was great fun. Eitan and Levi went to the market to select the food we would need. Talitha took Bilha to gather pinecones and break the petals open for the tasty pine nuts. I heard a steady thump-thump-thump as Bilha became adept at breaking the petals with a rock. Ariel went to the warehouse to pick a jug of white wine to complement our meal.

In the meantime, I prepped everything needed to cook. I waited until the children returned so we could cook together. We prepared a platter of goat cheese with figs, cooked lentils with mint and olive oil, sautéed couscous and mushrooms in olive oil, baked onions drizzled with olive oil and stuffed with pine nuts, and for dessert, sprinkled dried apricots with ground ginger.

\*\*\*

Everyone was excited and anxious to have his or her dish tasted. We set out about mid-morning arriving an hour later at a beautiful spot by the fast flowing river. Water danced over the rocks producing a range of tones from a deep bass to a high-frequency gurgle among the smaller rocks; both complemented by a muffled staccato as wind-carried spray fell back on the rocks.

We found a level area under a huge oak tree. To the northeast, we could see the snow-covered Hermon. It was a beautiful day with small clouds racing across the sky casting shadows on the valley and adding dark patches to the glaring white snow high on the mountain. Birds flitted between the trees singing their own songs in sonorous soprano voices. A hawk flew in wide lazy circles high overhead. It was a day that would always remind me of peace, plenty, and happiness.

Ariel and I followed the children to the riverbank to place the wine in the icy-cold stream to chill. Filling a small jug, we all drank the pure water. Ariel leaned over and kissed me. The children pointed, laughed, and said that *Aba* kissed *Ima*.

We ate under a tree. Each described the dish they had helped to prepare. Talitha and Bilha thought the onion was stuffed with the tastiest pine nuts in the whole world. Eitan told everyone how he and Levi selected only the finest vegetables and fruit at the market. Ariel said he was the most fortunate man in the world to have such a talented and wonderful family. We all blushed.

As the children ran to the stream to play, Ariel and I slowly sipped a magnificent wine. I leaned against Ariel feeling his warmth, and he put his arm around my waist. I wanted this day to last. I wanted Ariel to hold me forever.

"Elisheva, we are so lucky. We have wonderful children and a good life. I hope our children will be as happy as we are."

Before I could answer, Eitan ran up to us. "*Aba, Ima* a group of gazelles have come to the river to drink. Come see."

Talitha, Levi, and Bilha stood still and watched as the gazelles looked around and then lowered their heads to drink from the stream. They drank, looked up, drank, and quickly looked around. Deciding we were not a threat, they moved away from the water and seemed to be playing. They were gentle creatures delighting in the warm sunshine. They jumped straight up with all four feet leaving the ground, took a few steps, and again jumped straight up. It was an elegant playful dance expressing a joy of life. After they moved away, the children imitated their staccato like motions. It seemed to me that I could fashion a dance from the rhythmic motions of the gazelles and the beauty of life.

# BOOK FIFTEEN—DESTINY

My family and all of Israel prospered in the year 3692; the following year promised to be even better. For several years, harvests were bountiful in the Galilee. We were all healthy and our business successful. Our children grew so fast that I felt in the midst of a whirlwind. It was wonderful watching them mature and learn about the world. Why though did it happen so fast?

Ariel introduced Eitan, now nine years old, to the business just as his *Aba* did when he was young. It seemed not long ago that Eitan was a little boy, who sat in the corner playing with different shaped pieces of wood.

Eitan went with Ariel and Itai to the warehouse. He helped keep the wine properly stored, rotated the jars periodically, and made sure the floor was clean. He assisted in taking inventory while learning about the different wines: when the grapes were ready to be picked, how they were made into wine, and what distinguished one from another. It was still too early for Eitan to travel much beyond Dan and several years before he would be ready to assume major responsibilities. Eitan felt proud to be joining his *Aba*, and he was eager to become a partner in the business.

Talitha and Levi delighted in discovering the world around them. As twins, they seemed to have a language all their own. Sometimes, they only touched or looked at each other to know what the other thought. Their bond was strong. Each was the others best friend.

They already helped me prepare our evening meal. They enjoyed reading stories. Levi even started keeping a journal of all his ideas. When we went to the market together, they helped me pick the best fruit and vegetables. As I did when I was their age, they would look at the scrolls for sale and invariably ask for money to buy a new adventure story, a collection of poetry, or a story about one of our prophets. I never refused. They had discovered the same pleasures I did as a child. As *Aba* and *Ima* constantly encouraged me to learn, Ariel and I encouraged our children.

Bilha is a joy. The twins are closer in age to Eitan, and they naturally play together. They all adore Bilha and often will play or read to her. Most of the time, Bilha walks around the house happily talking to a little cloth doll that I had made for her. She looks up and smiles at anyone who talks to her. Once, I was angry after she broke one of my favorite dishes. I started to tell her it was bad, but she looked at me and smiled. All I could do was hug her tight. Often, Bilha, wide-eyed, smiles at people, and even if they are angry or in a bad mood, they smile back. Her soul radiates a special tranquility and joy.

I am fortunate to have such a wonderful family. Ariel is, and will always be, the love of my life. A special magic binds us, especially when the day is done and we sit next to each other—sometimes in silence when all we hear or feel is the beating of our hearts—or sometimes in passionate political discussions of our little world in Dan. I like to sing to him. He closes his eyes to listen more intently. Sometimes without thinking, we move toward each other and embrace.

Dan has been peaceful. The Galilee, even in bad times, is a rich area that supports us well. The Merom Valley is the most beautiful area of the Galilee, which except for the Garden of Eden, has to be the most beautiful place in the world. Anything we could want is grown nearby, fished from our streams and seas, or hunted along the Jordan or on the Golan. Our workshops produce the finest manufactured goods in the world. I hug myself with happiness when I think of my good fortune to live in paradise.

We have several grand festivals, theater, and often community singing. I love to dance and laugh with the children and want to introduce it as a community activity. Ariel enjoys taking children with him to hike in the surrounding fields. During special times of the year, large areas are covered with red, white, and occasionally blue poppies, pink cyclamens, bright yellow daisies, and waist high mustard. Along with the children, Ariel runs through the fields delighting in the magnificent colors that grow from the rich soil.

Ariel and I spend time helping those who, despite hard work, never seem to have enough to eat. Giving money is easy, but Ariel says for true charity we should give of ourselves. Often I will cook extra and bring the dishes I made to a family to "taste" my new creation. Sometimes I will buy extra food at the market and ask if they could use it as Ariel is away and I bought too much. When I can, I bring the children with me to visit families in need. They need to understand that we all are part of one community. Ariel has convinced many in Dan to join with us to help people in addition to providing money.

All my life, the whole community—men, women, and children—work together at harvest time. We build shelters in the fields. Until the end of the harvest, we eat and sleep in the shelters. At night, we hear families singing songs of praise to God—sometimes all singing the same song, sometimes a cacophony of melodies. As a child, I loved this time, as do my children now.

My parents delight in their grandchildren, but they tire easily now. It still shocks me to realize how much they have aged. *Aba* has difficulty walking, and *Ima* is often forgetful. Sometimes she looks at me as if she does not know who I am.

Adah and I take turns on Fridays bringing all the family together for the Shabbat evening meal. My parents sit at the head of the table. *Aba* blesses the wine and bread as he has done his whole life. It is the best meal of the week, special and full of joy. The evening always seems noisy, happy, and chaotic. Our Shabbat evening meal is a perfect way to end a hectic week, start a day of rest, and delight in being together.

On clear nights, even in winter, after eating, we might go outside to walk around Dan. We greet neighbors with wishes for a peaceful Shabbat. Some nights are particularly beautiful with millions of stars projecting a brilliant panorama in a pitch-black sky. Looking up, as Abraham once did in a foreign land, we could imagine an infinite number of shapes, figures, and sometimes a meaning to life.

After our rest on the Sabbath, we are ready and even anxious to start the new week. I will never forget one especially cold Sunday morning. I could see patches of low clouds drifting slowly over the Naphtali range and filling the wooded ravines with a blanket of white while a gray-white layer of fog hid the valley floor. Eventually, the sun would evaporate the fog creating a brilliant—even if painfully cold—day of sunshine.

I was baking bread for the day when Ariel and the children came to the warm cooking area for the morning meal. I had already made fresh rolls that I kept warm next to a pot of wheat porridge mixed with dried peaches and date syrup. A pot of boiling water for mint tea hung over the fire next to the porridge pot. It would be a busy day for all of us, but now we sat together enjoying the hot food and the warmth of our family.

Levi told us about a scary dream he had during the night. Suddenly, we heard the alarm bell. Ariel and I jumped up. "Eitan keep the children in the house. Do not let them out for any reason." We would be back as soon as we know what happened.

As we started to leave, Talitha ran after us. I took her hand, walking fast to the main gate as people streamed from their homes. Alarms were rare. There had not been one since the bandit raids long ago when I was a child. I sensed an underlying tone of nervousness and fear.

***

Three soldiers entered Dan through the main gate. One wearing a black cape over dark leather armor spoke. "With great sorrow, I bring terrible news."

There was complete silence. Everyone looked around confused not imagining what the news could be. The North was safe. Our defenses were strong. The army prepared. Enemies did not threaten us since Queen Shlomtsion negotiated treaties with Armenia and Rome. Relations were excellent with Cleopatra in Egypt as well as with the desert kingdoms to our east. We looked anxiously at the soldiers.

"I have the sad duty to inform you of the death of Queen Shlomtsion in Jerusalem on the third day of the week just past. May her memory be blessed. King Hyrcanus II, according to her will, has succeeded her. Long live the King."

We were stunned. Not a sound was heard. No one moved. It seemed as if everyone stopped breathing.

Then a lone voice screamed, "No. Please no."

I stood motionless. Talitha tugged at my sleeve. "*Ima* what is wrong? *Ima* what happened?"

"Our wonderful Queen died. This is a sad day, Talitha. Her son is now King, and we will be fine. Do not worry. I am just so sad. She was a wonderful Queen, and I will miss her."

"Was she a friend of yours, *Ima*?"

"I met her once. She told me she wanted to come to our home to have a meal with us the next time she traveled from Jerusalem to the North. She was always so busy looking after the whole country, that she was not able to come."

"I would have helped you cook, *Ima*."

"I know, Talitha. I know you would have helped me."

No one moved. No one spoke. In the history of Dan, I do not think there was ever a time as sorrowful as this. In a world so filled with chaos, Queen Shlomtsion kept us safe. She was a good woman, a pious woman, a righteous woman, a woman who believed in charity and equal rights for all, a woman who believed in peace, and a good Queen. We loved her. I held Talitha's hand tightly and looked around me. Men, women stood quietly crying. It was the deep pain of an unbearable sorrow.

We mourned her. For a month, there were no parties; weddings were delayed, and men did not trim their hair or beards. Women wore no jewelry nor colored their eyes, lips, or cheeks. It was longer still before we felt joy again.

Her name would always be blessed in Dan and in the Kingdom of Israel.

Several years have passed since our Queen's death. It has not been a quiet period, and the news is either bad or worse. I was optimistic when Hyrcanus II became King. He was Queen Shlomtsion's eldest son and supported by the Pharisees. We prayed wise leadership and prosperity would continue.

Ariel and I worry about our children's future. Despite Queen Shlomtsion's stated wish, Aristobulus challenged his older brother for the throne. The conflict between the two was bitter; the ensuing chaos exposed our country to new threats.

I watched in complete disbelief as a terrible tragedy unfolded. Within a year, Aristobulus II defeated Hyrcanus II, King and High Priest, in a vicious battle at Jericho. Aristobulus II assumed the throne and office of High Priest. The intrigue continued as the brothers, each seeking advantage, created competing alliances with Rome. The treaties negotiated with great care and wisdom by Queen Shlomtsion were violated. Israel now became a pawn in a far bigger power struggle—one convulsing Rome.

So far, we were fortunate. Ariel's business continued to flourish. Five years earlier, Rome had annexed Crete. Pompey, taking command in the east from Lucullus, vanquished King Mithridates VI, and defeated King Tigranes. Since King Tigranes acted with honor, Pompey, despite destroying his army, allowed him to continue to reign as King of Armenia. Syria became a province and protectorate of Rome. Surprising to us, the strong Roman presence in Syria led to a greater demand for Kedesh wine and Micah's ornate wine cups.

Late at night, we often sat in our courtyard garden planted years earlier. We whispered to each other the news reports about the warring factions. We tried to keep our fears hidden from the children. I had no doubt the sorrow

Queen Shlomtsion would feel if she knew her sons fought over the throne and destroyed the peace she spent so long nurturing between the Pharisees and the Sadducees. We both thought it was dangerous, foolish, and stupid to solicit help from Rome.

Last year, our worst fears came true. Pompey, at the request of Hyrcanus, declared Israel to be a Roman protectorate and moved his army into Israel. He captured Aristobulus, whom he sent to Rome as a prisoner, and restored Hyrcanus to the throne. We had lost our freedom.

Still, life continued in the Galilee without great changes. Although apprehensive about the future, we prospered. We feared Rome, in time, would impose harsh conditions on us. Ariel and I made sure to increase our hidden savings. We were nervous and glad we had saved in the years of plenty.

Despite being focused on the danger growing around us, one day Ariel asked me if Eitan felt well.

"Why do you ask?"

"He just is not himself of late. Do you think he is ill?"

"Ariel, I would not be surprised if our son has met a young woman. Whenever he speaks about his friends, he always talks a lot about Tsipora. I think our son has the same illness you and I had a long time ago."

"Elisheva, I still have that illness. You still make my heart beat faster."

"I know the young girl. Her *Aba*, Daniel, makes the stylish sandals I favor. He is a true craftsman. I speak to his wife in the shop and see her in the market. A few months ago, Tsipora joined my dance group. She is pretty with black hair and green eyes. Her dancing is full of expression; she has a natural rhythm and smooth, graceful movements. I notice they often dance next to each other."

"Now, I remember. Daniel is in my study group. At our last meeting, he raised a question that still puzzles me. We discussed the story of the flood. He asked why the animals had to die for the sins of man. At first, someone said animals kill and therefore are evil. I answered that we also kill for food, same as the predators. Another said animals have no souls. This puzzled all of us for a long while until someone asked whether fish have souls since they survived. I added,

227

from my experience with the bears on my first trip to Dameseq, that animals have families, and parents protect their young. I think they have feelings, show responsibility, and maybe love. Why did the giraffes drown? They are peaceful creatures and hurt no one. Their deaths must have been agonizing.

"What do you think of inviting them for a Shabbat evening meal? I do want to continue our study group discussion with Daniel. We could see for ourselves whether there are special feelings between Eitan and Tsipora. I think we know the signs."

Smiling, a bit mischievously, I asked, "What signs are those, Ariel?"

"I will invite them in the next few days. Perhaps we are mistaken."

A few weeks later, Daniel and Esther came to our home for a Shabbat evening meal. We were not wrong.

The evening meal was wonderful: somewhat awkward at the start, as it was the first time we had invited Tsipora's parents to our home. We all guessed why we were together—except of course Eitan and Tsipora who had no idea. Throughout the evening, when they thought nobody noticed, one would glance at the other and look away. Even Bilha noticed.

Later, she asked me, "*Ima*, why did Eitan look at Tsipora so much?"

"Well Bilha, I think Tsipora also looked at Eitan."

"Does that mean they will get married?"

"If their destiny is to marry, then yes, they will marry. But, we do not yet know if it is their destiny."

"How did you and *Aba* know it was your destiny to marry?"

"The first time I saw your *Aba*, I was two years older than you. I knew we would marry. I just knew it. And, it was our destiny to meet again years later and marry."

"Do you think my destiny is to marry?"

"Yes, Bilha. But, not for many years."

"Well, I already know I want to marry *Aba* when I get older."

Late that night, Ariel held me close and we whispered about the first Shabbat evening meal when we sat opposite each other so long ago. Ariel said he, as did I, remembered everything about that evening. How I had helped my

*Ima* prepare a meal fit for a King and served the food so graciously.

"I could not stop looking at you, Elisheva. I knew that night I wanted to marry you and be with you forever. Even though we spoke few words to each other, I hoped you knew what I was thinking."

"And, my husband I hoped you could hear what I thought every time I looked at you."

"My wife, if our son is as happy as we are, he will have a good life. Tsipora is a wonderful girl; they appear well matched."

"I guess now we know what our parents felt when they saw us together. It is good, is it not husband?"

"Yes, wife, it is good."

Time flew by as Eitan and Tsipora learned the steps of the ancient dance first begun in the Garden of Eden. Two years later, during a period of tension and uncertainty, they were married. Everyone in Dan attended and celebrated the formation of a new family with a special joy and gladness.

The following year, our first grandchild Tamar was born. Ariel and I, in a life filled with happiness, health, and prosperity, had never known such joy. I wished our parents had lived to celebrate the birth of such a beautiful great granddaughter.

"Micah, Miriam I am so happy to see you. I planned a special meal for us tonight. It has been far too long since we have been able to sit together and talk. Excuse me while I give the children their evening meal. I think they are bored with our discussions and more than happy to have their meal first. I will join you in a few minutes."

"Take your time. While you are busy, we will try some of Ariel's wonderful wine."

Ariel smiled, "I have an exquisite wine I brought from Dameseq. At first, when the supply of Armenian wines stopped, I worried it might be hard to obtain good imported wines. Not so, since Pompey occupied Syria, there has been plenty of excellent Roman and Greek wines. I myself favor our Kedesh Valley wines, but try this aged Roman red. I think it is superb."

Micah sniffed the wine and tasted. He raised his eyebrows. "Oh my, this really is good."

"Micah, your wine cups made a great impression on the new Roman rulers in Syria. Not only do they want cups for their households in Dameseq, they also send sets back to Rome. They favor your cups despite the many good glass manufacturers in Rome. They say your designs are exceptional and your workmanship extraordinary."

"That is nice to hear. I have you to thank."

"Micah, you have an international reputation. Since Pompey returned to Rome, I expect even more Romans will want your cups, and I hope good Kedesh wine to fill them."

"Ariel, if you have time next week, stop by my workshop. I have been using a new technique that lets me create multiple layers of glass. The layers can be different colors. The effect is dramatic."

"I can come in two days."

"Excellent. I look forward to it."

"Micah, when we first met, Elisheva told me you are the most talented person she knows. She was so right. You always surprise me with your ideas and creations."

"I owe a lot to Miriam. Whenever I am stuck, she helps me reason out new methods. In our family, she is the talented one. Besides, she can do the important work."

"I know what you mean, Micah. Elisheva has a keen mind for business and special insight. I ask her advice whenever I face a difficult problem. We are lucky to be married to such wonderful women."

Tell me, Ariel, "what do you think will happen now that the Romans control our country?"

"I do not know. I am apprehensive since Pompey left. The increase in taxes we pay to support the Roman occupation and the tribute sent to Rome are not the worst of our problems. I worry that Rome will erode our beliefs and the quality of our life. I doubt replacing King Aristobulus II with King Hyrcanus II was good. The animosity between the Sadducees and Pharisees continues. Both Hyrcanus and Aristobulus are mere puppets of Rome—one favored by Julius Caesar and the other by Pompey. We are now trapped by internal Roman politics."

"This is depressing. Let us change the subject."

"Tell me, Micah, how are you feeling? You look tired. Are you working too hard?"

"No, my hip pains me a great deal. Sometimes, the pain is unbearable."

"I am so sorry. Is there anything I can do to help? I know a good carpenter who can make you a chair that might alleviate some of the stress on your hip."

"That might help. I should see him—it might make it easier for me to work. I guess, my friend, it is not easy to get old. It certainly is not for the weak."

"I hate to see you in pain. I am glad you are strong, Micah. I want us to be friends until we are one hundred and twenty years old."

"Hmm, as old as Moses when he died. That would be nice."

"Let me pour you another cup of this wine. Our sages write that wine gladdens the heart. If we drink two or three cups, not only will our hearts be glad, but it may also lessen your pain for a short time. Now that I think of it, Elisheva tells me that she has read about a special potion made from poppies that the Greek physician, Hippocrates, used to lessen pain. It is a strong medicine, and may restrict how much you can work. It may be worth trying."

"Yes, I think so. I want to be stay as active as possible now that our son, Gideon, is about to marry Itai's daughter, Dina."

"Elisheva told me how happy she is that we will now be family. You know she has always loved you and Miriam. I think of you as a brother."

"I know, Ariel. I know."

"Speaking of family, excuse me for a minute, I see the children are ready to leave."

Ariel put his arm around me as we told the children to be home early. Joining our guests, Ariel brought me glass of wine and refilled Miriam and Micah's cups. He said, "Micah told me the good news about Gideon and Dina."

"Is it not wonderful that now we have even more to bind us together? Miriam, let's leave the men to solve the problems of the world while we cook." Winking, I added that at least something would be accomplished tonight. "I have prepared a new dish. I hope it turns out well. I marinated thin slices of goat meat in white wine with dried peaches and apples. I will cook the meat over an open flame, and brush it with a mixture of apple juice and honey adding either a touch of vanilla or perhaps cinnamon. I also thought a dash of hot pepper might add an interesting contrast. What do you think?"

"It sounds delicious. I think the cinnamon would be best with the apple and honey. Adding a small amount of hot pepper for contrast is a great idea."

"I agree. Cinnamon is the better spice. Vanilla might have added an interesting background taste in the marinade. If the dish succeeds, I will experiment with the marinade next time."

Miriam, "Micah looks tired. Is there a problem or is he just working too hard?"

"He won't admit it, but he has trouble seeing. I can tell by the way he holds his work close and squints a lot when he makes jewelry. I worry about him."

"Miriam, our men are strong. Come let us join them and try this new dish. I hope they will like it. I described the dish to Ariel, and he picked a superb wine to complement the marinated meat."

We sat at the table and talked about everything and anything. The children came home and went to sleep while we remained at the table. The change from our daily worries worked wonders for Ariel and me.

Later that night, Ariel held me and kissed me with a passion that made me think of the nights many years ago when we held each other late at night and listened to the soft whisper of the wind.

"Ariel, now that our children are married, why not work less and give more responsibility to Eitan and Levi. We could be together more. Time seems limited now, not the infinity of forever when we first met."

Ariel looked at me surprised by the simple truth of my words. "You are right. I would like nothing more than to be with you all the time."

"I would like to see the Great Sea again, visit Jerusalem, and perhaps Petra. Remember when you gave me this Elath stone?"

"I remember. It was so many years ago. I could not stop thinking of you. I wanted to send you something to remind you of me. I was afraid you would forget me."

"I treasured it all these years. Maybe we could go to Elath and see where the stones are found. I read the sea is a brilliant blue with a reef of many colors near the shoreline. It must be a beautiful place. I also read it was an important historical site. King Solomon kept a navy in Elath to protect the trade routes to Arabia and Africa."

"I plan to go to Dameseq next week. I will take Eitan and Levi with me and introduce them to the traders. They are certainly ready to assume control of the business. I will make one more trip to Tyre with our sons and then decide how to divide the responsibility between them. Then my wife, we can be together all the time."

Ariel left early Sunday morning with Eitan and Levi for his final trip to Dameseq. I watched as our sons began the climb to the Golan with the strength and energy of the young.

They stopped and made camp for the night in the same place Ariel had stopped years ago with Gershon and my brother, Yoav. The fire was warm, and they shared the excellent meal Eitan's wife Tsipora had prepared. I am sure Ariel enjoyed Tsipora's meal as much as Gershon enjoyed the meal I had made.

They stayed up late talking about Dan, Jerusalem, and the world. Ariel tired first. "Time for me to sleep if we are to make an early start tomorrow. Good night, my sons."

The dawn sky was extraordinary. A bright pink contrasted with gray bands streaked with thin lines of lavender heralded the start of a good day. They ate a quick meal and set off in the cool morning air toward Dameseq.

They had traveled half the morning when Ariel saw Levi walk between a bear cub and his mother. Unaware of the danger, Levi continued talking to Eitan. The bear lifted her head and rose on her hind legs. She felt her cub was in danger.

Ariel yelled, "Levi, look to your right. Do not run."

Levi panicked; the bear went for him. Ariel picked up a large rock and threw it at the bear. She then turned to Ariel as Levi distanced himself from the cub.

He threw another rock. It did not stop the bear now closing on Ariel. Eitan threw rocks at the cub. The mother reached Ariel and slashed with her paw just as a large rock struck the cub. The cub cried out. The bear turned and ran toward her cub. Eitan and Levi ran to Ariel.

The danger had passed. Eitan tore his shirt and pressed it to his ribs to stop the bleeding. Levi did the same. They gathered moss and put it on the wound. Ariel lost consciousness.

They brought him home. I was frantic. I sat next to his bed until he regained consciousness. "Well, my husband, are you feeling better?"

"What happened? Why am I here?"

"A bear attacked you on the Hermon. Eitan and Levi carried you home. You have a deep wound on your side and maybe one or two broken ribs."

"It doesn't hurt, so it cannot be too serious."

"I gave you medicine made from poppies. You were delirious and in agony. The bleeding has stopped, and you look much better today."

"How long have I been asleep?"

"Two days. I made some chicken broth; try to eat; I will hold the spoon for you. You will be fine. I will take care of you."

For the next three days, I did not leave Ariel's side and hardly slept. He improved and each day ate more. The worst was over.

"I worried about you, husband. I thought we would lose you at one point."

"No, Elisheva, we will be together for eternity."

The next morning, after Ariel did not join us, I went to see why the delay. He lay in a pool of sweat. I opened the bandages. The wound oozed blood and pus. As calm as I could, I returned with boiling water, cleaned the wound, and spread a layer of honey over the infected area before bandaging it. I kissed his forehead and whispered, "Sleep now, Ariel."

Shaking, I sent for Eitan. "Bring me zatar and aloe. We need a lot of each. *Aba's* wound is infected. We have to treat it immediately."

Over the next two days, the fever worsened. I kept the wound as clean as I could, applied zatar, and changed the bandages. The wound started to turn green. Ariel worsened and lost consciousness. Eitan, Talitha, Levi, Bilha and I did not leave him.

I held his hand the whole night. I must have dozed for a few minutes and woke when I thought he squeezed my hand. Maybe I dreamt it.

He died before the sunrise.

I sat next to him for a long time. I saw the young boy who carried my packages home from the market, stood next to me under the wedding canopy, held our babies, kissed me tenderly, spoke to the Queen of Israel, honored the commandments to help the poor and weak, and held me each night before we slept.

Oh, my husband. My beautiful husband. I love you so much. I kissed him a final time.

Then, the tears came.

Since she was a little girl, Bilha watched me write in my diary. She asked what I wrote. I explained that life holds so much and I wanted to write everything to keep the memories alive. Someday, you might want to read it to your children. Bilha stood for a moment looking at the diary. Then she asked if she could write something about *Aba*.

I hesitated. It was the story of my life with Ariel as I saw and lived it. Yet, Bilha too had memories that were part of our life story. I agreed.

The words seemed to pour out of her. She wrote the following:

*A year has passed since Aba died. He saw my brothers and sisters marry and have children. Talitha followed Eitan and married Itamar three years previous in 3702. Levi married Hannah a year later, and two years later, I married Samuel.*

*I miss Aba. He left a hole in my heart that will never be filled. He was the source of my strength. My sweetest memories are the times when, as a child, I sat on his lap, and he told me stories of faraway lands, the magic of Jerusalem, and how he met Ima. When I was older and explored knowledge of the world and the history of our people, we talked about everything. I never met a wiser man or a more gentle soul.*

*Aba liked Samuel. He admired that Samuel worked the land, although he would have been happier if we lived inside the walls. We do not have a lot of land, but we have enough. We do not have a lot of money, but we have enough. We have good food, and we are happy with all we have. Aba gave us money to add to the house that Samuel planned to build. He wanted extra rooms for many grandchildren and one for Ima and him when they visit.*

*I am happy living close to the land. The smell of the rich soil evokes distant memories that lie deep inside me. It speaks to me and binds me to my ancestors. I trust that the rains will come at their appointed time, and the land will support us as it has for more than a thousand years.*

*We have several fruit and olive trees that give shade and food. Ima often sits with me under one tree in particular near a flourishing jasmine plant that mixes its sweet smell with the pine-scented wind that flows down from the Hermon.*

*She carries a perpetual sadness I fear will never heal. She does enjoy being with her grandchildren, but it seems tinged with regret that Aba is not with her. Tamar, now five years old, was the first grandchild followed by Talitha's sons, David and Raphael, and Levi's children, Saul and Avigail.*

*Often, I find her holding my baby, Ariel, named after Aba, and staring the length of the Merom Valley. She seems to be waiting for Aba as she did so many years ago. As she holds Ariel and points to Jerusalem, she whispers in his ear.*

*It is nice in the shade of the olive tree. It is nice with Ima next to me. It is nice looking at the richness of our land. Our land soaked with the blood of so many who died to keep it free. Free, so that we could hold our faith and flourish. It is good to see Ariel play on the land that binds us to our history. It is good that the land supports us well.*

*It is my home.*

*It is the land where my Aba is buried.*

Bilha closed the diary and handed it to me. She hugged me, and I held her close. She looked at Ariel and smiled.

CHAPTER SIXTY-THREE—FOREVER—3717 (43 BC)

I often stand on the walls of Dan for hours watching the light and colors change. This land has all my memories, all my joys, and holds my children's future. It still gives me an extraordinary sense of peace and quiets my soul. Often it is dark when one of my grandchildren comes to bring me home.

I fear much. My parents and Ariel's parents worried they were leaving us a chaotic world with many dangers—much more than they experienced. I sense our children and grandchildren face a far more violent and dangerous world than we did.

Yet, the world has always been filled with terrors. More than a thousand years ago, King David wrote timeless psalms about solace and tranquility. They comfort me to this day.

Still, evil forces abound. They are far more powerful and threaten us more than ever. Queen Shlomtsion protected and kept us safe. Ariel and I prospered in a golden age. I wish she had lived and continued to reign. I am grateful, though, we had such a woman as Queen. Now, danger closes in on us. I fear the Romans. There is an underlying savage brutality in their culture.

I know our children and their children will fight to protect our country, religion, and way of life. They are strong. What started in the desert fifteen hundred years ago is worth protecting. As we were and those before us, they too will always be one with this land and our God. It is our destiny

Of late, I tire easily and sometimes feel pain in my chest. I have lived long and had a good life. Perhaps, now is my time. I wish Ariel had not died before me, and we were together now. We raised good children, and their children are indeed a blessing. I tell them about their grandfather, what a good man he was, and how happy we were together.

I miss his arms about me, the love of life in his eyes, and the joy of being together. I miss when at the end of every day and the earth was silent with only the whisper of the wind flowing down the mountain, he held me and I felt the hardness of his body against the softness of mine. Moments forever etched in my memory. So much so that I can no longer tell the difference between what is real and ethereal.

I know our dance together was written in the beginning of time. A dance meant to last forever.

Soon, I will again lie next to my beloved, and we will be together for eternity.

# BOOK SIXTEEN—FREEDOM

Israel awoke to headlines reporting the discovery of a diary at Tel Dan written by a woman called Elisheva more than 2,000 years ago—about 150 years before the destruction of the Second Temple in Jerusalem. The little that had been released about the diary caused great excitement. Radio talk shows, TV news programs, and newspaper editors scrambled to find experts who could give meaning to what was ostensibly one of the major archeological finds in the Middle East.

The early reports by scholars, and scholars who knew scholars, and experts who knew experts, told of a rich life in Israel long before the Romans destroyed the Temple and exiled the people of Israel. It described a prosperous society based on the laws of Moses with a deft government, good relations with neighboring countries, and an educated population. It told of a golden era during the reign of the stellar Queen Shlomtsion. It also described the huge political mistakes of Queen Shlomtsion's heirs— mistakes that proved catastrophic.

Many editorials were written about Musa who discovered and hid the scroll until now. Several condemned him for keeping a national treasure from the country. Yet, his ready admission of guilt and shame that has haunted him since that day as a young man when he took the diary to show his fiancé and then did not return the scroll, provoked a mixed response— anger and sympathy. In the end, after revealing his ready acceptance of the consequences of his action—including prison—so that he could help his family, his story touched a compassionate nerve in Israel.

Government ministers offered interviews on how the coalition support of archeology and the police enabled the discovery of this rare and priceless diary. Opposition leaders, in a surprise to all, supported a government proclamation and praised the police in recovering the diary. They added, however, the public should understand the reasons why Musa tried to sell the diary, and the court should be lenient.

The debate to help Syrian refugees had been difficult. Most favored accepting some Syrian refugees. Many Israelis, themselves or their relatives, had been refugees and victims of war. The feeling of compassion and desire to help a people suffering such horrific devastation was strong. Even right-wing government ministers were torn. Despite the desire to help, Syria had been a brutal and implacable long-time enemy. With surprising reluctance, the government decided it would be a mistake to allow an enemy to settle in Israel.

This was different. At issue was a man willing to suffer all to help his family. Here was a case that spoke to compassion and mercy. After much debate, ordinary citizens responded with an outpouring of sympathy.

The largest morning newspaper in Israel opened a special bank account and made the first contribution to hire a lawyer to defend Musa, even though he had admitted his guilt and agreed to accept any prison term. The fund would also support an effort to help Musa's family escape from Syria.

The response was overwhelming. Money poured in—some donations as small as five shekels, some as large as five thousand shekels. A famous criminal lawyer from Ramat Aviv volunteered to represent Musa. A former minister promised to use his connections with his counterpart in Jordan to locate Musa's family. A lawyer from Haifa, specializing in immigration and work visas, pledged to help Musa's family obtain a residency visa to live in Israel.

At the same time, a pronouncement from Damascus sent a chill through Israel. The Syrian Government announced there was no need to help a Syrian family. The government would take care of them.

The hunt was on for Musa's family.

Musa felt numb. One morning, without notification, the Police transferred him along with Ratib and Doron to the Nazareth District Court. He knew this court tried serious crimes leading to prison terms of more than seven years. The recently completed courthouse, housed in an imposing building, was a state-of-the-art prison facility. Despite the improved conditions, Musa was even more alone and even farther from his family.

Musa thought it was good news when his lawyer informed him that the prosecutor decided to separate the trials. Ratib and Doron faced charges additional to trafficking in antiquities. His trial would follow those of Professor Shlomo, Ratib, and Doron.

Professor Shlomo would be tried in the Tsfat Magistrates court. Without any hesitation, he agreed to testify against Doron in return for a reduced prison sentence. The Professor's lawyer requested probation claiming the Professor had no knowledge of illegal activity. He assumed his task was to appraise a scroll for a private collector.

Anticipating the defense strategy, the prosecutor brought Musa to testify. He related how Professor Shlomo questioned him about when and where he found the scroll. It was clear he knew all along the scroll was illegally taken from the Tel and that Doron wanted to sell it. As an accessory to the attempted sale of an antiquity, he was sentenced to five years in prison. The University suspended him without pay; he would be fired and his pension forfeited if the Supreme Court rejected his appeal.

The trials of Ratib and Doron were held in separate courts on the same day. Both rooms were filled with newspaper, TV, and radio reporters anxious to hear the details of the police investigation and their arrest. During the trials, reporters posted a constant stream of news on the Internet. A summary of the trial was the lead story on the evening news programs. Ongoing analysis—albeit mostly uninformed—of the diary supplemented the trial coverage.

The defense lawyers for both Ratib and Doron claimed police entrapment and maintained they were innocent of all charges. Methodically, the prosecutors in both cases presented the wiretap recordings and surveillance results dating back more than a year for Ratib, and more than two years for Doron.

Musa testified that Ratib had enlisted Doron to have the scroll appraised and to find a buyer. Following the appraisal, wherein Professor Shlomo called the scroll "the greatest find since the Dead Sea Scrolls" and assessed that it was priceless, Doron paid Musa 55,000 shekels for the scroll.

The trials lasted two weeks. Several days later, the two courts convened and sentenced both men to ten years in Shata prison. Built during the British Mandate, the prison population consisted of hardened criminals convicted of serious crimes. For the first time since their arrest, both men were afraid. The stood with bowed heads and looked at their lawyers as if there was some hope they could change the sentence. Both men knew that Shata well deserved its reputation as the toughest prison in Israel.

Two weeks later, the trial of Musa began in the Nazareth Magistrates Court. Musa had already agreed to accept any sentence the court imposed. Nevertheless, his lawyer felt it necessary to tell Musa's story before the Judge pronounced the sentence.

The trial judge asked both the prosecutor and Musa's lawyer to present an overview of the charges and the terms of the recommended plea arrangement. The prosecutor had assumed the agreement would be read, Musa would agree, and the recommended sentence imposed. Something had changed. For a moment, he was puzzled, but he regained his composure and requested a delay of two days to prepare his arguments. Without a moment's hesitation, the judge agreed and dismissed the court.

The reporters stood still and did not say a word. They had assumed in return for his sincere regret and testimony for the prosecution, Musa would receive a minimal prison sentence. To their great surprise, it appeared the judge may not accept the prosecutor's agreement or might impose a full sentence.

The lead story on the evening news programs reported the government's refusal to honor an agreement made in return for testimony in three criminal trials.

For two days, legal experts and government ministers argued whether the judge acted properly by insisting the trial go forward.

Some maintained that Musa's crime deserved the most severe sentence the country could impose. The theft of part of Israel's heritage could not be allowed or tolerated. A few ministers, however, conceded it was unusual for a judge to reject a plea agreement.

Others maintained that second-guessing a prosecutor's judgment was a great disservice to the legal system. They asked loudly and often, "What are the consequences when the word of a government prosecutor cannot be trusted?" Many pointed to Musa's contrition and said Israeli society should recognize his regret and treat him with compassion and mercy.

The arguments raged in opinion pieces, talk shows, and Internet blogs for two days. The trial became an international event with human rights organizations lining up to condemn the lack of justice for Arabs in Israeli society.

The trial moved to a bigger courtroom to accommodate a much larger press contingent. The judge asked the prosecutor and defense whether they were prepared to proceed. Both responded in the affirmative, and the trial started.

The state prosecutor said. "I will be brief your honor. I call Musa to testify."

Musa's attorney protested. "Your honor, the prosecutor is supposed to prove guilt, not call the accused to testify against himself."

The reporters snickered. The prosecutor wanted the accused to convict himself. This was going to make great headlines.

Musa put his hand on his lawyer's arm, stood up, and said, "It's okay; I do not mind answering his questions."

"Musa, I have only two questions. First, did you take the diary from Tel Dan and hide it until now?"

"Yes, I took the diary, and yes I hid it until now."

"Did you attempt to sell the diary?"

Again, his lawyer objected. "Your honor, this is beyond unusual. It is reprehensible."

Musa again answered, "Yes, I did."

The judge looked at the prosecutor and said, "Finish this now."

I have one more question. "Musa, do you think that you should you be punished for your crime?"

"Yes."

The reporters looked around. In a voice a little too loud, one of the reporters provoked laughter in the gallery saying, "I counted four questions. I trust the judge is better at arithmetic than the prosecutor."

Now it was time for the defense to make its case.

One reporter wondered aloud, "If Musa testified for the prosecutor to convict himself, is he allowed to testify for the defense to acquit himself?" The trial was turning into a circus.

The defense rose to address the court, "Your honor, I too will be brief. I intend to call two witnesses for the defense." Smiling, he added, "Musa is not one of them."

"Proceed."

"I call Hakim Azzam.

"Mr. Azzam, tell us where you are from and what is your profession?

"I am from the village of Ghajar. I am a lawyer."

Now, the prosecutor objected. "Your honor, I fail to see why the defense calls another lawyer to testify. This is highly unusual."

"Well, let us hear what he is to testify about before you object. Proceed."

"Mr. Azzam, where did you study law?"

"I studied at Bar Ilan University and passed my exams in 1971. I am a member of the Israel Bar Association."

"Please tell us how you know the accused."

"A few weeks after I opened my office in Ghajar, Musa came to me to draw up a will. His son was just born, and he wanted to make sure his property was distributed in accordance with Israeli law."

"Tell us if there was anything unusual about his will?"

247

"Yes, I have permission from Musa to disclose one of the terms of his will. He told me that he had a valuable scroll hidden in his house, which he had found at Tel Dan. If he were to die or become incapable of managing his affairs, I was to give the scroll to the Israel Museum."

"Thank you, Mr. Azzam."

"One final question, if I may. Were you directed to request payment for the scroll?"

"No, it was to be given and any payment, if offered, refused."

"Thank you.

"I now call as my final witness, Dr. Ephraim Ben-Shalom. Dr. Ben-Shalom, please tell the court your position and education."

"I am a Professor of Archeology. I received my Bachelor and Master's degrees from Tel Aviv University and a Ph.D. from the University of Chicago in the United States. I am a member of the team deciphering the diary of Elisheva."

"I am sure, Professor, it is interesting."

"Yes, it is fascinating even though we have barely managed to decipher one-fourth of the diary. We are learning a tremendous amount about life at that time. Elisheva herself is a fascinating and captivating woman."

"My question then might be premature, please bear with me. Based on your work to date, could you tell us what Elisheva would do if she had to compromise a strong tenet to save a life?"

"I can answer that most assuredly. In the beginning of the diary, she relates how, as a young girl, she risked her life to save her friend from being captured by bandits. In our religion, saving a life takes precedent over commandments. It was true thousands of years ago at Dan, and it is true today. For example, a clear commandment compels us to honor the Sabbath, yet the Sabbath can be violated to save a life. Elisheva risked capture and her life to save her friend. I submit that risking your life to save another is akin to violating a sacred law. Life is sacrosanct. That is part of our code of life, part of our heritage. It seems to me Musa, in his way, did the same as Elisheva, despite the consequences—which he does not try to avoid. He does not seek profit for himself; rather he acted unselfishly to save the lives of his relatives."

"Thank you, Professor Ben-Shalom."

"Do you have any more witnesses?"

"No, your honor."

"Court is adjourned. We will reconvene on Thursday for my final judgment and sentencing."

***

## Judgment

The courtroom was full. A large press contingent was present in the gallery with even more in an adjacent courtroom to watch a live feed of the proceedings. Outside the courthouse, angry protesters carried placards accusing the state of a malicious prosecution, apartheid, and demanded Musa be freed. An equal number of angry protesters, separated by police barricades from the pro-Musa protesters, demanded he be sentenced to life in prison for stealing and attempting to sell a valuable part of Israel's heritage.

As the judge entered the courtroom, the reporters edged forward in their seats, sat a little straighter, and listened intently. There was complete silence. The only sound was a lone fly buzzing around the prosecutor's table. Sensing the tension, the reporters wrote cryptic notes to later describe the scene for their readers.

The judge slowly looked around the courtroom, cleared his throat and said, "I am satisfied the plea agreement entered by the State Prosecutor and the Defendant followed all the necessary protocols. Having heard the arguments by the State Prosecutor and the Defense, I choose not to approve the agreement. The law, in this case, is clear, and the punishment is well defined. Without question, the defendant committed a serious crime."

There was a palpable gasp from the gallery. Reporters, noting the judge's comments and the gallery's response, scribbled frantically. Outside, the pro-Musa demonstrators fell silent, while the other demonstrators cheered and chanted, "Justice, justice, at last justice."

The judge banged his gavel, paused, and continued. "But..."

249

Now everyone sat straight up and focused on the next words. There was absolute silence.

"It is clear to me that this was a mistake of a passionate young man that has tormented him his whole life. The fact that, from the beginning, he has shown genuine remorse and never intended to profit from the sale of a national treasure, recommends that justice recognize a higher duty and moderate the sentencing mandates. It is my judgment, therefore, that you be sentenced to two years in the Hermon Prison. I further recommend that you be considered for parole in twelve months." Looking at Musa, the judge leaned forward and said, "The prison system maintains a program of free university education. I strongly urge you to take advantage of that program. Court is adjourned."

For a moment, there was silence. Then the room erupted in shouts at the surprise judgment that lessened the prison term previously accepted by both sides in the plea agreement.

Before rushing out, the reporter from *Israel Today* asked if anyone knew what the Hermon Prison is like.

"It is a new low-security prison, located near the village of Mugar. Most of the prisoners are in the final stages of rehabilitation before their release. I heard the conditions are excellent—for a prison."

The Za'atari refugee camp in northern Jordan is a dismal place. It is located just south of the Yarmuk Stream separating Syria from Jordan in an area known from ancient times as Bashan. The camp, a one-day journey from Dan, is not far from where King Alexander Yanai died and Shlomtsion started her reign as Queen of Israel more than two thousand years ago.

Spread over a barren windswept plain, the camp housed a large refugee population. People lived in utter despair, despite the best efforts of the Jordanian Government and the UN to make the place habitable. Winters are bitter cold and food in short supply. The refugees, arriving at Za'atari, survived a perilous border crossing often being ambushed and robbed of the little they managed to carry. The camp, as dismal and primitive as it was, offered life and safety.

Musa's family—Amir and his wife Hafa, their son Nida, and daughters Aini, Hiba, and Leila lived in a small one-room prefabricated building. They had no money. Hafa rose every morning at sunrise to wait in line for the daily bread distribution. The small allowance they received from the UN was barely enough to buy enough food every day. They had no heat, no running water, and used the communal bathroom facilities and kitchen. But, they were alive.

Amir and Hafa whispered to each other at night that they had to do something to save the family. There seemed no option other than to seek a marriage for Aini. They needed the dowry to survive the winter.

"Amir, how can we do this to Aini, my little spring flower?

"What choice do we have, Hafa? We are hungry and cold all the time. The children are barely surviving. They are good children, hardly ever cry

251

and are sad all the time. We have to do something so the family survives. Shukri is a good man; the money he pays will help us survive."

"But, Aini is fifteen, and he is forty-six years old. She will be little more than a slave. How can we let our little Aini marry him? What kind of parents are we?"

"I do not want to see her married either, especially to someone so much older than her, but it has to be. We have no choice; we must do what is best for the family. We will talk of this no more. I have decided."

The marriage was set for one month hence. Amir and Hafa always hoped that the marriage of their daughters would be joyous affairs. Now, it was a family tragedy.

One week before the wedding, they heard a loud knock on the door of their hut. Three Jordanian army officers entered. "Are you Amir and is this your wife Hafa?"

"Yes."

"Take your possessions, gather your children, and come with us."

"We have done nothing. You cannot take us. This is a UN camp."

"This is Jordan, not UN territory, and you will come with us or we will take you by force."

Resigned to their fate, the family looked around at their home and safety, such as it was, and like beaten dogs, they followed the soldiers out into the cold night.

"Where are you taking us? Please do not take us back to Syria."

"Quiet and follow."

They were brought to a small van. They were told to enter, and their meager possessions were thrown in the back. Amir and Hafa feared the worst. "We survived so many hardships only to be sent back. What did we do to deserve such a fate? Oh, our poor children. They never got to live and raise families. Why has Allah deserted us?"

*\*\**

The van traveled west through a pitch-black night. Trees, blown by fierce winds, appeared as menacing dark shadows trying to grab and pull them into the cold night. After an hour, they arrived at a border station near two bridges that spanned a narrow stream. The soldiers turned to them. "Out and walk across the bridge."

"Where are you sending us? We cannot go back to Syria."

"You are not returning to Syria. Our orders are to send you across this bridge to Israel."

"Allah protect us. The Jews will kill us. How can you do this to fellow Muslims?"

Shaking, they emerged into the cold night and started across the bridge. On the Jordanian side, the gate was lowered; they could not turn back. Spotlights illuminated the bridge. They had to move forward. Halfway across, Hafa stopped and hugged the children.

"I am so sorry, my little ones. I am so sorry."

She hugged her husband. "You are a good man, Amir. We will meet again in Paradise."

Slowly, numbly, they made their way across the bridge. A gate was raised. They held their breath as they saw soldiers holding assault rifles waiting for them.

*** 

Trembling, they were brought to the terminal. A female soldier with an M-16 on her shoulder handed Hafa a bouquet of flowers and said in perfect Arabic, "Welcome to Israel. We need to issue you temporary identification papers. I assume you are hungry. We prepared a meal, and even though it is late, we will complete the necessary paperwork after you eat."

The soldiers led them into a small dining area in the deserted terminal. A woman approached them. "Hafa, we have never met. I am Aisha, Musa's wife from the village of Ghajar."

Hafa stood uncomprehending. She thought she was in the midst of a nightmare—no, it had to be a dream. I must be in paradise. I have flowers in my hand, and my cousin Aisha is holding my hand.

"Hafa, this must be your husband Amir. Musa has told me so much about him. These beautiful children must be Nida, Aini, Hiba, and Leila.

You know children, you have many cousins anxious to meet you."

"I do not understand. Have we all died? Are we meeting in heaven?"

"No. We are meeting here in Israel because of Musa. It is a long story that started thousands of years ago. You must be hungry. Let us eat. There will be plenty of time to talk later."

"Will the Jews kill us?"

"No, Hafa. They raised money to find you and bring you here."

"I do not understand. Why would they do that for us?"

"I will explain everything to you later. We still have a long way to go tonight.

"Will you come with us?"

"Yes, I will stay with you. You are safe now. You do not need to worry."

The registration complete, a taxi waited to bring them to Nahariya hospital. Tired from a long and traumatic night, they stared out the window of the minibus as they passed through towns—several of which had prominent minarets signifying a Muslim population. On their right, towering mountains sheltered the lower Galilee from the cold northern winds.

They saw towns rising on mountain slopes with lights twinkling against a dark sky, rich farmlands, well-kept olive groves, neatly pruned orchards, shopping centers, and despite the late hour, traffic indicating a busy prosperous society. Nida pointed out that the signs announcing villages were in Hebrew, Arabic, and English.

***

They pulled into a modern hospital. Israeli's, Jews and Arabs, sat together waiting to see an Emergency Room doctor. They continued past the emergency room and to another treatment room located in the hospital basement. A receptionist told them in Arabic that many Syrian soldiers and civilians received treatment here. They are guarded to ensure peace. She assured them they did not have to worry. "The guards are only a precaution. We haven't had any problems with the combatants."

She explained that both the government and rebels leave their wounded near the border knowing that Israel will provide them with medical treatment.

"Since we do not ask what they did or for whom they fight, we need to ensure there will not be any problems. All we do is care for the wounded. When they are better, we return them to the border so they can go home."

"How could that be? Why do you care for your enemy?"

"They are people. We help. Do not worry. You are safe here."

After several days of medical checks and treatment for malnutrition, the family was brought to Ghajar. The entire village welcomed them. The following year, Musa was released from prison. Returning home, he embraced his cousin and sat at the head of the table as his entire family enjoyed their Sabbath meal. Amir, Hafa and their children eventually became Israeli citizens. They blessed their escape from the horrors of Syria and would forever honor Musa and his country.

תם ונשלם

# ABOUT THE AUTHOR

Richard D. Small lives in Metula, the northernmost point of Israel, not far from Tel Dan and Tel Kedesh. He has a Ph.D. from Rutgers University. His career has been in science, with his work internationally recognized and featured on *60 Minutes*, *National Press Club*, TV, radio, magazines, and newscasts. Biographical sketches are included in *Who's Who in America* and various scientific *Who's Who* listings. He has written numerous scientific papers and one technical book. He served in the Israeli Army and is an avid student of history. His passions include cooking, opera, building cabinets, and gardening. This is his first novel.

91334041R00152

Made in the USA
Middletown, DE
29 September 2018